# Waxed

Also by Robert Rave

*Spin*

# Waxed

*Robert Rave*

St. Martin's Griffin
New York

WAXED. Copyright © 2010 by Robert Rave. All rights reserved. Printed in the United States of America. For information, address St. Martin's Press, 175 Fifth Avenue, New York, N.Y. 10010.

www.stmartins.com

Library of Congress Cataloging-in-Publication Data

Rave, Robert.
   Waxed / Robert Rave. — 1st ed.
      p. cm.
   ISBN 978-0-312-54437-9
   1. Sisters—Fiction.  2. Female friendship—Fiction.  3. Self-realization in women—Fiction.  I. Title.
   PS3618.A935B37 2010
   813'.6—dc22

                         2009047576

First Edition: August 2010

10  9  8  7  6  5  4  3  2  1

*Blanche: Barbara, Dorothy tells us you're an author.*

*Barbara Thorndyke: Malamud was an author. I'm just a writer.*

*Rose: I thought Malamud's were chocolate cookies with marshmallows in the middle.*

*Dorothy: Those are Mallomars, Rose.*

—The Golden Girls

*Dedicated to Andre Mello*
*for reminding me to stay in the moment*
*and to enjoy the life that is in front of me*

# acknowledgments

*Silent gratitude isn't much use to anyone.*

—G.B. Stern

SEP 1 0 2010

Heartfelt appreciation and love to my parents, my sister, and my brother, who have never faltered in their love, support, and belief in me.

I feel incredibly blessed to work with such a talented and patient editor as Sarah Lumnah at St. Martin's Press. Thank you, Sarah, for everything. I've learned so much from your guidance. It's so comforting to know that you're in my corner.

Very big thanks to Sally Richardson, Matthew Shear, John Murphy, Ann Day, Victoria Hajdu, Elizabeth Catalano, Jason Ramirez, and all the immensely talented people at St. Martin's Press. To be included on your roster of writers is truly a gift to me. Thank you.

To my friend and literary agent Jason Allen Ashlock, who not only understands (and often shares) my vision, but knows how to make that dream a reality.

To Paul Aaron—thanks for all of your support and for

not having me locked up when I'm pitching you my latest outlandish idea.

To SuChin Pak for being the voice of wisdom, offering me endless encouragement, and reminding me to have fun along the way.

To Alejandro Cardenas, I'm honored to have your art on the covers of my books.

To Marnie Black and Lisa Hancock-Jasie for your PR wizardry.

To Luigi Picarazzi for being the digital media manager/guru that you are. To Greg Baldwin for answering my countless marketing questions.

Very special thanks to the following people who I could no doubt write a book of gratitude for each and every one of them: Scott Seviour, Marc Malkin, Eunice Jordan, Blaire Bercy, Laurie Jacobs, Michelle Jubelirer, Bryan Jacobson, and Richard Chung.

A humongous thanks to Jen Lancaster, who was kind enough to write a blurb for *Spin* and recommend it to her legions of fans.

Thanks to Amanda Goldberg, Ruthanna Khalighi Hopper, and J.J. Salem for their incredibly nice words about *Spin*.

To the two little snoring machines that are my Xanax, Stanley and Freddy.

And finally, thank *you* for shelling out the dough to buy this book and for all of the wonderful e-mails, tweets, and Facebook messages. This is a dream for me.

Now, on with the show . . .

*It's the most important decision I've had to make
since 1978 when I decided to get a bikini wax.*

—Arnold Schwarzenegger on running for governor


*These greens are so fast they must bikini wax them.*

—professional golfer and sports
commentator Gary McCord


*A man will go to war, fight, and die for his country.
But he won't get a bikini wax.*

—comedian Rita Rudner


*I dropped out of Oxford, and now I only speak
Russian with the woman who gives me a bikini wax.
See what Hollywood does to you?*

—actress Kate Beckinsale

# Waxed

# in her shoes

irst steps can be a real bitch. Few things terrify like the unknown. And so most prefer the status quo—even if it means scraping by in an unfulfilled life, being stuck in a loveless relationship, or existing in a constant state of denial. Until one day just before drowning in the cliché that life has become, you take those first steps to a new life.

Just make sure you're wearing the right shoes.

On a very busy Monday morning, amid a sea of khaki and black, a pair of fuchsia-colored Christian Louboutin ankle boots weave their way through a bustling city crowd. No doubt chosen to accentuate the jaw-dropping long legs onto which they had carefully been slipped, the boots are sumptuous without being brash, perfectly complementing the fabric-challenged garment with which they had been paired.

*Clack. Clack. Clack.* Boots like these make their own kind of melody.

The young woman in an onyx and ivory-swirled Biba minidress is a special creature—a model perhaps, or a film star caught by a camera no one sees. For no mere mortal could pull off such a short, blunt coif. Yet on her it works. On her, it's *poetic*. Her face is ethereal, speckled with a glimmer of pale pink lipstick that looks both soft and acid-sharp. She towers over other women—the smart suits that would make Hillary Clinton proud, the calculated-to-seem-uncalculated bag lady look inspired by Mary-Kate Olsen—and she practically walks shoulder to shoulder with the army of Brooks Brothers knockoffs falling over one another to steal a second look. Her taut, olive-hued calves hint ever so subtly at her twice-a-week yoga class at Jivamukti on East Broadway.

*Clack. Clack. Clack.* Heels on concrete never before sang such a song.

It's eighty-five degrees and the clock doesn't yet read eight thirty. The humidity's so thick that the underwear of a million women clings to the backs of their butts within thirty seconds of closing the front door.

But this woman, of course, isn't wearing any.

The mugginess of this morning is profound, and there's no amount of Frizz-Ease that can tame the tiny shrubs that rest on the tops of many heads. She, however, is no ordinary girl. With the silk scarf wrapped round her head and the matching oversized sunglasses on her nose, she pays homage to her style icon, Jackie O.

It's an iced-cappo-frappo type of morning. And it seems

2

the rest of the bustling neighborhood is on the same page, judging by the winding line at Starbucks that at this moment is simply too much for her to deal with in the early-morning heat of the early-morning hour. If the collective sweltering weren't enough, the uncollected garbage bags piled on the street corners release an odor that permeates the cotton of her dress: a foul stench akin to placing three-day-old curry in the microwave on high for twenty minutes. The city feels tropical, but not in a good way—more like Guam. To make matters worse, a thick layer of polluted city air hangs just above, trapping the heat. Despite a majestic blue sky and billowy clouds that normally would offer some respite, commuters seem more irritable today than usual, shoving and grunting their way through the masses, rushing to get to their offices by nine.

Welcome to summer in New York.

Unwavering, she swiftly *clacks* her way through the steady pedestrian stream flooding the narrow city sidewalks. Walking with pomp and determination, she doesn't have the time to be distracted. She is quintessential New York, a blur of skin and confidence.

The clacking intensifies. *Clack.* Pause. *Clack.* Pause. *Clack.* Pause.

It's as if some tragically hip sound track plays with every pop of her Louboutins against the paved concrete—the kind of music that pipes out of a downtown hipster hangout. As she approaches the corner, the fictitious music builds with her every step: the bass thumps louder, the tribal rhythm pounds, encouraging her to continue down her outdoor cat-walk. Then come the horns, and the subtlest shake of the hip. She's in a world all her own. As the imaginary rhythm nears its passionate and powerful crescendo—*Clack. Clack. Clack. Clack. Clack. Clack. Clack.* Pause. *Clack. Clack!*—the music comes to a screeching halt, and the sinfully vibrant pink heels with the bloodred soles turn left.

That was not our girl. And this street is not quite Manhattan.

Oh come on! Don't do this to me. It's my favorite part of the song!" a voice spouts among the mob of strangers marching down Fourth Avenue in Brooklyn bound for the F train into the city.

Anna Ligano shakes her green iPod in the hopes of kick-starting the music again. It's too late. The moment, like so many before them, is gone. A few suits roll their eyes as they scurry down the stained subway stairs, slipping by the diminutive Anna. Her ill-fitting navy Banana Republic suit grips her five-foot-three-inch frame. The pants had rested on a hanger for so long that they have a permanent crease at the knees. Unlike the Chanel, Prada, and Cartier sunglasses that zoom by her, Anna's sunglasses display teeth marks on the ends. Her hair is an entirely different mess. In short, it's in dire need of a gallon of extra strength conditioner to resurrect it from its scarecrowlike state. Her plain, black ballet flats work to support all 155 pounds of her. It's the first morning in a long while that Anna has dressed in anything other than sweatpants—or anything without an elastic waist, for that matter—before noon.

"Friggin' iPod," she says, throwing it into a tattered canvas bag she got from the Strand years ago, as she quickly descends the decaying steps. A nervous excitement washes over her as she reaches the steamy subway station. She's dreamt about going back to work a countless number of times, and now the day is finally here. "It will be a new beginning," she's told herself so often, practically adopting it as her daily mantra. Standing on the platform, she stares into the dark tunnel and attempts to hum the same electronic beat that was on her iPod just a few minutes prior. But like most things in Anna's life, her version is slightly off rhythm.

She takes note of the stylishly dressed men and women around her, and ponders how both the morning commute and New York fashion have become foreign concepts to her. The aisles at Target are more familiar than the racks at Barneys, and she can't remember the last time she's seen more than the Christmas windows at Bergdorf's.

Anna never anticipated moving to Park Slope. But she finds it suits her organized—*routine*, she dared not say—life. Unlike the tremendous weekend crowds on the Manhattan sidewalks, in Park Slope her family's biggest obstacle is maneuvering around the plethora of strollers being pushed by expats from the Upper West. She had staked her claim in a large, rent-stabilized building and welcomed the increase in the neighborhood's police force and the extra garbage pickup.

A few remnants of the preparenthood lifestyle remain—enough for Anna to maintain a vision of herself as youthful and urban, despite her non-Manhattan zip code. She sometimes meets up with her younger sister, Sofia, for bellinis over brunch Saturdays in the city. They'll walk the market and laugh like a decade hadn't passed. Sundays, however, are strictly reserved for family, a tradition she's carried over from her own childhood. She'll take her three kids, Fabiana, Michael, and Ariel, and their six-year-old French bulldog, Greta, to Prospect Park—even on the most bitter of East Coast winter days—and they'll pretend the world will not change.

On the surface, Anna's life thrives on what many would consider the mundane. But for Anna, there's nothing mundane about what's hers. And she knows nothing is ever as it appears on the surface.

It's standing room only in the subway car, and space is at a premium. Anna balances her weight by locking her arm around a shiny metal pole that's oddly similar to those found at strip clubs, a thought that makes her smile. In one hand, she holds her deli coffee and bagel while occasionally raising her left wrist to her nose, temporarily blocking the stench of the homeless man who's been standing next to her since Carroll Street. The subway slows down to a crawl followed by a hard brake that causes her to clench the pole with her elbow, and spin halfway around—just barely saving her coffee from becoming an accessory to someone's outfit. Pleased with her recovery, she turns to the man on the other side of her, and says, "A stripper's got nothing on me, right, Father?" The bearded man in the collar stares at her blankly. Her twelve-year-old son, Michael, would be mortified. Anna shrugs and takes another slurp from her coffee.

"You've got something on your jacket," a twentysomething woman sitting in front of her says politely. Surprised, Anna glances down at her lapel. She sees the faded milky white spot on the navy fabric, shaped somewhat like a drooping daisy. She eyes the remnants of her breakfast, primarily the cream cheese oozing from her toasted sesame bagel, lifts her collar, and bends her head to smell.

"Ah, okay." Anna nods knowingly, while the commuter waits for some type of explanation. "Thanks," Anna says with a smile.

"Cream cheese?" the woman finally asks.

"Or vomit." Anna sniffs the jacket again, then eyes it, her chin on her neck. "Looks like vomit," she says matter-of-factly. "My youngest daughter Ariel's got the flu."

The young businesswoman looks at Anna as though she just vomited on *her*, and turns her head in disgust. Anna offers her an off-kilter smile and pulls out a tissue from her purse to wipe away the creamy stain. Sadly, the newly wet tissue simply pills all over her suit jacket. She's interrupted by three chimes from the subway speakers.

"Ladies and gentlemen, we're delayed due to a sick

passenger at the Delancey Street station. We should be moving shortly."

Anna's face drops. She looks at her yellow Technomarine watch, a gift from her older sister, Carolina, on her thirty-first birthday four years ago, and the only thing that hints at trendy on Anna. It reads 8:53.

*Damn it*. She can't be late. Not today. Of all days. What will *she* say? Her eyes fall to the floor and she sees the tiny, faded silver buckle sitting crooked on her left shoe.

Wearing only her powder blue bra and panties, Sofia Carnahan lazily picks through her closet. She's on a mission: to find the perfect shade of lilac to complement her newly highlighted hair. She reaches for a Prada slip dress that she got on consignment in NoLita last spring. Consignment: defined here as "the only thing that keeps Sofia from bankruptcy." She shops on a whim, as her MasterCard bill would prove if ever an archaeologist were unearthing her apartment, looking to chart the behavioral patterns of a twenty-six-year-old Manhattan female. Her most recent impulse buy included a caramel-colored Carolina Herrera leather jacket and a set of Versace luggage—in metallic purple. Thank God and the consignment shops of SoHo she's not paying full retail. She's a self-admitted product of the *Us Weekly, People, Star Magazine*, and *E!* generation, an amalgamation of corporate influence and personal taste. As she slips the dress over her tanned shoulders, she hears his voice.

"Something about this isn't right. Oh yes, you're supposed to be getting *un*dressed," Scott says. Her husband of the last fourteen months is lying on the bed in only his Calvin Klein tighty-whiteys. Sweet, kind almost to a fault, and with a body that would make David Beckham want to do a few extra crunches at the gym, Scott looked more like an action star or the third baseman for the Yankees than an I-Banker. His gorgeous, wavy dark hair and strong Italian features made Sofia's stomach flip every time she looked at him. She never believed people actually got butterflies when they fell in love. That is, until she and Scott met on a blind date four years ago. They went to Chelsea Piers and played a round of golf in a simulated golf course. To Scott's dismay, Sofia spanked him on the green. He liked her love of sports, and she liked his love of her.

Sofia smirks at him as she reaches for a pair of heels. "God, I love watching you in the morning," he says.

Sofia was striking. A beauty noticeable enough to have gotten her stopped a dozen times everywhere from Equinox Gym to Au Bon Pain by the heavily cologned men and their promises of a lucrative career in the modeling industry. She gave up on dreams of becoming the next Cindy Crawford or Gisele Bündchen after a nightmarish experience at a modeling "school" that left her with a comp card that was more reminiscent of a different Cindy—Lauper, that is—and regret for paying out the three thousand she'd worked all summer for at the little Chinese place on Forest Avenue.

Their bedroom is clutter-free, a reflection of Scott's maniacal need for things to be always in their proper place. Black-and-white photos hang on the sage green walls, images of the cosmopolitan couple on various vacations: Rio, London, Cape Town. A striped upholstered chair rests in the corner near the closet, balancing the room. On a linen-covered corkboard—serving as a chic version of a dream board—rest various images torn from magazines; it's the only item in the room that displays any kind of disorder. Not surprisingly, the board belongs to Sofia.

"Only in the morning?" she asks playfully as she sits on the edge of the bed, putting on a pair of shoes that would no doubt make a dominatrix quiver in agony and pleasure. Scott kisses her arm up to her shoulder, sliding the strap of her dress down.

"What are you doing?"

"If you have to ask, I guess I'm wasting my time." He smiles and continues on, kissing the tops of her breasts. Sofia can't stand it anymore and finally gives in and kisses him passionately. To her surprise, Scott pulls away and lies back in bed; his olive skin a stark contrast to the crisp white Frette sheets. He pats his muscled chest, a prod for her to lay her head down.

"Feet first!" This request for Sofia to lay her entire body down on him was part of their ritual, a way to extend the time to cuddle. However, it was usually Sofia doing the asking.

"I'm going to be late," Sofia protests.

"Come on, when was the last time I was home at this hour on a Monday morning for fuck's sake?"

"You're supposed to be at a funeral."

"That place will be so packed. I'll swing by at the tail end, stand at the back, and everyone will think I was there the entire time," he says.

"He was one of the partners," she argues. "I just don't want you to get in trouble."

"Why don't you spend that energy worrying about something, well . . ." He gets that famous devilish grin and smirks. ". . . something more productive." He wraps his hand around the back of his head causing his biceps to tighten. He's pulling out the big guns.

She looks down at Scott's intense brown eyes. "I wish I could spend all day in bed with you."

"So do it," he says matter-of-factly.

"That would go over well with *her*," she says, rolling her eyes.

Scott sighs. "You know, I don't get you. You always swore that the minute after you said 'I do,' you'd be through with work."

"I said 'I do' to Carolina long before we met, babe. Try divorcing *your* sister, then come talk to me."

"She doesn't scare me. Your unwavering allegiance to her is what scares me."

Sofia glances at Scott, unable to say he's wrong. So instead, she places her feet on the bed and kisses him on the lips.

"Feet first," Sofia says sweetly. Scott kisses her passionately, then begins to pull the straps down on her dress. "I'm so going to be late this morning."

"Uh-huh," he says, caressing her neck.

"My nine o'clock is going to be pissed."

"Let her wait," he says, rolling Sofia onto her back.

Sofia reaches for her foot. "One second, let me take my shoes off."

"Leave 'em on," he says, and kisses her again.

Monday-morning traffic in Midtown is nightmarish. Ambulance sirens blare, taxis honk, and commuters pour out of the Fifty-seventh Street subway station, rushing, running even, to arrive at work on time. To the naked eye, it's a backdrop of surreal yet familiar images, like wandering off the set of *Law & Order* only to find oneself on the set of *Sex and the City*.

The ironically named Brooklyn Diner on West Fifty-seventh Street in Manhattan buzzes with the breakfast rush. Near the back, in an oversized booth, a pair of black Derek Lam open-toe t-strap ankle-wrap sandals tap incessantly. Dressed in vintage Chanel, Carolina Impresario is Michelle-Pfeiffer-as-Catwoman hot, and as such has the majority of the restaurant glancing at her between bites of their scrambled eggs and turkey bacon. It's no wonder: She's impossibly skinny, and her hair is impossibly blond—in contrast to her natural (and obsessively hidden) Italian roots. Carolina rarely dresses in anything other than black, including today's ensemble. To the delight of the mostly male patrons, she maximizes her assets, revealing just enough of her perfectly shaped body to attract admiration while avoiding the garish.

At the tender age of eight, when across America most little girls dreamt of growing up to be schoolteachers or astronauts, Carolina declared to her schoolmates and her family that she wanted to be surrounded by very attractive people and very attractive clothes—in that order. Though this dream was not well received in her blue-collar Queens neighborhood, Carolina nevertheless remained steadfast. She didn't know the how or the when, but she knew her beautiful dream of beautiful faces and fashion would one day be her beautiful reality.

Thirty-five years later, Carolina lives her dream. Beautifully.

Copies of *New York*, *The New York Times*, the *New York Post*, *Fast Company*, and *The Wall Street Journal* are stacked on the faux-marble table according to their appropriate size and dimension. Carolina's silverware, water, and plate of egg whites with broccoli are within millimeters of being in a perfect line.

"Can I get you a refill, sweetie?" the waitress asks, nodding at Carolina's half-empty coffee, and leaning ever so slightly against the table. The pressure shifts the stack of periodicals a few inches, and Carolina is forced to bite the back of her lip to keep from going over the edge. "Hon?" the waitress says again.

"No," Carolina says coldly, continuing to stare at the

periodicals, which are now slightly askew. The bubbly server politely nods and moves on to the table of music execs at the booth across from Carolina. Carolina fixates on the table, on the symmetry that now has been slaughtered by carelessness. Her shoes tap even faster, now in a kind of syncopation. She often indulges in these eccentric rituals under the watchful eye of strangers. She quickly readjusts the stack of papers and realigns her off-white plate and water glass.

Carolina's obsessive-compulsive disorder has grown intense in recent years. Fortunately, these self-described "quirks" haven't led to any serious complications in her life . . . yet. Her inability to handle the unknown, to allow for any flexibility, has made the lives of all who walk in her orbit miserable. Her employees christened her "Carolmeana," a nickname that would bother Carolina greatly—if she actually gave a damn what her employees think.

"Carolina?" A red-haired woman in a peasant blouse and tight jeans places her hand on Carolina's shoulder.

"Oh. Hi, Willow," Carolina says with half a smile. She has for some time been unable to look directly at Willow, as the caps on Willow's teeth are so large that it appears as though, with every word, she is threatening to devour her listener. Carolina originally assumed that Willow's friends had decided that it would simply be too rude to inform Willow of her dentist's malpractice. But after getting to know her, Carolina quickly realized those friends were taking a special joy in her freakish appearance.

"Eating solo?" Willow asks.

"I am." *But your shrill voice and enormous teeth have destroyed that dream.* "Ron had an early meeting."

"I'm just so exhausted from the Lindells' house party in East Hampton on Saturday. I don't even know how I'm talking to you," Willow says with a bit of a laugh that unfortunately forces open her lips.

"And yet somehow you are."

"Of course, Glorious Foods did the catering. You know how Tori loves them. I'm like 'There are other caterers besides Glorious Foods, Tori. This is the Hamptons not the Jersey Shore!' But she didn't want to hear it. She said they're the best." To Carolina's horror, Willow leans in closer, her arm mere centimeters from the magazines. "But I will say: The quail spring rolls were a-MAZ-ing."

Willow's gargantuan teeth are only inches away from tearing into Carolina's skin. *It could happen at any moment.* Carolina slides over a few inches to avoid the possibility of rabies.

"How nice for you."

"I'm surprised I didn't see you there! Oh, but that's right, you're open on Saturdays. Such a worker bee! I don't know how you do it." The condescension is as subtle as her teeth. "Speaking of which, do you think you could squeeze me in this week?"

"I don't—" Carolina clears her throat softly. "I don't know what the schedule looks like."

"It'll take like five minutes. Honestly, it'll be a quickie." She giggles. "I'm sure you like quickies!" Willow says, with too much appreciation for her own lack of creativity.

"No, actually I don't. They're empty and unsatisfying," she says, looking directly at Willow.

"This will be your first good quickie then!" *Oh, the poor thing tries so hard.*

"Right." Carolina knew that a quickie meant anything but. Moreover, Willow never paid for Carolina's time, playing the friend card even though a relationship built on occasional kisses at charity events and corner commentaries at wedding receptions meant that there were only so many of those cards in the deck. Carolina's compulsions did not stop at magazines and dishes, however, and her obsession with keeping her relationships with the social elite at the right angles meant she would never raise a fuss.

"I'll see what I can do."

"Here's my card—"

"I have your card."

"Oh, but I just picked these up from the printer this morning! You're the first to get one! So call me, and we'll set it up!"

Carolina freezes, her hand with the card hanging between them. "I'm sorry. I think I misunderstood. You want *me* to call *you* to set up an appointment?"

"I think that's easier, right? Just have your girl call me." She glances at her phone and slides her chair back gracefully.

"No problem."

Willow leans down and kisses Carolina on the cheek. "Talk soon! I gotta jet!"

Willow turns to leave, then suddenly turns back around.

"I almost forgot! Eve's school is doing a fund-raiser for the Environmental Research Initiative. I'm on the host committee, and . . . anyway, just read this!" Willow grabs a green flyer from her oversized purse and hands it to Carolina.

"Environmental Research Initiative? How old is Eve again?"

"Seven! She's so—"

"I'll send a check."

"Oh, great! See you later! Call me!"

Carolina sighs, weary of the woman who speaks only with exclamation points, and reaches for her pocket-sized bottle of Purell. She squirts it all over her hands, methodically wiping every crevice. She looks at the clock on the wall. Fifteen minutes to make it downtown, two minutes for a smoke. With her thumb and forefinger, she grabs a crisp twenty from her wallet and places it on the table.

Carolina walks outside to the concrete courtyard, puffing on a Marlboro Light. Her OCD notwithstanding, she does manage to flood her lungs with nicotine without much thought. In the distance, she spots Willow standing on the curb waiting for a cab, talking on her cell phone. Willow waves and Carolina begrudgingly returns it. She listens to her voice mail while taking a drag.

"Hey. It's me. Can you do dinner with TJ and Debbie tonight? I told them I'd have to check your schedule. Call me." Carolina deletes Ron's message, just as she spots a brindle-colored boxer squatting by a nearby fountain. She shakes her head in disgust. Dogs shitting all over the pavement at all hours of the day. A shiver runs down the back of her neck. But she can't seem to take her eyes away from the canine. A few seconds pass, and the big dog shakes a leg and begins to walk away, pulling his middle-aged owner toward Seventh Avenue.

To her horror, the pile of poop remains.

"Hey!" Carolina shouts. The man continues walking. "HEY!" she shouts louder.

Finally, he turns around, and Carolina points at the pile of shit that resembles the top of an ice-cream cone. He shrugs and is pulled again by the overweight boxer.

"Asshole!"

Carolina shakes her head and walks around the plaza looking for an available maintenance man to take care of the "situation." She simply cannot let it remain in the open. But it's not quite nine o'clock, and there isn't a handyman in sight.

After much internal debate, she takes Willow's green flyer and places it delicately on top of the dog poop.

"Carolina!"

It's Willow, turning suddenly as if she's just remembered something. Carolina stands in front of the pile, hiding her indiscretion.

"My cell is the only number on my card! I should give you my home number, too!" she shouts across the courtyard.

"That's okay. Your cell should be fine," Carolina answers, willing the woman to leave.

Carolina spots a woman getting out of a taxi ten steps away, and she quickly jumps for it. "I've got to get to work. See you soon," Carolina says, slamming the door to the taxi and speeding off down Seventh Avenue. Within seconds, she's lost in the morning traffic.

Anna finally arrives at 161 West Fourteenth Street, and barrels up the front steps and into the small lobby. She quickly spots the elevator doors sliding closed.

"Hold that!" she yells, flailing her arms. "Hold the elevator!"

She raises her voice and reaches for the doors, bag flopping at her side. The doors' shiny gold plates slip together mere inches from her fingers. Her morning's luck has not improved. She grunts and shakes her head, looking to the security guard standing at the nearby podium for sympathy. He shrugs and returns to his sudoku. Exhaling loudly, she heads to the corner of the sleek, understated lobby—more reminiscent of a boutique hotel than a typical office building—and opens the small door. Four flights. She stares at her flats and, wishing she'd worn sneakers but with little choice left, begins her journey up.

Inside the elevator, Sofia is practically pressed against the door. Unbeknownst to her, the clunky, topknotted aubergine Sissi Rossi shoulder bag she's carrying is resting on the breasts of the woman standing behind her. She sips her grande-soy-mocha latte and stares directly into the gold doors, oblivious to the other passengers. Her phone chimes (old-school George Michael's "I Want Your Sex"), indicating a text message from Scott. She glances down at her phone: *Luv u*, it says. She smiles as the doors slide open and she steps off onto the fourth floor, the sound of her heels echoing off the bare walls.

Sofia pushes open the frosted-glass door to reception and enters Impresarios, still emanating a postcoital glow. Instantly, the smell washes over her: the wick of a single jasmine candle resting next to a white orchid on an entry table. The calming earth tones on the walls and the smooth, bright lights keep the scene natural and comfortable— soothing enough to relax, but not dark enough to fall asleep. Ninety percent of New York's in-the-know female population come to this room, paying top dollar to be plucked, pulled, tweezed, and waxed—all within a six-to-eight-inch patch of flesh.

Ask your average man, and he'll liken this type of salon to a medieval torture chamber. Ask your average New York woman, and she'll tell you something very different: Impresarios is the crème de la crème of the city's waxing salons. There's no other place they'd rather go to have their pubic hair ripped out. Impresarios' high-profile clients go by first names—Naomi, Kate, Gwyneth, Jennifer, Victoria (and those are only the names the paparazzi have caught leaving)—and have inspired countless women to go bare down there. Everyone—*every*one—from suburban moms to business executives passes through the lobby on any given day.

Behind the reception desk hangs an original Andy Warhol, a painting of a giant handgun, owning the eye. It was a gift from the president of American Express—one of Sofia's clients. A stock image of American male violence, Sofia is known to say (since that's what her hippy-chic client Gail Gordon told her it represented), but no one passing in or out seems to recognize the irony.

The phone rings continuously, the tone soft and perfectly pitched, and a woman in her early forties with a wireless headset does her best to wrangle the constant aural flood. The salon boasts an extremely loyal following among the landing-strip ladies of Manhattan, averaging approximately 230 clients a day, earning the salon a very pretty penny.

"Impresarios, can I help you?" The receptionist's throaty, raspy voice is either sexy or disgusting, depending on the sentence. She pauses for a moment. "We book six to eight weeks in advance. Forty-five for a regular bikini wax; eighty for a Brazilian. We also offer a 'betweeny.' A little more than a regular bikini but not quite a Brazilian."

"Morning, Candace." Sofia drifts past the desk.

Candace's mouth drops as her eyes move up and down Sofia's body. Candace raises her hand, telling Sofia to halt. Staffers scurry behind her.

"The next appointment I have is August 14 at seven with

Janelle." She covers the mouthpiece of her headset, and says, "Loving the Prada in lilac. The highlights are popping! And those shoes? Total fuck-me pumps. You look insanely good."

"Really? It's not too much?"

She releases her hand from the headset. "I'll need a credit card to hold the appointment." She puts her hand back on the mouthpiece. "I'd go gay for you. Seriously. Never had an urge for vag before, but I'd do it for you. Damn, you look amazing!"

"Um, okay. Thanks?" Sofia smiles demurely and makes her way back to the staff room. Candace returns to her call.

"We'll see you on the fourteenth then. Impresarios, hold please. Impresarios, please hold." Her eyes glaze over. "Impresarios. We're open till seven."

Seconds later, Anna explodes into reception like a grenade with the pin already pulled. Out of breath, with a thin, shiny layer of sweat covering her round face, she approaches Candace, who ignores her.

"Impresarios, please hold." Anna senses a break in the action.

"Hi there!" Candace stares at her blankly and remains silent. Undeterred, Anna tries again. "Hi there. I'm Anna—"

"Impresarios. Let me transfer you."

"Okay, I'll just give you a minute," Anna says politely, and takes a step back. She sees the white-leather sofa, feels the heat of her feet, and plops down.

"Sugaring is less painful than waxing. It's this ancient

technique that combines sugar, water, lemon juice, and a few other secret ingredients. Think of it as your mom's special pasta sauce."

Anna grimaces, and says under her breath, "Not like any pasta sauce I'd want to eat."

"Hi. Can I help you?" Candace says.

"I'm here to see Carolina. I'm—"

Candace points to her headset.

"Right. Sorry." Back to the couch.

Sofia returns to the lobby, looking decidedly less glamorous than a few minutes before. Her beautiful Prada dress is now concealed by a beige overcoat, which looks part doctor's uniform, part bathrobe. Her glamorously highlighted hair is pulled back into a ponytail, and her exquisite gold bracelet and chunky David Yurman knockoff ring are gone. Her wedding ring is all that remains. She'd transformed from incredibly fabulous to surprisingly drab—just as the client prefers.

"Anna?" she says with surprise. "What are you doing?"

Anna turns to Sofia, and says calmly, "Sofia. Hi."

Before Sofia can reply, the door flies open, and Carolina enters the room. Passing the receptionist desk, she extends her arm, and, perfectly on cue, Candace places into her outstretched hand a stack of messages. She thumbs through them as she walks away until she suddenly stops.

"What," Carolina snaps, "is that putrid smell?" Anna looks at the remnants of dried vomit and Kleenex on her jacket, and Candace does, too. As Carolina and Candace meet eyes, the latter points without subtlety toward Anna, who sinks deeper into her business casual attire and deeper into the couch.

"I was talking about the candle, Candace."

"Oh! Carolina, I'm sorry. It's just that it's been so crazy in here this morning. I haven't even had a chance to help this woman who has been so lovely and been waiting patiently all this time."

"No. It's fine," Carolina says, her tone expertly blasé. She eyes Anna's stretched and stained navy suit, focusing momentarily on the uneven shoulder pads, the deep creases across the knees, and the odd stain on the lapel. Her eyes flash for a moment before she looks at Sofia, then back at Anna. "She's our sister."

"What?" Candace exclaims.

"Don't," Carolina snaps. "You've mastered kissing the asses of two sisters for years. What's one more?" Candace closes her mouth slowly and presses a button on her phone.

"Impresarios."

Carolina looks at Sofia. "Get her a smock. I will not let her walk around in that dreck she's calling a suit. And for God's sake, don't tell anyone we are related until you find her some heels."

"Good to see you, too," Anna says softly.

Carolina had already turned on her four-inch heels and headed toward her office. Sofia puts her arm around Anna's shoulder and smiles nostalgically. For a moment, they are two teenagers again.

"Let's go, ladies!" Carolina orders from down the hall. Sofia and Anna snap to attention and walk quickly past the employees to the back room.

Sofia's eyes are on the ground as they walk, a habit she knows she needs to break. "One question, though, Anna." She looks into her sister's face. "What's with the flats?"

"Shut up."

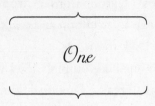

*One*

# bikini boot camp

The Tuesday before Memorial Day at Impresarios Salon is the beauty equivalent of going to the mall the day after Thanksgiving—sheer insanity. This particular hysteria is thanks in part to the coming Great Exodus of Manhattanites to Suffolk County, New York, or, as it's more commonly known: the Hamptons. Before packing their Mercedes or Range Rovers with weekend bags and sandwiches from Dean & Deluca, New York's elite clamor for a place in the schedule at the city's hottest salon—of a different sort—before the official kickoff of the summer social season. Impresarios' estheticians tend to the unwanted hair of everyone: society women who prefer full bikini waxes; young heiresses and future socialites who like to leave the initials of boyfriends (and sometimes girlfriends) in the most intimate of areas; and celebrities who are scheduled to shoot the cover of *Maxim* magazine in

26

three days. The steady stream of black town cars on the brick-lined street evokes the feverishness of a movie pre-miere rather than the lackadaisical vibe of a salon. Tourists staying at the nearby Gansevoort Hotel and a few stray paparazzi circle the block on foot in hopes of spotting one of their favorite stars in front of the meatpacking district's beauty mainstay. It is a cyclone of frantic energy. And un-fortunately for Anna Ligano, it's also her first day of work.

"Hello, Ms. Thang? Anna! Pay attention! Hello?" The girl curls her lip, showing off her ultrabright white teeth. She reminds Anna of a young Rosie Perez, about twenty-one, she guesses, with her curly brown hair highlighted blond, and green eyes. She is a loud and proud Puerto Rican, and she would tell anyone who asked. And many who don't.

Anna is visibly overwhelmed. Her inner mind is a reflec-tion of the salon's frenetic pace. She searches her brain for the attractive Latina's name. Though she's spent the last two hours shadowing her, she still keeps forgetting.

"Sorry." Anna winces, and then exclaims, "Kiki!" as she suddenly remembers the fiery Boricua's name. "Sorry, Kiki!" she repeats. Judging by the dark circles under Kiki's eyes, she was out last night and is in no mood to train someone new. If there were a minute to spare, Kiki would have scowled at Anna's paralyzed stupor, but—fortunately for Anna—there are no spare minutes.

Kiki has worked at the salon for only a year, but her ar-rogance makes it seem like she's been working here since the salon opened its industrial-design doors. For the previous three months Anna's been taking classes part-time and studying for multiple exams to prepare for this day. That she had prior experience and already held her cosmetology license wasn't good enough; she was still required to spend a certain amount of time shadowing another Impresarios employee, per Carolina's strict instructions. Anna had worked hard, and she felt prepared until the cocky twenty-one-year-old standing in front of her made her feel every last minute of her thirty-five years.

"I need you to run to the supply closet and grab more strips, sticks, and toners and meet me back in my room in exactly four minutes."

Anna hears, but she is frozen. The constant ringing of BlackBerries and iPhones, the continuous flow of hip, soothing spa background music—was that Enya or Dido?—drowned out by the sounds of miniature Yorkshire terriers yapping as their owners went to and from the reception area, constitutes a sensory overload. Especially for a woman whose daily stimulation up until now had consisted of watching *Foster's Home for Imaginary Friends* with her six-year-old.

"Oiteh?" the girl asks.

"Oh, yes, I heard you," Anna answers politely. Anna's Queens upbringing made her fairly fluent in Spanish, and that nearly always caught people off guard. Anna wishes she could pull the family card so she wouldn't have to go through this training, but the reality was that Sofia had to practically beg Carolina to hire their middle sister.

Carolina and Anna's relationship had soured when Anna chose the domestic life over launching their childhood dream of owning their own business. Anna had always been known as the creative one, Carolina the entrepreneur. Anna had dreamed big, too—of working at the salons on Madison Avenue, of everyone wanting an "Anna do." While the pair attended beauty school, Anna got a really sweet college-student model who wanted highlights. Carolina got a really awful middle-aged wannabe society woman who took herself way too seriously, despite going to the beauty school for a freebie cut. Anna's client left the salon with burns on her scalp. Carolina's client, on the other hand, got a gorgeous cut. But she was painfully unhappy with it. When Carolina's client complained to the teacher—"I came in wanting to look like the model in the picture!"—Carolina shot back, "It's a comb, lady, not a magic wand."

Needless to say, their dreams of doing hair were quashed with their grades.

So Anna set her sights a little lower: mani/pedis, and facials sometimes. These she did until she got married. Now her sights were set even lower: she was going to be doing "bikini-cials," as her fifteen-year-old daughter Fabiana called them. Anna looked confused, until Fabiana explained: "Mom, it's a facial for the who-ha."

Back at the salon, Anna was getting a makeover of her own—a "make-under" to be precise.

"Oh, and fix your smock," Kiki says in a condescending tone. Anna looks down at her bland robe and tugs at the sides in an attempt to make it lie flat against her body. Unfortunately, medium was the only size left in the stockroom and Anna teetered on the line between large and extra large. In her beige robe, Anna looked like a giant hamburger stuffed between two miniature buns. And she felt like one, too. The clientele at Impresarios are fast, fashionable, and fierce. Anna had not had these adjectives attached to her—ever.

Kiki quickly disappears into one of the salon's many cavernous hallways while Anna stands in the center of reception, her head spinning.

Anna takes a deep breath, and speaks her new mantra, "Each breath I inhale fills my body with strength and power." She learned it in therapy and was trying it on for size. She pokes a passing Impresarios employee and asks where the supply room is located.

"Down the hall, first door on the left," Renata, a fiftyish Hungarian woman responds in a loud, curt voice before disappearing into a treatment room. Anna quickly moves to the cramped supply room and swings open the door. She grabs a few toners, a couple of cans of wax, waxing strips, and a bundle of stirrers off the methodically organized shelf and throws them in a small pushcart, a *jolly trolley*, as the staff calls it. In this makeshift trolley rest the essential ingredients for providing the best bikini wax humanly possible, which results in merriment for all: the client, the esthetician, and the client's potential sexual partner. Anna's got just enough time to make it to Kiki's room before the client arrives. She begins to push the trolley out as Tiffany, a blond-

haired, green-eyed Midwestern transplant sporting bright
MAC Twink Pink nail polish, enters the tiny room. Anna
vaguely remembers meeting her earlier that morning, and
knows she's some sort of assistant manager. Something with
a title. She doesn't have the time now to figure it out, so she
smiles politely and attempts to squeeze by.

"Where are you going?" Tiffany asks, her tone terse.

"Hi. I'm running these to Kiki before her next appointment arrives."

"No. You're picking up this mess you made. Carolina
values order and uniformity in every area of the salon, including the closet. I'm sure you wouldn't want to give off
the impression that you're above the rules, you know, since
you're family," Tiffany says with a patronizing smile.

Anna, rarely violent, suddenly feels like smacking the
smile right off Tiffany's face. "Of course not." She rushes to
the shelf and straightens the boxes of eliminating peel pads
so that they are perfectly centered. Then she picks up three
boxes of toners and places them on the shelf.

"That's not how you do it," Tiffany chirps from behind
Anna.

"I'm sorry, what?" Anna says, nearly in a panic because
she's going to be late to Kiki's appointment. Tiffany reaches
for the four containers of ingrown-hair-eliminating gel from
a larger box that rests on the floor and stacks them neatly
on the shelf. She makes certain that the packages are aligned
just right; labels facing out and no more than four boxes in
a single row.

"That is how you do it," Tiffany says. "Carolina hates odd numbers!" she continues in a Joan Crawford, no-more-wire-hangers kind of way.

"I really have to go, but I sincerely appreciate all of your help," Anna says, returning the condescension.

Wheeling the jolly trolley like Speed Racer back into the crowded reception area, she's met with several stares. The eyes are staring just above her forehead.

*Damn! The hair!*

The humidity from being trapped in the hot supply closet has caused Anna's hair to frizz immensely. She looks like a contestant on *Rock of Love* or Joan Cusack's double in *Working Girl*. She places one hand up to feel how far she's expanded, and her fingertips touch frizz a good ten inches from her head. She doesn't have the time to care, and moreover, there is something subversive about it: Her bridge-and-tunnel appearance could be her way of protesting the fact that at thirty-five she's a newbie again. *Why did her sister have to be the type that was above nepotism?* she thought. Before being stoned to death for the ultimate salon faux pas, Anna wheels the trolley down a hallway, and opens a frosted-glass door, revealing a whole new dilemma: a row of twelve nondescript, identical doors.

"Oh, Jesus!" In her frenzied morning, Anna has forgotten which door leads to Kiki's treatment room. She can't go back to the receptionist—it will be too embarrassing, and she feels stupid enough as it is. She stares long and hard at each of the doors, hoping something will jog her memory.

Nothing. Blankness. Each door looks exactly like the one beside it and the one beside that. A thing of absurd beauty, actually, but there's no time to appreciate the kind of obsession that would make for such uniformity.

Suddenly she thinks of the number three. She doesn't know why, but she can't ask questions. *Follow your gut.*

Anna pushes the cart down the long, low-lit hallway. She takes several deep breaths, soaking in various smells: rubbing alcohol, Cedarwood Candles, hot wax. She stops and says a little prayer to herself, begging the fates of follicles that she has picked the right room. As she quickly opens the bleached wooden door to room three, she offers a polite "Sorry, I'm late."

The jolly trolley barely makes it inside before she spots a man in his early fifties applying wax to a woman's extremely pale, borderline-translucent, rotund body. Anna's eyes widen as she notices the woman writhing in what could only be a mixture of pleasure and pain. Her stomach begins to churn. *Oh my fucking God! Holy Shit! What is going on in here?*

"I see some stray hairs, would you like the tweezers, Gary?" Anna suddenly hears Cynthia, the esthetician. She must have been standing behind the man with middle-aged hands. Cynthia immediately spots Anna, frozen, mouth open, cart wobbling.

"What the hell are you doing in here?" Cynthia asks. Surprisingly, neither the ghostlike woman nor the older man bats an eye.

"I'm so sorry! I'm looking for Kiki!"

"Well, she's not here!" Cynthia screams. Anna quickly gets behind the cart and starts to shove it through the door, but the quick rattle of the cart bumps loose a bottle of toner that tumbles to the treatment-room floor. "Get out!" Cynthia says in a Russian accent.

"Sorry!" Anna hurriedly picks up the bottle of toner, her eyes not leaving the ground, and quickly backs out of the treatment room. She shuts the door, utterly shell-shocked. She leans against the wall and breathes heavily, contemplating calling it a day and stopping by Starbucks for a job application. It may have only been a husband waxing his wife in that room, but it just felt . . . dirty. Her thoughts quickly shift to her three kids, to the intermittent, unhelpful check from their father, to the bit of sick on her lapel.

"I accept abundance and prosperity into my life," she says aloud, breathing deeply and moving the jolly trolley to the next room. She knocks softly on the door.

"Kiki?" she whispers loudly.

The door opens a fraction and Michelle's face appears in the crack. Michelle is tall and Brazilian—a lethal combination in Manhattan. Her hair is slicked back into a ponytail and despite her understated appearance, her natural beauty beams. Clients book eight months in advance to spend a mere eleven minutes with her—especially after *Allure* named her the waxing wunderkind of New York.

"She's in the room across from me," Michelle says with a smile. *Finally, a friendly face.*

"Thank you so much. I'm so sorry to disturb you."

"No problem, honey!" Michelle looks down at Anna's cart. "Do you mind if I nab one of those Tend Skins, a lemon verbena toner, and a baby powder," she says in a hushed Carioca accent.

"Everything okay?" a very recognizable voice from behind the door calls out.

Anna catches a glimpse of a quarter of a woman's thigh through the doorway as Michelle takes the supplies. She wonders which celebrity could possibly be draped across Michelle's table. Scarlett? Jennifer? Kate? Anna momentarily gets lost in the excitement.

"Thanks!" Michelle smiles at Anna.

"Sure. Have a good day," Anna says, snapping out of her momentary excitement. Michelle closes the door, and Anna crosses the hallway, finally reaching Kiki's room.

Anna quietly lets herself into Kiki's station, and sees Kiki extremely focused. Jemma Young, the granddaughter of the CEO of one of the biggest cable channels, relaxes on the cushioned table. And though the summer season hasn't officially started, her toned body is already a golden brown, courtesy of Portofino tanning salon at East Seventy-fifth and Third Avenue. She was, as they said at Impresarios, *on the circuit.*

For many of the Impresarios clientele there exists a kind of beauty glamour tour: Portofino for tanning, Jean at Frédéric Fekkai for a haircut, Tomas at Oscar Blandi for color, Artisan Spa for manicure and pedicures, Eliza's Eyes for the perfect eyebrow shaping, and, finally, Impresarios for the final magic.

Anna whispers, "Sorry."

"Anna, if you're going to be helping me, it means you actually have to *help*," Kiki snaps. Anna doesn't respond. Perhaps because she doesn't feel like sharing her sad adventure with some kid who would dish out the details of her ineptitude to the staff in the break room. Or maybe because she wants to save her energy to scream at Carolina for putting her through hell day. Or maybe because, in this moment, Anna's simply too emotionally spent to talk. She merely nods.

Anna hears muffled music and looks at Kiki curiously. Kiki nods at the iPod lying next to Jemma's naked body. "She didn't want to hear anything. The anticipation and the ripping sound freaks her out." Kiki continues, "I'm not sure why. The girl is hopped up on Vicodin, so it's not like she's feeling anything."

"What in God's name? Lemon juice?" Anna gasps seeing the bottle on the table.

Kiki shrugs. "I know. It stings like a mutha, but these women who are into their natural, organic, holistic shit like to use it as a toner for ingrowns. It doesn't do shit, but they like to think it does."

"Jesus!" Anna says, putting her hand over her groin. "I don't think I'll ever look at lemon juice the same way." She quickly puts the rest of the bottles on the shelf.

Kiki laughs. "God, you're green. And I don't mean eco-shit. You're cringing now, how are you going to look at some of the stuff we see here on a daily basis? And trust me, we see A LOT."

Anna feels her palms begin to sweat. "Spare me the nauseating details."

"Okay, go on. Get it out."

She's at a loss. "Get what out?"

"You just need to get it out and deal with it. I'm not sure if you're aware, Anna, but we look at coochie all day long."

"I'm aware. And do you have to speak about it like that?"

"Like what? Coochie? Honey, you need to just say every bad slang word you can think of because it's going to be sitting in your mind every day you come to work until you do. You need to purge it—*desensitize*. Like a kid with a video game."

Anna wipes her hands on her smock and pretends to be observing Kiki's work. "That's an interesting request," Anna says, looking at Jemma's vagina.

"Junk, Pussy, Twat, Bearded-Clam, Peekachu . . ." Kiki bursts out like someone who has a very particular kind of Tourette's. Jemma drifts in and out of consciousness, in a daze only possible after a marriage of Vicodin and Coldplay, blissfully unaware of what the two women are talking about or even that a second person has entered the room.

"STOP! I already know the various monikers, thanks." Anna bristles at the sudden change in direction the conversation has taken. It's clear that Kiki is taking a certain pleasure in embarrassing her.

As Kiki stands back to observe her work, checking for perfect symmetry, she looks down at Anna's unfortunate shoes and grumbles. "I may not have the most money, but you at least need something somewhat fashionable if you want clients to respect you—and more importantly, book you."

"I have kids," Anna says.

"And I have cats. At least buy yourself a decent pair of shoes. Not these Payless wannabes. They don't have to come from Barneys, but your appearance should at least look like it." Kiki opens her robe to reveal a blue flowery sundress that she paid eight dollars and ninety-eight cents for at Filene's Basement in Union Square. She was too proud of her bargain find not to show it off, even if Anna was too distracted to notice. "The dress might be cheap, but I'm not." Anna stays quiet; she doesn't feel like talking laboriously about her divorce and the expense of raising three kids and why her shoes are, as they were called earlier, fugly.

Anna stirs the wax mindlessly and hands the stick to Kiki. To her surprise, Kiki says, "Put two drops there—just above the center." Anna follows her direction and Kiki hands her a waxing strip. Anna presses down and yanks. She's pleased with herself as it's a clean tear. "Now take the stirrer and dab just a bit of wax on the tip of it, then dab it on her. That's it. Now stretch it out, and add a slight curve upward," Kiki continues. Like a star student, Anna does as she's told, then rips off the paper. Jemma doesn't react at all, but Anna gasps for the two of them.

"She asked for that?"

"You have no idea some of the things we're asked to do," Kiki replies.

Anna takes a giant step back and takes it all in—in all of its fabulous and bizarre glory. And there it is, staring up at her from between the golden brown legs—a smiley face of pubic hair, the size of a half-dollar.

"It's kind of . . . cute," Anna confesses. "In a weird sort of way."

Kiki has no time for the postgame show. She rummages through the jolly trolley. "Where's the Tend Skin?"

"Oh, Michelle asked—"

"Jesus Christ! Don't get it twisted—you're working with me, not Michelle!" Kiki balks.

"Sorry. Would you like me to go get you another one?"

"If you think you can be back in the next five minutes, then yes," she snips.

Anna opens the door and slides out of the room without Jemma ever knowing she was there. She stops in the hallway momentarily. *A sex fantasy, a major celebrity visiting for maintenance, and a smiley face. So many secrets behind these doors.*

At least her sisters were the only ones who knew her biggest secret, and she'd only revealed it to them a few months ago: the real reason Christopher had left her. Of all these closets, Anna was willing to bet the skeleton in hers was the biggest. So far.

# rip it. rip it good.

Stacy Reich lies on her back on the leather massage-style table in Sofia's tiny but plush cubicle-sized room. Much to Carolina's dismay, Sofia had personalized her workspace. The walls are a rich buttery yellow and the light emanates from an orange-and-rust-colored linen pendant light, set on dim, hanging from the ceiling, rather than typical fluorescent lighting. The space is maximized, which means a lot of shelving and cubbyholes for storage. In addition to Sofia's beauty certification, a few framed photos of Sofia and Scott hang from the wall. Thankfully, there are no windows. Otherwise, Sofia would be in a constant state of distraction. This room, the size of most of her client's walk-in closets, is Sofia's office, and her second home.

With Stacy's every twitch, the exam-table paper crinkles, causing the introverted twenty-three-year-old to panic even more. Stacy had recently gotten a lap band around her stomach that resulted in a quick shedding of ninety-six pounds. In the semidarkness of the room, Sofia notices that despite the extreme weight loss, Stacy's features are still quite large for her shrinking body, and the overall appearance seems disproportionate. This makes Sofia feel a certain sadness. She doesn't know exactly why.

Stacy's a waxing virgin, and like 90 percent of her peers who come to Impresarios, she has come to see Sofia. Known as "soft Sofia," Sofia's reputation precedes her among the just-out-of-college and first-job set. It's widely known at the salon that Sofia has the gentlest touch in all of Manhattan, resulting in the least amount of pain for her clients as is humanly possible.

Stacy's more attractive and overbearing best friend Alyson holds Stacy's hand as if she were about to go into labor. Sofia stands a few steps away, stacking several waxing strips on the small counter.

"Would it kill someone to get us a couple of Grey Goose and cranberries in here?"

"Alyson!" Stacy snips.

"What?" Alyson asks incredulously. "I had a Harvey Wallbanger two weeks ago when my legs were around my head." Stacy shakes her head in disbelief. "Oh please, you'll be fine. I was out at APT later that same night sipping on a glass of Veuve."

Sofia glances at Alyson.

"APT is a club in the meatpacking district. It's short for apartment—but pronounced separately: A." Alyson takes a dramatic pause, then, "P." One last pause follows, and finally "T."

Sofia knew the exact club Alyson was talking about. In fact, she knew the doorman and had breezed past the velvet rope during the club's opening four years ago. However, there's an unwritten rule in the service industry: Make the clients feel like they're superior even when they're not. Sofia quickly learned this when she told a client about eating at Nobu with Scott. No client wants to hear that the woman waxing her vagina frequents the same places as she does—as far as they know the employees eat in some sort of dingy cafeteria, McDonald's even. It didn't matter that Sofia took home more money than most of her young clientele. What mattered was the comfort they felt in believing that, even though they might not be where they want to be in their lives or careers, at least they were better than the service-industry workers. Sofia knew this and knew to keep in line if she wanted to continue building her business.

"I haven't heard of it. I don't really go out much since I got married." Mentioning her marriage was the only way Sofia could subtly dig at her snobbish customers. It drove these young spinsters nuts. Alyson looks at the picture of Scott and Sofia on the wall.

"That's him?"

"Yes, that's Scott." She beams.

"He's hot. Does he have a job?" Alyson sneers. Sofia smiles politely at Alyson but doesn't answer. Scott was exactly the type of guy these girls dreamt about: gorgeous, smart, and a very successful investment banker. "Any babies?"

"I don't know. I'm not really in a place where I think I should have kids simply because it's the thing to do. I'm not even sure I want kids."

"Oh," Alyson says. Her tone is one that Sofia is familiar with—the type of tone within the segment of society that feels like if you're a woman, and you don't have children, there's something inherently wrong with you.

"So can you get us a drink?"

"Alyson!" Stacy says horrified.

"No, it's fine," Sofia smiles politely. "We have white wine if you'd like a glass."

"Really?"

"Some of our guests feel that it relaxes them."

"Then absolutely. Yes, please," Alyson says before giving Stacy a chance to answer.

"Sit tight. I'll be back in a sec."

Not even a minute later, Sofia emerges with two glasses of wine.

"Is this a Sauvignon Blanc?" Alyson asks, grabbing the glass out of Sofia's hand.

"Alyson, I mean really?"

"It's a Pinot Grigio, and no one's complained about it yet," Sofia says, doing her best to remain polite. Alyson sips the wine and shrugs as Stacy downs her glass in one fell swoop. She hands the empty glass to Sofia and snatches the remaining wine out of Alyson's hand.

"Jesus!" Alyson says, too loudly for the moment.

"I'm dulling the pain."

"She hasn't done anything yet."

"Fine. The pain that's coming." She's seen this hundreds of times. Sofia turns her back and smirks.

"Okay, I think it's time," she says, staring into Alyson's eyes.

"I'll be right here. You squeeze my hand as tight as you need. Wait, I better take off my rings." Alyson takes off three rings and sets them on a countertop. She stares at her Cartier watch and decides that had better go, too. Finally, she grabs Stacy's hand and squeezes.

"We're ready," Alyson declares in an overly dramatic tone.

"Okay, then." Sofia stands in the corner and wheels over a contraption a little bigger than a toaster and turns one of the knobs upward. She takes a Popsicle stick and begins to stir a thick, jade green, gel-like substance.

Then suddenly, a look of panic washes over Stacy. Sofia turns her back to give Stacy some semblance of privacy despite the fact that in less than three minutes she would see the most private of Stacy's areas. Stacy hands Alyson her pink Juicy Couture sweatpants. Stacy clenches her La Perla underwear with her right hand.

"Smart you went with the sweats. You don't want to chafe," Alyson says, folding the sweats.

"Not helping!"

"So are you going for the full Brazilian?" Sofia asks in a monotone-yet-soothing voice.

"I don't know. What do you think? Should I just clean it up? I mean, I don't really have to go with a Brazilian."

"A landing strip perhaps?" Sofia asks as if she's offering a choice between a latte or a cappuccino.

Stacy looks at Alyson, but before she can say a word, Alyson chimes in, "No, she wants the Brazilian." Stacy laughs nervously.

"I don't know Al, maybe I could just go with a landing strip. I like landing strips . . . Is it warm in here?"

"If you're not comfortable with a landing strip, I could do a small and basic triangle," Sofia offers. "Small and Basic?"

"That could be good. Don't you think?" Sofia looks to Alyson like a daughter searching for her perfectionist mother's approval.

Alyson rolls her eyes. "Would you say my father is successful, Stacy?"

"Huh?"

"Just answer."

"I guess, I suppose so. Sure."

"He's one of the most successful real estate agents in the Five Towns on Long Island."

Sofia stirs the wax again as Alyson talks. Neither Sofia nor Stacy is sure where this is going.

"One of the first things he tells his customers is that curb appeal makes or breaks a deal," Alyson continues. "People won't even go near a house if that's off. He tells them, if you want to sell your home, you have to invest in some landscaping."

"Alyson, what does this have to do with—"

"Invest in some landscaping, Stacy. Mow your lawn, and you'll see just how quickly your house sells."

Sofia smirks. This is one even *she* hasn't heard before.

Stacy takes a deep breath in summoning as much courage as she can and exhales. "Okay, I'm ready."

"It's going to be quick. I won't lie: It's going to hurt. But I'm going to do the best I can to make it as quick and painless as I can, okay?" Sofia does some preliminary preening of the "lawn" before bringing out the mower. She stirs the wax one last time.

"Could you slide your right leg over just a bit?" Sofia asks. Stacy complies, and Sofia places the hot wax at the top of Stacy's vagina. Whereas a nonprofessional would be visibly jarred by the stretch marks that paint Stacy's legs, buttocks, and lower stomach, Sofia doesn't bat a beautiful eye.

"Oh. That's not so bad. The hot wax feels kind of good. Like when you get one of those paraffin manicures at the nail salon," she says anxiously, nodding. Sofia sees that Alyson wants to make a comment and raises her eyebrow. The last thing she needs is for Stacy to be even more tightly wound.

Sofia places the paper on top of the wax, smoothing it on all corners so she doesn't have to go back to the same area unnecessarily. In one swift motion, she grabs a tiny corner of the paper and YANKS.

"OH, GOD!" Alyson shouts. Sofia's head peers up from between Stacy's legs and shoots Alyson a cold stare.

"What? I'm having sympathy pain."

Stacy is surprisingly quiet except for a deep exhale. Sofia rubs Stacy's calf to let her know she's doing great. Sofia applies a smidge of wax to the other side, and once again TEARS the paper, removing a mound of hair. Alyson drinks the remaining sip of wine that Stacy missed.

"You're doing so good," Sofia smiles.

"Thank you." Both young women answer simultaneously.

"Okay, we're halfway there. How are you doing, *Stacy?*"

"I'm surprisingly okay."

"You're doing better than I normally do—I'm usually in tears at this point in the program, and you haven't even gotten to the worst part!" Alyson chimes in.

"This part of the program? It gets worse?" Stacey begins to sweat again.

"Much."

"Maybe your friend wants to wait outside for this next part?"

Before Stacy can even answer, Alyson interrupts. "Yeah, I think you're doing great. You don't need me for this part. I love you, honey, but I don't need to see any more, especially her waxing your labia, then your ass. I'm more of a preshow kinda girl." Stacy nods, and Alyson grabs her oversized purse and exits the cramped room.

"All right, Stacy. You can do this. You're almost up the hill," Sofia says, utilizing her countless hours of listening to Tony Robbins. It was in moments like these that Sofia told herself the high price tag for the CDs paid for themselves tenfold.

"Just give me a minute."

Stacy turns her head and faces the wall, glancing at a black-and-white photo of Scott and Sofia looking impossibly cute on the beach in Miami. "That's such a cute picture," she says, trying to sound polite but disinterested. Her speech is unexpectedly much looser.

"It is. That's Scott," she says. "We went to South Beach on a whim."

"What's it like . . . ?" Her voice trails off.

"I don't know. It's hot, invigorating, and sexy. But it can be cheesy—it is Miami, after all."

"No, I meant to have a man love you." This catches Sofia off guard. She wonders if the white wine has already had an impact on Stacy in the short of amount of time they've been together.

Without the slightest hint of judgment, Sofia answers. "I don't know. It's hot, invigorating, and sexy. But it can be cheesy." Sofia laughs, breaking the heaviness in the air. Stacy smiles.

"I've had a couple of guys as hot as him." Stacy's tone shifts.

"I'm sure you have." Sofia returns to stirring the wax in order to avoid clumping, or even worse, hardening.

"Oh come on. Who are you kidding? You wouldn't believe a hot guy would screw someone like me." If there was a doubt as to whether Stacy was feeling the alcohol prior to this moment, it had just been erased. "Let's acknowledge the elephant, or should I say former elephant, in the room—me."

"I'm not quite sure we should be having this conversation," Sofia says.

"No one thinks girls like me can land a hot guy like that." She nods at Scott's picture. Sofia was used to these types of secrets being revealed before her very eyes. There was something about the vulnerability of a client that made her feel as if she was in a confessional or at her shrink's office. Sofia usually indulged the client—to a point.

"I think 'someone like me,' to quote you, can have anyone or anything she wants."

"Spare me the political correctness," Stacy begins to slur.

"Do you want me to call your friend in here?"

Stacy ignores her. "You know how girls like me get guys like that?" Sofia shakes her head. "We let them do dirty things. Humiliating things," she says, as the corners of her eyes moisten. "And for that one second . . ."

Sofia stares at the picture of her and Scott, and as much as she feels for Stacy, selfishly she's relieved that she never had to endure the kind of suffering that Stacy has.

". . . anyway, one day," Stacy says as she wipes her eyes.

"Oh come on, you gotta toughen up, girl." Stacy is clearly confused by Sofia's lack of sympathy. Sofia refuses to accept "the poor fat girl" mentality that Stacy is serving up. "You want to talk about pain and humiliation? Let me tell you about the first time I got my kitty cat waxed." She goes for the obvious smirk. And it works.

"I was eighteen, and I was petrified. My older sisters sent me to this woman—what was her name?" She pauses, then quickly remembers. "Mrs. Mickic! They knew her from their cosmetology courses in Queens. I trekked to this woman's house in Brighton Beach, Brooklyn. Did you hear me? I said *her house*! Not a spa—a house! It's one thing to go to a friend's to get your bangs trimmed or maybe a few highlights—and that's pushing it—but for this, come on!"

Stacy's smile begins to return. "That's pretty, um, unconventional."

"Unconventional? Ha! It gets worse. When I rang the door, this old gray-haired Russian woman answered and didn't say a word, just pointed behind me. She quickly stepped outside and shut the front door—clearly hiding me from someone or someone from me. She led me back down her front steps and into her garage."

"Her garage?" Stacy gasps, leaning back in her chair, the tension and painful memories of her past sexual history slowly beginning to dissipate.

"She opens the door and there is this old, coffee-stained sheet that separated a beat-up old Buick from the rest of the garage. She pointed at two card tables stuck next to one another and motioned for me to lie down. Again, she didn't say a word. I'm not even sure she spoke English. I removed my miniskirt and reluctantly climbed up on the wobbly tables. Honestly, it was so disgusting—dirty with dried wax and various stains so gross they looked like you could catch an STD simply by looking at them." Sofia's mind goes back to the grungy garage, and she can feel her skin against the rough wood. She inadvertently begins to scratch the base of her neck with her index finger as if she feels the reused wax scraping against her bare flesh.

"I sat there with my panties on and waited as Mrs. Mickic put a saucepan on an old electric hot plate and melted some wax. She looked like she was cooking Sunday dinner! She told me to lie back flat, so I did. And the next thing I know, she's ripping my panties off without warning. Then she turned on the AM radio, and it was some preacher talking about the sins of the flesh."

"Nooo! It's like a horror movie!" Stacy is into it now.

"Tell me about it. Here I am, lying naked on a table, about to have my privates tidied up, and there's some preacher screaming about the evils of sex. A few seconds later, she slopped the wax on with a BUTTER KNIFE. Yes, I said a butter knife. I will only eat foods that can be cut with a fork to this day." Sofia pauses and pictures the tarnished, silver knife dripping with glue, and quivers. She snaps out of it, and continues. "Then she began to rip the paper off with no advance notice. At one point, I thought she ripped my entire lady bits off with the paper." Stacy grimaces. "Anyway, she continued to go back and forth from the electric plate and dripping the hot wax both on the floor and my inner thigh. She was silent the entire time. Until . . ."

"Until, what?" Stacy says, eyes widening.

"All of the sudden, in broken English, she starts singing *Rip it. Rip it real good* to the melody of the old eighties song

"Whip It" by the group Devo. You know the one, right?" Sofia sings the melody and Stacy nods in excitement.

"Shut up!"

"Never. You know the part where they shout out 'crack that whip!'? In her bad English and all of her gray-haired glory, Mrs. Mickic sang "'Wax that Strip!'"

"GET OUT!"

"How could I make something like that up? Really, it's far too priceless to be made up. She had this half smile, half-dazed look on her face as she sang. I went into autopilot because the oddness of the situation was just too much to deal with." Sofia stops and shakes her head.

"It wasn't until I got home that I realized she'd given me a full bikini wax—not what I went in for!" Sofia puts her hand on her hip, and sighs. "My sisters have quite the sense of humor." She pauses for a moment, reflecting on that day. "Or at least they used to." She stares at the picture of the three sisters on the wall next to the photo of her and Scott and gets lost in the memory.

"I'm ready," Stacy says through clenched teeth.

Sofia looks up as if she's just discovered Stacy lying on her bed. "Hey! All right, I need you to extend your right leg." Stacy extends her leg, and Sofia moves in closer, positioning Stacy's leg to rest on Sofia's hip. Sofia readies the area, then places the strip in the general vicinity of the labia. In a soothing voice that's akin to a masseuse, Sofia says, "On the count of three, I'm going to remove the strip." Stacy nods. "One. T . . ." and without warning Sofia yanks the strip off Stacy.

"You said three! What the hell happened to three?"

"You would've clenched up in anticipation of three and trust me, then it would've really hurt."

"Okay," Stacy says with newfound enthusiasm. "It was easier than the other one."

"Good. Only a couple more."

"More?"

Sofia waxes the few remaining spots and quickly pulls before Stacy has time to anticipate or worry.

Stacy breathes heavily. "So did you get everything? Are we good?"

"Turn over on your stomach and please spread your cheeks."

"Oh. I'm not really, well, it's not like I'm in porn, ya know? Nobody's going to be going back *there*. Not again anyway," she says under her breath. "I don't think I really need it."

"Turn over."

"But . . ." was the best Stacy could manage.

"Like your friend said, it's all about landscaping. What would you think if you went to the Hamptons' house of this guy you really liked and the front yard was this incredibly manicured, beautiful, and immaculate sanctuary. Then when you got to the backyard expecting something as equally dynamic—it was overgrown, unruly, and a breeding ground for all types of bugs and bacteria."

"STOP! Okay, I get it!" Stacy says while reluctantly turning over on her stomach. She crosses her arms and rests her head on top of them. "I've never been so mortified in my entire life."

"I got my first bikini wax in a garage. I still trump you."

"But I . . ."

"Wax on an electric hot plate."

Stacy sighs. There's just no winning this one. Sofia ignores her and places the heat of the wax in the place where the sun don't shine. The intense heat makes Stacy squirm.

"Stay still." Stacy presses on the waxing strips and PULLS.

"OH MY GOD! That's honestly the weirdest sensation I've ever felt." Stacy has a look of guilt on her face. "I think I kind of liked it." Both women laugh at the absurdity of the situation.

Sofia rubs some Tend Skin on Stacy's backside to prevent any chafing or ingrown hairs. The cold liquid sends a shiver through Stacy.

Sofia moves to the front of the table so she can look Stacy in the eyes. "Okay, just sit tight for a minute and let this dry, then you're good to go. You did wonderful."

"Thank you . . . for everything. Sorry about my little freak-out."

"If that's what you consider a freak-out, hang around here a little longer, and you'll see what one really looks like."

"You're so damn cool," Stacy says, still a bit inebriated.

"Well, thanks." Sofia smiles.

"You should totally come out with Alyson and me this weekend. We're going to Dirty Disco on Fourteenth Street.

It's pronounced *Dur-tee*," Stacy says, mocking Alyson's earlier condescension, "*Dis-co*."

Sofia laughs, then instinctively covers her mouth in embarrassment. Since she was a child, she'd always placed her hand in front of her face when she laughed, as if she was afraid to show off her smile. "I would love to, but I think my going-out days are over."

"You're not even old yet—how many years until you're thirty?"

"Four."

"Then you have to come out!"

"Scott and I like to have quiet nights at home. What am I going to a bar for? We both know that the primary reason anyone goes out to the bars is to meet someone—whether they choose to admit it or not is a different story." Sofia often repeated this to herself in an effort to quell her desire to go out. The reality was that she and Scott rarely had quiet nights at home. Scott typically didn't return home from work until after eleven—stuck at the office or at a client dinner—and Sofia spent most of her nights curled up on her couch on East Eighty-ninth Street eating Korean food from Buddha B B Q around the corner. Sofia felt that's what married women do: wait at home to greet their husbands. Her mother rarely met her father at the door, and Sofia vowed that it would be different for her.

"Are you sure I can't convince you? I know Alyson would

love it if you came. She can seem a bit rough around the edges, but she's a lot of fun."

"I'm certain, but thank you for the invite." Even if Sofia had wanted to go out, she'd rather stick pins in her eyes than spend an evening with that she-devil Alyson.

"Okay, then, I'll see you next month."

"It's a date."

With Stacy relaxing on the table, panties still in her hand, Sofia grabs the trash bag full of wax strips and hair while singing . . .

*"Rip it. Bare nare nare nare narnt. Rip it good."*

# Three

# white

n 1956 Eero Saarinen was named the world's most re-
nowned architect by *Time* magazine.

Fifty-plus years later, the white Formica table designed
by the legendary innovator doubles as Carolina's office desk,
and its owner takes great pride in possessing such a pristine
piece of furniture. The exquisite craftsmanship is lost on
the employees of Impresarios, since no more than one of
them has heard of Saarinen, and only a smattering of her
clients are vaguely familiar with his work. Despite having
worked at the salon since its doors first opened, Candace
only noticed the table last winter, when she was delivering
a tray of gourmet cookies from Dean & Deluca to Carolina
from one of her clients. To Carolina's utter disgust, Candace mentioned having just seen a similar table in *Us Weekly*
when they did a fluff piece on one of the girls from *The
Hills*. In fairness, Carolina had never heard of the designer

either until her ex-husband, Barrett, educated her on the essential tenants of good design.

Carolina met Barrett Hartley while she was working as a color assistant at the famous CHOP salon on Madison Avenue. For Barrett, it was lust at first sight. Their twenty-one-year age difference—she was nineteen, he was forty—mattered little. One year and one extravagantly expensive courtship later, the pair were married in a lavish ceremony in St. Barts. He was a slightly jaded multimillionaire who loved the innocent excitement that Carolina exuded with every breath, and he would tap into it by surprising her often with weekend trips: one to Paris to study French Impressionists, a jaunt to Italy to learn about architecture, a trip to Buenos Aires to learn how to tango. Barrett reveled in Carolina's ebullient youthfulness: After all, this was a girl from Queens, sweeping up hair, and that was precisely why he adored her so. Carolina might not have attended college, but Barrett gave her an education that no school could offer.

A girl could only take so many trips before she wanted more—the side effect of education, he knew—and soon the dream of her own business couldn't be ignored. Carolina knew the needs of Manhattan's high society and soon pitched her very bold idea to Barrett. "The Bergdorf Goodman of waxing salons!" she said. Barrett responded with a laugh. After he realized that she was, in fact, quite serious, he agreed to finance the salon—viewing it as nothing more than a project to keep his young wife occupied. To his great surprise, Carolina's little business quickly became a giant success, and like most successful people, when one area of their life catches fire, another begins to smolder.

Carolina returned home one day to find Barrett diddling a Russian call girl.

The divorce, much to the press's chagrin, was amicable, with Carolina remaining grateful for her time with Barrett. She kept him as a silent partner in Impresarios, and the Saarinen table, a gift from Barrett, marked the time the duo once spent together far better than a photograph in a dusty frame.

Carolina's office is bathed in white. The large oval dining table, like everything else in her workspace, has its designated place. The Alpine white Herman Miller chair sits in perfect proportion under the desk. There's a wireless keyboard (in a custom-built drawer), a sleek flat screen computer monitor in stark white, and pens, paper, and Post-it notes (specially ordered in white) stored in another custom-built drawer. Carolina's office is meticulous in both its scarcity and organization, and can be jarring to those first entering. After Sofia complained of the room's lack of color, Carolina perfectly aligned three orchids to sit on a shelf behind her desk to make her visitors feel more comfortable. The deep purple of the flowers—Sofia's color choice, not Carolina's—pops brilliantly against its white canvas.

Several of her employees speculate that the ubiquitous use of white represents something much deeper about Carolina, that perhaps there's a metaphysical motivation behind the design. In hushed whispers in the break room, with one person standing lookout at the door, they offer that for the spiritually minded, white represents an energy balance, a natural restoration to all living things. Carolina, some say, must simply be balancing her energy. Though cloaked in analytic chatter, it is really only an expression of hope: that one day, perhaps, balance would be achieved by their boss, and she would arrive in a warm and pleasant mood, forever shedding her "Carol-meana" nickname. When Carolina heard this, she cackled for at least five minutes: the longest she'd laughed since childhood. "How big is the bullshit you people serve up out here?" she asked her staff. The message was clear: To Carolina, white meant nothing more than exposing every last speck of dirt.

It's been almost four weeks to the day of her younger sister's arrival, and the sun is blazing through the modest-sized window in Carolina's corner office, bouncing and reflecting off of nearly everything in the room. The room is so bright, it's almost blinding. Carolina feels the warmth of the sun against her skin and stares out the window: Suits swish past, returning from their lunch break, intermixed with tourists from Peoria taking pictures of Manhattan's latest neighborhood du jour—the meatpacking district. Carolina smirks as she sees a group taking a picture in front of Stella McCartney and feels a certain satisfaction knowing that she no longer is relegated to only window-shopping at pricey boutiques. She momentarily forgets that she's on the phone with her boyfriend but quickly remembers why she drifted off in the first place.

"Ron, are we seriously having this discussion?" Carolina says as she leans back in her chair. She fidgets with the frayed edge of her black Phillip Lim cropped jacket. She stares at the back of her hands and wonders if she's beginning to have old-lady hands. *Maybe Dr. Eric can Botox my hands?* Her long fingers are also another issue of insecurity— oftentimes she hides them under her suit jacket to avoid attention. Like many of Carolina's purported flaws—her neuroses would give Woody Allen a migraine—she was the only who knew they existed.

"Do you realize how ridiculous you sound?" she says, rocking herself upright in the chair and becoming gradually more annoyed as the conversation drags on. She sips water infused with fresh cucumbers from a crystal tumbler.

"Who cares if some guy named Steve didn't add you as a friend? You haven't spoken to this person since college. Jesus, it's a social networking site designed for twenty-year-olds! You're more than twice the age of their target demographic."

As Ron rambles on about being slighted in his virtual world, Carolina peruses the gossips: Perez, Go Fug Yourself, Page Six, A Socialite's Life, and finally the NY Social Diary. It's the party pictures she's searching—she and the very successful man on the other end of the phone were often featured within. She felt embarrassed and dirty for reading such trivial muck: A woman her age wasn't supposed to care. Hell, she felt juvenile calling Ron a boyfriend at her age. Every book she'd ever read said that once a woman hit forty, she would finally know herself and wouldn't need validation like she did in her twenties and thirties. Unfortunately, no one told Carolina's ego that.

"I have work to do," Carolina says as she spots a picture of herself from the Central Park Conservancy party she went to last week. She studies it for a long minute, deciding that never again will she listen to Tony, her hairdresser, when he tells her she needs to "shake things up."

"Yes, I'm listening," she lies. She can't take it anymore. "Look, you're getting paid obscene amounts of money to work for some of the top entertainers in the world, and you're asking me about bullshit. I want you to take a real hard look at the people on that friend list of yours and ask yourself how many of these people you would meet for a drink." Carolina pauses and lets the silence hang. "Exactly. Your number of computer friends is not an indicator of your actual social status."

Most men in Ron's high-powered position and social standing would be threatened by someone like Carolina, but not Ron—he *delights* in it. Carolina was the first woman to call him out on his bullshit. She didn't need him; she was a successful woman in her own right, content as a solo act. She might have *wanted* him, but she certainly didn't *need* him—and there was a monumental difference between the two. And at that very moment, Carolina was calling Ron on the very bullshit he was so accustomed to spewing.

Anna enters Carolina's office unannounced, holding a bottle of pomegranate tea and a bag of french fries from Pop Burger down the street on Ninth Avenue. She sits down, or rather balances herself, on an egg-shaped chair. It doesn't matter that Anna has been in the office on numerous occasions, she's always blinded by the blazing sun that reflects off all the white surfaces. She nearly falls off the hipster chair because of the bright light. Carolina stares intently at the bright red liquid in Anna's hand and the grease from the fries, and feels her heart rate rise at the idea that even a drop might touch her unspoiled office. For Anna, eating lunch with Carolina was about as much fun as eating lunch in her divorce attorney's office.

Sofia follows a few steps behind, enters the room, and leans against the radiator, adjusting the blinds to soften the sunlight. Carolina catches one last look through the closing slits: a nondescript white truck unloading meat to a neighboring restaurant, and considers for a moment the irony. All of Manhattan's meat once came here to be packaged and shipped—it was a hub of flesh and blood, what the fish markets are to the South Street Seaport. Now the meat was delivered from somewhere in rural New Jersey, and the meatpacking district was that in name only, a convenient setup for an overused joke. Change was constant, and even the most basic change unnerved her.

"I have to go, Ron. I'm having lunch with Sofia and Anna," Carolina says, still staring at Anna's bottle of tea. *A giant stain waiting to happen.* She sighs deeply, then looks up at Sofia and Anna and begrudgingly says, "Ron says hello."

"Hi, Ron," the younger sisters respond like two schoolgirls at a slumber party. Carolina rolls her eyes but can't help smirking.

"Happy now? What? Fine. Yes, I love you, too. Okay then, I HAVE to go." Carolina pauses, then suddenly explodes. "No I don't want to play Scrabble with you online! Good-bye!"

Anna and Sofia laugh discreetly. Carolina pretends to ignore them and goes back to work on her computer. Whether she actually was or not, Carolina always portrayed an image of being engrossed in something that demanded she type very quickly.

"What's that smell?" Anna asks, sipping her tea. Carolina can't take looking at the pomegranate tea any longer and stands up, grabs an oversized white cup from a cupboard, and snatches the bottle out of Anna's hand and pours a conservative portion into the big cup and hands it back to her. Carolina then grabs a straw from her drawer and hands it to Anna. Neither sister says a word, as though Carolina has done this for years, and Anna has learned to live with it.

"Is that your perfume?" Anna looks at Sofia. Sofia shakes her head. "Its like a mix of mint, tangerine, and ginger. It reminds me of that potpourri Mom used to have in the living room—honestly, I don't think she ever changed it.

Do you have potpourri in here, Carolina? Where are you hiding it?" Anna jokes.

"It's Armani," Carolina groans.

"Armani makes potpourri? What's it called?"

"Do you take a special joy in irritating me? No, Armani doesn't make potpourri—and do I look like a potpourri person?" Anna shrugs, which annoys Carolina even further. "It's my perfume. It's called *White*."

"Of course it is." Anna tugs on Sofia's dress, and quietly asks, "Where are the padded walls?" Sofia smiles but conceals her laughter. These were the types of comments that only a sister could get away with, so perfectly aimed to land beneath the skin, so perfectly crafted that Carolina often felt that her two younger sisters were conspiring against her.

"It's my signature scent."

Carolina regrets saying it the minute the words leave her mouth.

"Your signature scent? Wow," Anna says, too earnestly.

"Come on, you don't have one? Even I've got a perfume that I pretty much wear habitually except when I run out," Sofia explains. Anna's face reveals her unhipster-like naïveté.

"The closest thing I ever had to a signature scent was when I found your old Strawberry Shortcake dolls. I rubbed the Blueberry Cheesecake all over my neck so I'd smell like her," Anna says, a twinkle in her eye.

"I don't remember that," Sofia says.

"You'll remember the hives. I woke up from my nap with

Spike licking my neck almost raw. I had hives for three days," Anna explains.

Sofia finally takes a seat next to Anna in the other haute couture, egg-shaped, glorified beanbag. After several regrettable mishaps resulting in face-first falls, Sofia's mastered the art of sitting in the oblong chair.

"Where are the photos of the kids that I sent to you?" Anna asks, looking around the room. Carolina lets out a deep sigh and temporarily stops typing. She opens up one of her drawers and digs through some file folders, and produces a stack of photos that Anna's sent to her through the years. Anna is dumbfounded. Carolina flashes the photos in sequential order at Anna. Anna smiles warmly, looking at her babies growing up, but before she can enjoy their faces, Carolina stuffs the photos back into the folder and places them back into a drawer. Anna is horrified.

Carolina notices Anna's shock. "What? I need things to be pristine."

"There's pristine, and then there's crazytown. And you, dear sister, are its mayor."

Carolina goes back to typing. There's no getting Carolina to loosen up, and the more Anna tries, the angrier Carolina becomes. Anna looks at Sofia, who's nibbling on a bag of Soy Chips, then back at Carolina. "You're not eating?"

"No, I've got too much work to do. I'll grab something later from Cosi," Carolina says, still focused on her computer.

"Well, why the hell did we come in here for lunch then?

Sof and I could've gone for some fresh air," Anna says, picking at her french fries.

"I'm running a business here. What do you want me to do?"

Anna sees an opening. "You can let me start working on some clients! I mean honestly, Sofia, you *know* I can do this. I was better at it than you if my memory serves me."

"You know the rules. Every employee has to shadow until she's ready to be on the floor."

"Is she reading this from an employee handbook?" Anna looks at Sofia—who stuffs another Soy Chip in her mouth to avoid the fray—and then fixes her stare back at Carolina. "This is bullshit. I'm your sister!"

"Which is precisely why I'm having you do the trainee program! Did you expect me just to let you come in and start on a client after you haven't done this in God knows how long? These women pay a lot of money to receive top-notch service from seasoned professionals—not a hack job by someone who just got her beauty license back. Do you know how many fires I had to put out from your first two weeks here? I had clients threatening not to come back and employees wanting you nowhere near them."

"Hack job? I'm so glad I spent my lunch break in this iceberg."

"I'm sure you can find something deep fried around here."

"So did I tell you Mom Skyped Scott the other night?" Sofia nervously interjects, desperately trying to change the subject. "She knew I wouldn't pick up. But, of course in typical Lunetta fashion, she wore a T-shirt two sizes too small. Scott was so embarrassed he didn't know what to say. I mean, could you imagine what that had to look like?"

Neither Carolina or Anna say a word. "She just loves that Skype," Sofia continues.

Carolina collects herself and looks at Anna. "I think perhaps you're just a bit rusty. You're not ready for the big dance yet."

Anna sits in silence, then takes a deep breath and closes her eyes. She takes three more deep breaths and exhales loudly.

"Oh God. What are you doing?" Carolina asks.

"Channeling my anger," Anna says, her breathing slow and measured.

"Now that is definitely something that Lunetta would say. You always have been just like her," Carolina says. Carolina couldn't stand the unorganized, bohemian, and often loose-lipped way about her mother, and instead of calling her Mom, Carolina referred to her by her first name. Carolina fell in line with her father, a methodical perfectionist, in everything.

Unconsciously, Anna pulls at a string on the quasi chair, rubbing it between her fingers, causing the thread to grow exponentially. Carolina immediately notices and becomes infuriated, her eyes widening. Seeing her older sisters nostrils flare, Sofia jumps in, talking too loudly.

"Oh my God! You have to come with me to my 'Buddha Camp' class at the gym!"

"I'm sorry, what? 'Boot camp'?" Anna asks.

"It's kinda like boot camp. But more spiritual. Think enlightenment on steroids." Anna is obviously clueless, but she has stopped pulling the string, and Carolina's eruption has been postponed. "It's a mixture of yoga, tai chi, Gyrotonics, and a little Pilates. You do it while chanting."

"It sounds . . . awful." Anna laughs. "I think I'll just save the cost of a gym membership and sit in silence and channel my anger. It's one of the only beneficial things I got out of therapy with Christopher."

"Channeling your anger? You're on the wrong coast for channeling. We work on the East Coast—there's no time for your Deepak Chopra woohoo bullshit. Channeling your anger is not a luxury that anyone in this salon, especially you, Anna, can afford. If you want to channel anything, how about someone like Stila or MAC? At least *they're* at the top of the beauty heap."

"I can't. You won't let me do my job," Anna says as she snaps the tiny string off with her fingernail.

"Is this meditating/channeling thing something new for you?" Sofia asks, now desperate.

"I saw it on *Oprah*. I figured it couldn't hurt."

"And are you less stressed?"

"I am. I suppose—you know, *considering*." Anna tugs at her chestnut-colored hair. She's had a rough sixteen months.

She can still remember the exact spot she stood in when Christopher told her he couldn't stay in the marriage any longer. She remembers studying the tiny cracks in the grout of her kitchen backsplash. *I need to get that fixed* she had thought, while the man she gave everything up for gave up on her and their kids.

"I hope I have even a tenth of the strength that you have," Sofia says.

"I think the strength is in all of us—we just don't realize it."

"You're way too modest. Ariel is lucky to have such an incredible mom like you," Sofia says, squeezing Anna's knee.

"Thanks, honey, and thanks for calling her by her new name," Anna says. Her face is tight, as if she could burst into tears if one more word is uttered.

"Honestly, you give in to every demand of that child," Carolina says.

Anna can feel her body temperature rising as her cheeks flush and she digs at the cuticles in her left hand.

Sensing another potential altercation, Sofia shifts the topic yet again. "Maybe we ought to take a meditation class," she offers. "The three of us." Sofia considers herself a peace-maker, but she's simply a topic changer, switching direction whenever there's a threat of raw emotion. "What do you think, Carolina? You could even write it off as a company retreat. I think I read about one in the Catskills."

"I'm simply saying that you have to be very careful how

you raise your kids," Carolina says calmly, staring at her computer screen.

"Says the woman with no kids," Anna huffs. Anna practically shovels the remaining french fries into her mouth and glances at a nervous-looking Sofia. "Always a pleasure to eat lunch with a woman in a shitty mood."

"I'm in a mood? Could it be because I'm e-mailing my manufacturer in the Netherlands so I can launch my product line at Sephora in the fall? Or did you think I'm in here texting love messages to Ron's BlackBerry all day?" Carolina says.

"I think I liked you better when you just did bikini waxes," Anna says. Carolina is noticeably infuriated. Before Anna can say another word, there's a knock at the door.

"WHAT?"

Jody Kerrick, another receptionist from the front desk, nervously enters. "Sorry to disturb you, Carolina, but there's a Jacqueline Powers on the phone wanting to confirm her appointment for Thursday. I don't have her on my book, but she was pretty insistent that you told her she had an appointment."

Carolina rolls her eyes. "Yes, JJ Powers. I know who she is—she's a complete lunatic. She cornered me at the Lenox Hill fund-raiser. Damn it. The last thing I want to do is go to her house."

Anna whispers to Sofia, "I thought she doesn't work on clients anymore."

"She doesn't. At least I don't think she does."

"Tell her I won't be there," Carolina says pointedly. "But that I'm sending Anna."

"Anna?" Jody asks.

"It's about time!" Anna interrupts.

"Yes, Anna," Carolina says. Jody nods and quickly disappears. Carolina has become reinvigorated, almost giddy over her new idea, and her eyes are glimmering oddly. "I think JJ is going to be just perfect for your reentry into the business." There is something sinister in her voice, and Anna catches on.

"She's some raving bitch, right? She's got genital warts? She's eighty?" Anna laughs nervously.

"Oh, I wouldn't do that to you," Carolina says, like a fox inviting a rabbit to play. "Whether or not she's a bitch, well, that's subjective. I don't believe she has any STDs, but then again I've never worked on her. And she's definitely not eighty."

"Okay . . ."

"She's seventy-nine."

"I'm sorry?"

"Seventy-nine."

Anna glances in Sofia's direction and finds only horror in her eyes. Carolina's dead serious.

"At Impresarios, we don't discriminate," Carolina says, delighted at the beads of sweat that are beginning to form on Anna's forehead.

"But . . . I don't even know where to start . . . It's like— it's like giving Grandma a bikini wax. Oh God."

"You look a little ill, Anna. Did you have enough to eat?"

Sofia shoots Carolina a piercing look of disapproval. Carolina doesn't flinch.

"Don't get squeamish," Carolina says. "You'll mess up the office."

Anna, wobbly, stares at the orchids behind the desk, as she slips slowly into full-blown denial. Carolina swivels in her chair, picks up her BlackBerry, and glances for a moment at Anna, whose eyes have moved from the orchids to Sofia's dark brown eyes. Anna was inspired: She wasn't going to let Carolina get under her skin. Carolina was her boss, after all, and had this been someone else, there wouldn't have been the leisure of such a conversation.

"Sounds like fun," Anna says, to Carolina's surprise. The older of the two covers it well and immediately begins to bark orders.

"Sofia, I need you to teach her everything you know. All of your techniques. We just never know what JJ might ask for, and I want the Impresarios brand to hold true." Carolina's not joking anymore. "The hag is worth a fortune and a major player in the social scene. Don't screw this up."

"Carolina, why don't I just go?" Sofia asks.

"Because I didn't ask you."

"It's fine," Anna interrupts. "I appreciate the opportunity. Thank you, Carolina."

Neither sister knew how to respond. Sofia was dumb with suspicion, and Carolina was muted by surprise.

"So . . . I'll check in with you two later. I'm sure you have lots of work to do," Carolina says, edging her chair closer to her computer. Sofia stands up and opens the door, waiting for Anna, who remains fixated on Carolina.

"Thanks again for the opportunity. I won't let you down," Anna says graciously, and, standing up slowly from the egg-shaped chair, she places her cup, wet with droplets of moisture, upon the surface of Carolina's pristine, white Saarinen table, leaving an instant water ring.

"I like the table," she says over her shoulder. "Very chic."

*Four*

# the heart of every home

In New York, you know you've arrived when you come home—not to an adjacent garage or a grand piano or a roof deck—but to a large kitchen. In a city of closet-kitchens and tiny stoves, nothing suggests success like a Sub-Zero and a granite counter. Carolina had not only arrived, but she had done so in style, with a kitchen of Viking, Miele, and Bosch—the Holy Trinity of culinary design. A large island sits in the middle of her kitchen, surrounded by four low-back stools. The floor had been ebonized, making the entire surface one giant glistening piece—like a still lake in the middle of night. The countertops are white Carrera marble, and they complement the raven floors brilliantly. Vintage cookie jars—collected over the years at various flea markets—are displayed on wide plank shelves. The back wall holds Carolina's large collection of cookbooks, Nigella Lawson dominating the group, and Rocco DiSpirito pushed to the back (she bought his for the dish that was Rocco, not for the Italian cuisine within). The kitchen's divine order would inspire even the most unorganized of chefs. It's the kind of kitchen that makes Carolina's socialite acquaintances jealous with rage, and makes editor friends beg to photograph it. Yet despite its veritable beauty, Carolina's apartment feels young, sophisticated, even—surprisingly—relaxed.

Carolina sits at the island with paperwork and marketing plans spread out in three neat piles in front of her. It's only nine thirty in the evening, but it feels more like three in the morning. Her head is throbbing, and her stomach feels like one giant ulcer. Not helping her ailments is the half-empty glass of Grey Goose that stares at her—calling out to her to finish what she's started. The ice cubes have almost melted, prompting her to shuffle to the freezer to refresh her drink. Before putting the chilled vodka back in its proper place, she nabs a Cutie—a nondairy tofu ice-cream treat. She longs for the taste of real ice cream, but doesn't miss the bloatedness.

"Carol? You still up?" Ron calls from the living room. The freezer door obviously woke him up from his slumber on the sofa. She could hear Suze Orman's schizophrenic voice blathering on CNBC, causing her already throbbing head to nearly explode. Whereas most women would be perfectly content to hear the voice of a significant other calling from a nearby room (her sister Sofia among them), Carolina thinks otherwise.

*Oh Jesus. For the love of God, why are you talking to me? If you heard the freezer door, then why are you asking such an obvious question?*

Did he think some psycho had come in and sliced her throat in the twenty minutes he'd been asleep? Her alone time was sacred—space for her to grow reacquainted with her old friend Grey, the goose that lays frozen eggs.

And she hates it when he calls her Carol. It brings back memories of grammar school in Queens and all the girls from the neighborhood with their stupid skirts and braided hair and bony knees. She's been running from those girls her entire life. Running to the name *Carolina*, which implies a grand sense of style and glamour. *Carolina* says, "I vacation in Lake Como." *Carol* says, "I'm the woman who buys the year supply of Maxi Pads at Costco for twelve dollars." Nonetheless, Ron had chosen it as his nickname for her, no matter her protest.

Based on previous experience, she knows it is best to answer quickly—otherwise, it leaves the door open for more interruption. "Yes," she says softly, rolling her eyes dramatically, with the security of a wall separating her from the object of her current disdain.

"What are you doing in there?" he asks in a groggy tone.

*Figuring out a way to smother you in your sleep and get away with it.*

Carolina cannot precisely express why she feels such contempt for Ron, but if she'd given it more than a passing consideration, she'd probably credit it to the monotony and predictably that had come to define their life together.

"Just looking over the *Sephora* deal," she says, sitting down in her stool, waiting for Ron to return to Suze and her use of the word "girlfriend" for the umpteenth time. What the appeal was, she'd never know. Perhaps he had some sort of twisted crush on the doyenne of money. Better her than the "money honey" Maria Barti-what's-her-face, whom Carolina found to be unbearably smug. When the economy began its downward turn last year, she began to notice a slight smirk on Maria's face each time she delivered news of a quarterly loss.

"Do you want me to take a look at it?"

Carolina cocks her head like a confused cocker spaniel. Even though Ron has never worked in the beauty industry or on commercial products lines—handling acts like the Foo Fighters and Green Day—there's not, in his mind, a business deal he can't master. "I think I'm good, thanks," she says, quietly containing her resentment.

"I'm going to go lie in bed," he says.

"Mm-kay," Carolina answers. She holds the cold glass of vodka against her forehead to help with the throbbing. She stares at the marketing analysis in front of her, trying to decipher what is what.

"Aren't you going to come?" he asks like a young boy wanting his mom to tuck him in. But Carolina wasn't that type of woman and Ron knew this—so it infuriated her whenever he asked. They might have been together for nearly four years, but she wasn't his wife or his mother. That was precisely why she kept her *own* apartment, and at that moment she wished very much that Ron would wander back to his own place.

According to Carolina's schedule, she is already an hour late. She had counted the pages of the document and given herself a certain number of minutes for each page. And Ron's baby voice only promised to make matters worse.

"No."

"Oh," he says, with a hint of clueless surprise. Carolina hears the volume on Suze go way up—a passive-aggressive move crafted no doubt to send Carolina leaping from her sixth-floor window.

"Could you turn that down? I'm trying to finish this up."

"What?" he screams, as Suze laughs maniacally.

"TURN IT DOWN!" Carolina snaps, lifting her headache to an entirely new level of pain.

"Why don't you just come to bed?"

Carolina sighs deeply and places her head on the cool marble countertop. "Because I'm going to the cemetery tomorrow, and I'll only be at the salon for half of the day." Carolina's father, Vincent, died almost five years ago from lung cancer, and she makes it a point to visit his grave at least once a month. Eight months after he died, Carolina's mom, Lunetta, moved to a small beachside town in the Florida panhandle called Destin. Just one letter short of destiny, she had said. Caroline found it lacking much more than a "y."

"Oh, right. You told me that already. Sorry," Ron says,

acquiescing. It wasn't Ron's intention to annoy her, but this fact did nothing to alleviate her sense of frustration.

"It's okay," she says, her head still resting against the white marble.

"Do you want me to go with you?" he asks.

And so the queries continued for the twenty minutes that followed, as Carolina slowly began to bang her head against the marble, praying with each slap of contact that she would induce a brain aneurysm, and the questions would finally end.

Armed with a roll of paper towels and Mrs. Meyers lavender-scented, environmentally friendly, all-purpose cleaner, Sofia paces back and forth in her modest shabby chic kitchen. It is a standard New York galley kitchen, yet Sofia managed to infuse her own sense of personal style into the miniscule space. Its almond-colored walls, concrete countertops, and stone floors give the kitchen an urban-farmhouse vibe.

The whole place was the perfect starter apartment for Sofia and Scott. However, Sofia began tear-sheeting fantasy kitchens the day after Scott casually mentioned the next step up while reading the Sunday Real Estate section in bed. The plan was that since he was working all the extra hours at the office, the couple could buy a bigger place or maybe even a small country house in the Hudson Valley. Sofia lethargically sipped on her latte and pretended to be reading the latest Jennifer Weiner novel when he mentioned a bigger home. Scott had thought she hadn't heard him until the following week he found a file folder stuffed with more than fifty different styles of kitchens and computer printouts of homes in the Hudson Valley.

Sofia attacks the maple cabinets—on a search-and-destroy mission aimed at any remaining dust. She's been cleaning for the last forty-five minutes while waiting for Scott to get home from the office. She had stopped preparing elaborate dinners for him after six months of dating—and she was quite relieved. She'd never been much of a cook, and the idea of having to cook for someone *else* terrified her. But she longed to sit across a table from him and share a meal and a conversation.

She picks up a *Time Out New York* magazine and stares at the cover: "The Quintessential Nightlife Issue." *Time Out* and *The Village Voice* were at one time Sofia's bible for the nocturnally hip happenings of the city. She could have written the column, she felt, as she knew which clubs to go to on Monday nights and which to avoid on Thursdays. One of Sofia's clients, Mia Cadelo, was a publicist at the firm that repped some of New York's hottest nightspots and often offered to put Sofia on the guest list of any lounge she wanted. Yet Sofia never took her up on her offer, choosing quiet evenings at home, a dinner with Scott. She is embarrassed to admit it now, as she slowly wipes the top of the wooden bookshelf, that a part of her misses the nightlife—the excitement! the fun! She barely dares to think it, and can never say it.

As she wipes the chrome handle of the cabinet, the house phone rings.

"Hey babe," Sofia says, reading the caller ID.

"Are you ready to divorce me?" he asks in a playful yet repentant way.

"Well . . ." she says, "I'm beginning to wonder if you're calling me while you and some big-boobed blond hooker are holed up in the Four Seasons."

"Go on."

"Stop!" she yells with a laugh.

"What? You're giving me a chub."

"A chub? Oh God. I see you've been hanging out with the frat boys again." Sofia could barely stomach the alpha male fraternity mentality of Scott's coworkers. Sofia never went to the office to meet him for lunch like many of the company's other wives, girlfriends, or mistresses did. The obligatory company socials were as much as she could handle.

"Cute," he says. "So listen, don't wait for me for dinner. Gary, Dean, and I have to take this guy from Dubai out on the town. He's fuckin' loaded. Hundreds of millions. A major player. You know—Gary wants me to show him where all the good puss is at."

"SCOTT!" Sofia shouts.

"What?" he asks innocently.

"There's two things wrong with that sentence. First, you saying the word "puss" to your wife—"

"Oh come on, you work—

". . . Uh, NO!" Sofia interrupts him. "Second, how would *you* know where to get—" Sofia pauses, not wanting to say the word.

"Puss?" he says, purely to irritate her. The playful banter is a part of their interplay, and though she's loath to admit it, it's part of what turned Sofia on about him. He's one hundred percent man.

"Yes," she says, deadpan.

"Oh, come on. I'll take him to Marquee for a drink, then straight to Score's. The landscape hasn't changed that much since we got married, babe."

"Well, fine then, go! You're going to be missing out on a fabulous meal here. I was thinking of Italian," Sofia says, sliding open a drawer and pulling out a large three-ring binder filled with menus.

"And by 'making Italian' you mean ordering from Piccolo's," Scott says.

"You say order, I say make. Tomato, tomato," Sofia says.

"I'll make it up to you this weekend—promise." She sighs under his voice, aware of how very much in love with him she is.

"I want extra kisses when you get home."

"You'll be sleeping!" he argues.

"I don't care. I want them," she huffs.

"Done. I gotta run. I love you," he says. Sofia could hear the door open to the taxi and Scott jump inside.

"Love you more," she replies. She hangs up the phone and stares at the book of menus. "Looks like Chinese instead."

She dials the number to the Chinese restaurant on Third with one hand, while thumbing through the new issue of *Dwell* with the other. She spots a large kitchen in a Connecticut clapboard, and with practiced ease tears the page from its binding.

Could you clear the table, Fabiana?" Anna asks, squirting Windex onto the stove to begin the cleanup that always follows penne alla vodka. Her kitchen is exceptionally standard, from the white cabinets and white appliances, to the seafoam-colored mosaic-tiled countertops—clues that hint that this was at one time a stylish family gathering spot. Those days, however, are long gone.

"WTF?" her fifteen-year-old daughter growls.

"Don't text-talk me, Fabiana. I am not a mobile phone."

Fabiana begrudgingly stands up from the table and stacks the pasta bowls containing the remnants of dinner.

"And I know what it means, and should ground you right now for using such language."

"I didn't say it!" she shrieks.

"But you *implied* it," Anna says, spraying the counters with Clorox. Anna hated the mosaic-tile countertops from the moment she saw them. When she and Christopher bought the place nine years ago, they agreed the kitchen would be the first project. They didn't know then that the kitchen would stay, and Christopher would go.

Fabiana dumps the bowls into the sink and stares at her mother incredulously. "What are you doing with that?" Fabiana asks, staring at the cleaning spray.

"I'm cleaning."

"It's bad for the environment, and it's bad for us," Fabiana argues. "Have you not turned on a TV or read a newspaper in two years?"

"I've been cleaning with this since I was your age, and I'm still around, aren't I?" Anna counters.

"Yeah, but your organs are probably rotting."

"Wishful thinking, Ms. Smartie."

"I bet Aunt Sofia or Aunt Carolina don't use chemicals in *their* house!" Fabiana interjects.

"I'm not your aunt Sofia or aunt Carolina."

"I know," Fabiana says rolling her eyes. "Believe me."

Anna felt frigid and hot at the same time. She had been for years painfully aware that she would never be as cool and hip as Sofia, or as successful as Carolina. Rinsing the towel under the water from the kitchen faucet, she did not react to the terrible thought that her daughter was aware of this, too.

"Are you done with your homework?" Anna asks.

"Yeah. I'm just waiting for Dad to e-mail me back." The pair stare at one other. Anna tries not to let her emotion get the better of her.

"For what?" Anna asks.

"You're not any good at math, and Dad always helped me with it before."

Anna finds herself staring into space, her eyes blank, her mind frozen. Another discussion about Christopher would not be good for her—not now. She already felt like less than a person at work, she didn't need to feel like that at home, too.

"Okay. Where's your brother?"

"Which one?"

"Don't get cute with me, young lady," Anna snaps.

"He's probably playing Wii in his room. I don't know." Fabiana puts her hand on her hip and stares at her mom in all the glory of her fifteen-year-old mother-daughter angst-ridden life. *A Carolina-in-training*, Anna thought. "Can I go?"

"Sure," Anna says casually, as though she was not holding the counter to keep herself from slipping to the floor with weariness.

"TTYL," Fabiana answers as she walks out of the kitchen.

"Fabiana," Anna calls out flatly.

"Talk To You Later," she grumbles from the hallway.

Anna returns to her Clorox spray and scrubs the pink sauce from between the tiles. She notices Fabiana's schoolbooks strewn across the butcher-block island in the center of the kitchen, and gathers her voice to call her daughter to clear them away. She stops short of the first syllable and decides it's easier to move them herself. Grabbing the trigonometry and social science books, she stacks them on top of one another, and, spotting Fabiana's navy messenger-style book bag hanging from the back of the kitchen chair, she drops both books inside. The weight of the books in the bag causes the chair to topple, and it *THUDS* against the parquet floor.

*Can't I catch a friggin' break for once in my life?*

She knows the reaction is overdone, but she's too tired for self-editing. Anna picks up the chair and hangs the school bag around the back. Out of the corner of her eye she notices a photo has slipped to the floor, and she bends to pick it up. She sees that it's their family picture from four years ago the morning she had dragged everyone to Sears. The photo's wrinkled only at the corners, and as she stares at her three beautiful children, she begins to cry.

"Mama," she hears a voice say. Anna quickly wipes her tears and looks down at her youngest daughter, Ariel, in her soft, pink, Disney shiny, polyester sleeping gown. It's mildly tattered, a hand-me-down from Fabiana, but Ariel treasures it, its two tiny pink bows on each shoulder, its picture of Cinderella embroidered on the chest, its skirt a giant puff with pink tulle lining the bottom. Ariel's chocolate-colored shoulder-length hair is held in place by a dazzling tiara that rests atop her head. With her Sleeping Beauty jeweled slippers on her feet, Ariel is quite the six-year-old princess.

"Hi, baby," Anna says, trying to sound excited. Her voice cracks.

"Why are you crying?"

"Mama had something in her eye that's all. Some fuzz," Anna says.

"Like when I get fuzz?"

"Yes, just like that."

"Can you come play with me?" Ariel says wide-eyed.

"We have to think about bed," Anna says. Ariel's face drops. "But maybe you'd like me to read you a story?"

"Yeah!" Ariel shouts.

"Okay, you go pick out the book, and Mama will be there in a minute." Before Anna can finish the sentence, the young sprite has darted out of the room.

Anna glances at the photo one last time before returning it to Fabiana's bag. She fought with Christopher over the white-and-green-striped Polo shirt he wore that day. She had begged him not to wear it—she hated stripes. Her eyes move down to Michael, only eight at the time of the photo. His soccer game was immediately after their photo session, and they rushed to get him there on time. His team had lost three to one. The Tigers. Fabiana stood next to him, her hair braided. She had begged Anna to braid it, something Anna reveled in—it made her feel needed, something that had disappeared within the last year and a half.

Finally, Anna's eyes are drawn to the front of the photograph. No baby girl dressed in head-to-toe pink with all the accoutrements. Instead, a baby boy in a pale blue jumper with a teddy bear on the belly. He wore a navy-and-white Yankees cap on his head. While dressing the baby that morning, Christopher had told Anna—without any intention toward hyperbole—that he'd rather die than have his son be a Mets fan. So he presented his son with his very first

Yankees hat. The memories and the tears quickly return. She slides the picture into Fabiana's bag, between the textbooks to keep it flat. She wipes her tears.

For two years Anna has blocked from her mind the old photos, the mental images of her son. He no longer existed. He was now Ariel.

*Five*

# the model cometh

hate this shit. I'm such a fuckin' baby when it comes to pain." Dennis Hilding, the chiseled twenty-five-year-old lying nearly naked on Sofia's table, nervously laughs.

Less than two years ago, Dennis was working as a male model and earning roughly fifty bucks a day doing mainly promotional modeling work. If the latest energy drink wanted to hand out samples at Chelsea Piers, they'd hire Dennis to stand in front of an oversized, logo-emblazoned refrigerator and hand out free cans of the Vitamin B12-infused drink to gym members as they entered. He shared a one-bedroom apartment with three roommates and ate ramen noodles four times a day.

That life is a far cry from the black Marc Jacobs cashmere sweater, limited edition Pharrell designed Vans, and the Rock & Republic jeans that are folded methodically on the chair next to the table. Since becoming friendly with several top female models, money had started flowing. A friend fixed him up with a job as a nightclub promoter, and he had one task: bring models to the club, where they in turn would attract big-spending guys. This was practically stealing for Dennis, since the gorgeous models loved the comfort of being around a strapping, pugnacious man who didn't want anything from them, and he loved having beautiful women around him—even if they were a bit vapid. The models drank for free and avoided the lines at the city's trendiest nightspots—Kiss & Fly, Library Bar, 151—and the clubs paid Dennis in return. A little under a year ago, Dennis began pulling in about nine hundred dollars a night as the "image director" of Izzy, West Chelsea's hottest nightclub since Bungalow 8.

"So if you hate it so much, what are you doing here? If you don't mind my asking," Sofia says, prepping the wax. Dennis is not classically handsome. But he encapsulates a beauty that is simultaneously brutal yet artistic, dangerous yet protective, masculine yet graceful. He's Lower East Side with a splash of Chelsea, and Sofia feels an instant physical pull toward him that has her completely unnerved.

"My boyfriend," he says—*Oh, my gaydar is so off,* she thinks, feeling a flood of both relief and disappointment. She takes a deep breath and reaches for the strips of three-inch-wide waxing strips from the shelf. "He doesn't like any hair. *Anywhere.*"

"Oh. I see," Sophia says, expertly masking her surprise.

"So, here I am," he says anxiously.

"Well, if it's any consolation, my husband prefers the same." The minute the words leave Sofia's mouth, she instantly regrets them. What's gotten into her? She'd never told anyone such a personal and private fact—let alone a client. "Uh, I'm sorry, I don't know why I just said that."

Dennis laughs. "It's okay. Most women feel like they can tell me anything. It's like I'm a sister but . . . not a sister. You know what I mean?"

Sofia pulls the waxing cart closer to the bed. "I think I do, yes." Trying to avoid any additional uncomfortable moments, Sofia quickly goes back to business. "Can you remove your wrap?" Dennis obliges and disrobes. Sofia, tongue depressor in hand, reaches to dip the stick into the hot wax, when she stops abruptly, visibly shocked by the size of Dennis's manhood. Dennis zooms in on Sofia's flabbergasted expression as if he is used to this type of reaction.

"I know, I know. It's pretty crazy, right?" Dennis says, looking down at his crotch. Sofia's face turns three shades of crimson, one right after the other, in the space of five seconds. "It sucks. I can't wear Speedos in the summer. And jeans? Forget it. Unless they're a size bigger, you can totally see the outline."

Not quite sure what to say, Sofia offers, "That's unfortunate."

*Unfortunate? God, I sound like I'm sixty.*

Dennis laughs. "It's not so bad. Now I know what a

straight girls feels when a guy is staring at her boobs when she's trying to have a conversation with him."

Sofia places the hot wax a few inches below Dennis's stomach. She covertly glances over at *it* again, hoping he doesn't notice. She's never seen something so perfect. Scott certainly wasn't small by any means, but Sofia had never seen something so exemplary in length and width, and this was only in a flaccid state.

"It's very sweet of you to endure the pain of a wax for your boyfriend," Sofia says, trying to shift her mental focus from Dennis's dick. "If that's not love, I don't know what is. That's *commitment*." She smirks.

"I suppose."

"You suppose?" Sofia cocks her head.

"Well, the idea of commitment sounds, I don't know . . ."

"Permanent?" Sofia interrupts.

"Yeah. I guess what I'm saying is that I don't really mind if my boyfriend sleeps with other people. I don't *own* him. I'm just grateful for the time we do spend together." Something in the way that Dennis broke eye contact with Sofia made her doubt his sincerity. But if that's what he wished to believe, she wouldn't burst his bubble.

"I get it." Not being able fully to accept the pile of bullshit that Dennis was serving, Sofia adds, "Sort of." The pair laugh at the absurdity of the topic.

"I mean, come on, I'm twenty-five years old. I live in New York City. I could've hooked up at least four times on my walk over here. You can't tell me that doesn't happen to my boyfriend at least twelve times a day. It happens. I'm a realist. I may have an angel on my shoulder, but I've got a devil in my pants," Dennis says, winking.

"You're definitely something. I'm not sure what." Sofia smiles.

"Oh, come on, you're gorgeous! I'm sure as many opportunities presented themselves to you this morning."

"Um, I don't—" Sofia pauses, contemplating the idea of random strangers wanting to sleep with her. Her thoughts flash to Simon, her sixty-one-year-old doorman, then to the hairy-ear guy at the newsstand, and finally to the guy with cough-drop breath next to her at Starbucks. Repulsed by all of them, Sofia responds, "Hmm, I don't think it happens like that in my world. Most people I know in New York are going from home to work and aren't really looking for sex on the way." She spreads the wax on his inner thighs, places the strip on top, and then yanks his hair off.

"JESUS!" Dennis says, grimacing. "Come on, can't you at least humor me with some sort of random Manhattan encounter so I don't feel like such a man whore." Sofia is silent. "Fine. Tell me something to distract me from this goddamn pain."

"Okay, okay. Who knew a big strong guy like you would be such a baby?" Sofia teases.

"WHAT?" Dennis says aghast.

"Oh. I'm sorry I was only . . ."

"You think I'm a big strong guy? I love you!" he says, toying with her. Sofia shakes her head. "Go on. Tell me your story."

Sofia turns up the heat slightly on the wax and stirs. "It was about four years ago, before Scott, that's my husband, and I got married. We had just started dating."

"Uh-oh. It sounds like there could be some overlap here. Scan-da-lous! I love it!"

"Calm down or else I'm really going to tear the paper off nice and slow and leave you with a garden of ingrown hairs." This sudden liberation she feels around Dennis is exhilarating and slightly frightening.

"You wouldn't!"

"Keep flapping your mouth, and you'll see," she teases.

"All right, I promise."

"Anyway, as I was saying"—she takes a pause for a new dollop of wax—"every morning on my way to work, I transferred to the C train at Forty-second Street. I usually sat in the third car from the steps, and every day I saw him. He was much older than me—by at least fifteen years. He wasn't particularly handsome, but something about him was disarmingly sexy."

"He was ugly hot?" Dennis interrupts.

"I'm sorry?"

"Ugly hot. As in he's so not traditionally good-looking that he's actually hot in his ordinariness."

"I guess you could say that," Sofia says, unsure if she is

being offensive by stating such a thing. She paints a line with the green hot wax just above the base of Dennis's penis and yanks as she continues. "He had short, salt-and-pepper hair and he always wore worn-in navy work pants, with dark brown work boots, a light blue button shirt, and a brown Carhartt jacket."

"Blue-collar guys are the hottest."

Sofia ignores him. "We saw each other for almost three weeks before either one of us said a word. Until one day, he got off at my stop."

"I'm sure he did," Dennis chimes in.

"Stop! He followed me up the steps and stopped me before I crossed Eighth Avenue. We exchanged pleasantries, then, out of nowhere, he just planted the deepest, most passionate kiss I've ever had," Sofia says, her tone tantalizing, but not cheap.

"And then you went back to his place and fucked like rabbits?"

"No! That was it. That was all I needed."

"What do you mean that was it? This was someone you fantasized about, and you just left it at that? God, you need to hang out with me for a few hours."

"I had just starting dating my husband. I was in love," Sofia says demurely.

"Uh-huh. But you still made out with the maintenance man on Eighth Avenue."

Sofia tears the strip of hair along the side of the base of Dennis's penis with a little extra oomph.

"OW! Now, you're just being mean!" Dennis shouts, mock-annoyed.

Sofia laughs. "Oops, that's gotta sting."

Dennis recovers from the initial pain. His eyes are watering, not from the pain, but from laughing. "Do you want to go for drinks tomorrow night? There's this gay night outside the Hotel Gansevoort called The Garden of Ono or something very 'mo like that. And then afterward, I usually go over to dance at this club called Hiro. It could be fun!"

Sofia suddenly becomes very quiet. Something about the idea of going out with Dennis is both intimidating and exhilarating.

Before Sofia can answer, Dennis quickly jumps in, "If you're not down with going to a gay night, that's totally cool, but the gays would love you. I think . . ."

"I'll go," Sofia mutters—interrupting him.

"You will?" Dennis says, surprised.

"I don't think I'll make it to dancing afterward, but I'll be there for drinks."

"We'll graduate to dancing later." He laughs.

"Done," Sofia says. "Could you hold them up?" Sofia asks referring to the eggs in Dennis's basket. Dennis lifts them up, and Sofia places the hot wax just below them.

"It's a gay date!" Dennis declares with a devilish grin.

Sofia nods in agreement. She's not quite sure what it is she's just gotten herself into, but there's something about it that she likes. And despite the fact that she's in her tiny treatment room spreading wax on Dennis's taint, Sofia feels invigorated, as though the most popular boy in school just asked her to the prom.

The rain pelts the top of the bright red awning above Anna's head. The afternoon thunderstorm is a welcome relief from the humidity of the New York summer.

Anna looks at the address written on the back of an Impresarios business card, now smudged from the dampness.

42 E. 63rd Street. Between Madison and Park.

Candace had given her the address earlier that morning with a snicker. "Good luck with JJ. I bet that thing looks like a baby possum down there." Candace's comments were nothing out of the ordinary, and over the last few weeks she'd learned to ignore her effectively. The entire staff had been buzzing about Anna's first house call and the nightmare of JJ's advanced age. Everyone except Kiki, of course, who was jealous—house calls, she knew, tipped much higher than normal appointments.

Anna makes the turn onto East Sixty-third Street and the rain's anger finally begins to ease. The street is crowded and noisy with service and delivery trucks double-parked on both sides of the street. Several English Oak treetops reach just below the second floor of a row of town houses.

Anna spots number forty-two and takes a deep breath, unsure of what the next hour will bring. She slowly climbs the towering steps and stands between two perfectly manicured topiaries that bookend the landing. She straightens her beige Impresarios robe and catches her reflection in the glass door. The blowout she'd gotten last night on her way home from work is now unrecognizable. She feels like a wet dog just beginning to dry. *Take another breath. I am at ease with myself, and I am at ease with other people.* She steadies herself.

Anna takes one giant breath and lets it out just as the glass door flies opens. Anna shoots a burst of hot air into the face of a petite gray-haired woman.

"Hot dog from the vendor on Sixtieth?" the small woman says with guff.

She's about as tall as Sophia Petrillo from *The Golden Girls* and shares, apparently, the same zest for one-liners. "With mustard?"

*What is she, some sort of breath analyzer?*

Anna had thought that the two Altoids she had popped in her mouth would have removed any evidence of her dietary misstep. Her pulse quickens, and she feels the lump growing in her throat.

*This can't be her. No socialite answers her own door—at least not in the movies. Maybe this is her best friend who began working for her after her husband died in the war—or . . . Say something! She's staring!*

"Hi. I'm Anna from Impresarios Salon. I'm here to see Mrs. Powers," Anna says, raising her voice.

"I'm old, not dead," the woman shoots back.

"I'm so sorry," Anna starts. "I didn't mean to . . ."

"JJ Powers," she says in an authoritative New England, perhaps Massachusetts, accent while extending her hand. She may have the small frame of the sassiest Golden Girl, but she is chic and elegant without effort. Her white hair is more reminiscent of a crew cut than an actual hairstyle. Anna senses this was most likely the result of radiation or chemotherapy.

Anna shakes her hand. "Nice to meet you, Mrs. Powers." JJ's hand is surprisingly soft and smooth—not the callused claw she was expecting after listening to the salon chatter.

"Look, I'm clearly not a housewife preparing dinner for my husband and four children, and you're obviously no Girl Scout selling me cookies, so let's just cut the Mrs. Powers crap and call me JJ, okay?"

"Oh, okay," Anna stutters. *Okay. You can do this. She's not a sea monster. Just hold your breath and go to a happy place while waxing her.*

"And you're late," JJ says, walking into the parlor. Anna stands in the doorway speechless. Never one to let an uncomfortable moment pass, JJ says, "And you look like you had other expectations—thinking I'd be Big Edie from *Grey Gardens?*"

"Was that the Drew Barrymore or Jessica Lange character?" Anna asks without missing a beat. JJ looks at her incredulously, then continues walking.

Anna tiptoes behind her, trying not to knock anything over. The town house holds a gray cast, in part due to the heavy rain clouds, while the white-marble floors manage to keep the room from teetering toward the dark and depressing. The place is surprisingly modern in its décor, but comfortable, with a long-lived-in feel. To the right is a small office painted in a soothing lavender color. A white desk is pushed against the wall, with a plum pendant lamp hanging above a tufted-velvet eggplant-colored chair. Anna turns left and notices a formal dining room that's bigger than her first studio apartment. Down a long hallway adorned with large, framed photos of horses is a great room, where Anna notices a tall, thin, effeminate black man talking to a woman dressed in jeans and a peasant blouse. They both stare at a young woman in her early twenties, who is getting her makeup done. A man dressed in a navy suit with his back to Anna stands to their left.

JJ stops in the formal dining room, and asks, "So you're Carolina's sister?"

"Yes, ma'am," Anna answers. JJ arches her eyebrows. "Sorry. I mean JJ."

"She's tough," JJ says. "And that's saying a lot, coming from me." She laughs, breaking the ice. Anna joins in JJ's infectious laughter.

"Are you a regular client of Carolina's?"

"Oh God, no. I see Carolina at every last one of these social events looking just as miserable as me. She seems nice enough, but trendy salons, especially salons below Fourteenth Street, aren't the type of venue where you'll find an old lady like me sitting in reception. Honestly, when was the last time you saw someone my age at your salon?"

Without thinking, Anna blurts out, "I actually just started, but I'm certain there's women your age . . ." Anna stops midsentence to regroup. "What I meant to say was, I'm sure there are several of your peers that are clients of Impresarios'."

"My 'peers'?" JJ says with a laugh. "That's rich. The truth is you rarely see women older than sixty-five anywhere in this city. I think they take them to Central Park and shoot them. I'm waiting for the knock on my door. But I'm ready for them," she says with a devilish grin.

"What made you decide to make an appointment?"

"*New York* magazine," she says matter-of-factly.

"*New York* magazine inspired you to get a wax?" JJ shoots Anna a questioning glare. "I mean, I would have thought *Vogue, Elle, Cosmopolitan*, et cetera."

"Impresarios was named best luxury waxing salon by that magazine, so I naturally I had to give it a try. I'm trying everything on their best-of-New-York list."

"Wow!" Anna exclaims. "It's so, I don't know . . ."

"Pathetic?" JJ interrupts.

"Decadent. Exciting," Anna says, her eyes lighting up.

"Well, don't get too excited. It's my sad substitute for a 'hundred things to do before you're dead' list," JJ deadpans. "I'm sure you've heard of 'the bucket list'"—Anna nods—"This is my 'fuck-it' list."

Anna's mouth drops. "I'm sorry?" she says.

"Meaning, I'm about to die. So fuck it. I might as well try it," JJ says, poker-faced, then bursts into wild laughter.

Anna smiles small and feels the lump in her throat return.

"Thought I nipped this lil' sucker when it was in my breast last year. At least that's what that good-for-nothing-but-fuck-fantasy doctor told me. Now those renegade cells made it down south, and I got ovarian cancer. Haven't produced eggs in nearly thirty years, and I still get stuck with cancer there."

Anna feels her eyes burn. "I'm so sorry to hear that," she says, trying not to think of her dad lying in his hospital bed after several grueling rounds of chemo praying for God to take him.

*Don't cry. Toughen up. Pull it together.*

"Cancer's a real bitch," JJ says. "So are you ready for this? Because I sure as hell am not," she says, effortlessly shifting the topic.

Anna sets the bag down on the shiny marble floor. "You want to do this right here? Wouldn't you prefer to go some place a little more private?"

*Go to a happy place. Happy place.*

"It's my house. How much more private can we get?" JJ scoffs. "I'll just sit in the chair, and you can do me real quick."

Anna gulps. "Okay, it's your choice." She picks up her bag and places it on top of the long dining-room table. *Twenty*, Anna thinks, guessing at how many people it could accommodate. A far cry from Anna's modest kitchen table that barely held five. JJ sits down in her oversized chair and closes her eyes.

"Ready?" Anna asks.

"No, I'm just sitting here with my eyes closed as a meditative practice. Yes, I'm ready."

"I, uh, I'm going to need you to disrobe," Anna says softly in JJ's ear.

"Disrobe? I don't think so!" JJ says, her eyes bursting open.

"Mrs. Powers—JJ—I don't know how you expect me to wax your bikini area if you won't disrobe," Anna explains.

"My what?" JJ laughs so loudly that the people in the next room crane their necks to see the commotion. "Oh sweetie, I think someone's played an awfully cruel joke on you. I need my eyebrows waxed—what's left of them anyway, not my 'bikini area' as you called it." JJ bursts into laughter yet again.

*OH. MY. GOD. I'm going to kill her. In her fucking white office.*

"I'm so sorry! I—there—must have been some kind of miscommunication at the salon."

"Bikini wax! I haven't worn a bikini in fifty years. And I have never gotten a bikini wax in my life!"

"Something to add to the fuck-it list?" Anna says, attempting a connection, and sensing her inadequacy to make the leap.

JJ looks at her for a moment sharply, then relaxes. "We'll see."

A thin layer of sweat erupts from Anna's forehead. "I'm

so sorry. I just assumed you wanted . . . it is our specialty, after all. My apologies." JJ doesn't say a word and once again lets the awkwardness hang in the air like a heavy fog. Anna takes this as a sign to just shut up and do her job. She tries to breathe slowly to calm her nerves. She opens the small saucer with a hard layer of wax in the middle and plugs it into a nearby outlet.

"JJ?" a smooth male voice calls out.

"In here," JJ says.

The lanky black man glides into the room. "Ivy's taking a little longer than expected, so would it be a problem for you to do your own hair and makeup?"

"Elvin dear, I've done my own hair and makeup since before you were born, and I've always made it a point to be camera-ready at all times. So to answer your question, yes, I will take care of my own makeup, and perhaps you haven't noticed, but there isn't much hair for me to *do*. Unless, of course, you want me to run out and get some extensions," she says with a throaty laugh. Anna is speechless and a bit embarrassed for Elvin. JJ turns to Anna. "He isn't used to his subjects talking back to him; most of them claw their way to get into his magazine's pages."

"JJ, I . . ." Elvin starts.

JJ speaks over him. "They normally send him boxes of cupcakes from Magnolia or flowers from Ovando. I'm not the flowers-and-cupcakes kind of gal," JJ says, and turns to face Elvin. He's not the first to be surprised by such tough talk coming from a small woman. Some referred to her as a phenomenon many thought impossible: a tougher Shirley MacLaine.

"What's the holdup?" JJ continues.

"Ivy isn't pleased with her hair and makeup."

"I'll be there in five minutes to sort this out. Tell Ivy to get ready for me," JJ barks. Elvin flits away as quickly as he had appeared.

Fortunately, Anna came prepared for everything and has a wooden stick in the shape of a pencil in her bag. She dips the stick into the hot wax and outlines JJ's thin eyebrows. A full eyebrow wax wasn't necessary as JJ had only a few unruly hairs that a pair of tweezers could easily remedy.

"I don't know why I even agreed to this. The brain trust at *Quest* thought it would be a fabulous idea to pair an old socialite with one from this new crop of retards," JJ says.

Anna knew better than to correct JJ on her very un-PC diction. Instead, she ripped the wax off JJ's left eyebrow. *Perfection.* JJ didn't flinch. *Is she that tough? Or just immune to pain?* "And they paired you with Ivy Lane?" Anna asks.

"Yes. What kind of pretentious assholes name their child Ivy Lane?" JJ laments.

A member of the next generation of young socialites that sought and caught media attention for their every move, Ivy Lane had risen above the crowd. Sex tapes, prescription-drug abuse, staged photos without panties, YouTube videos trashing frenemies, and Facebook blogs chronicling it all— for most it sounds like fiction, parents' worst nightmares for their child's adolescence. For these girls it was Tuesday. Anna knew their names and faces, their latest exploits, through Fabiana, who emulated them whenever the opportunity arose.

Anna finishes the other eyebrow, and asks, "Would you mind if I used a little cover-up to eliminate some of the redness?" JJ simply nods—once—and Anna reaches in her bag for her concealer. Anna studies JJ's forehead and notices every imperfection; the deep lines from a life long lived, and the creases between her eyebrows that resemble the number eleven. She smiles at the wrinkles with a certain admiration and applies the makeup with genuine care despite having just met JJ. Unconsciously, she reaches for her blush and places a smidge just above JJ's cheekbones. JJ's eyes are closed, and Anna discovers a softer side of this woman who was barking orders just a few minutes ago. JJ's skin was unaltered, unlike the Botoxed women whom Anna came across every day at the salon who were half JJ's age. Anna finds the crevices in her skin glorious and beautiful. JJ now sits before Anna utterly vulnerable. Anna snatches the MAC lipstick and blots it on JJ's lips with razor-sharp precision. Anna can't help but beam. She takes a step back and examines her work. "There. I think we're good." Anna holds up a small hand mirror and shows her work to JJ.

JJ is taken aback by her reflection and lets out a gasp.

"I'm sorry!" Anna says, worried. "I may have gotten a bit carried away."

JJ pauses, looking at herself in the tiny mirror. "No. I

like it. You did good, kid. I actually don't look like a man anymore." She guffaws.

Anna exhales deeply, careful not to blow any of her hot-dog breath toward her client. JJ stands and walks into a larger living room, while Anna unplugs the hot wax and packs up her makeup. She did good, JJ had said. Not bad.

"Anna?" a deep voice says.

Anna looks up and a man in a navy suit stands in front of her. He's tall—maybe six-foot-one or -two—and no older than forty, with very serious brown eyes.

"I'm Tim Shaw, JJ's attorney. Actually, I'm more of a friend who looks out for her, but I'm a lawyer, nonetheless. At any rate, she's asked me to come in and see if you're available to stick around for the photo shoot. She'll pay you double."

"Oh." Anna hesitates. "I really don't know. I should get back to the salon probably."

"You must really hate me," he says, stone-faced.

"I'm sorry?"

"You must really hate me—if you want me to go and tell JJ Powers the word 'no,'" he says with a giant smile, revealing two Mario Lopez—sized dimples.

*Dimples? Really? This suddenly has taken an unexpected turn.*

Anna follows Tim into the living room, where several light boxes are set up, and a photographer is stationed in front of a large overstuffed couch. Ivy Lane perches on the long arm of the sofa, her face vacant, a cell phone in her hand. A makeup artist and hairstylist fuss over her, as the team from the magazine stands around, waiting. Anna and Tim lean against the wall in the corner of the room, peering out from behind editors and photographers and their ubiquitous assistants. The room is tense, but static, and everyone seems to be whispering.

Suddenly, JJ Powers pushes her way through a herd of loiterers and plants herself in front of young Ivy.

"How do you do?" JJ says, as the beauty experts flutter about the burgeoning socialite.

"Awful!" Ivy pouts. At that moment, JJ longs for the days of the inauthentic, when a person asked how someone was doing, and she'd reply, "Fine, thanks." Even when enduring a complete mental breakdown, one should have the common decency to keep her troubles to herself.

"I'm not sure if you've noticed, but I'm old as dirt, and I've been doing this sort of thing my entire life—since the day my parents, Adam and Eve, raised me in that big garden. I'm not quite sure what your problem is. It's not brain science. Get in front of the goddamn camera and let them take the picture. Then get the hell out of here so the rest of us can get on with what's left of our miserable lives."

Ivy is shocked into obedience. JJ's tone is not so rarely heard, it seems as if she enjoys it. She dismisses hair and makeup and pats the sofa, inviting JJ to take her seat.

"Okay, people, let's do this," the photographer shouts.

From the corner of the room, Anna watches Ivy unsuccessfully attempt to make small talk with JJ. As the photographer readies New York's most well-known socialites into position, Anna blurts out, "Wait!" The entire room turns to face her. "I need to fix Mrs. Powers's makeup," she says, her voice cracking. Tim glances at Anna curiously as she darts over to the couch.

"Hi," Anna says as she bends down and blots JJ's face with a tissue. Irritated, Ivy pulls out her BlackBerry and text messages feverishly.

"What are you doing?" JJ whispers.

"Blotting," Anna says.

"My makeup is completely fine, isn't it?" JJ says.

"Yup."

"Then why are you over here, dear? You're the waxing person not a makeup artist."

"Because you deserve someone to fawn all over you for a minute, too," Anna explains.

JJ is silent. With the exception of Tim, she can't remember the last time someone actually gave a shit. "Well?" she asks.

"Yes?" Anna replies.

"How do I look then?"

"Like a supermodel," Anna says, and darts out of the camera frame.

JJ raises the corners of her mouth slightly, smirking at the wax girl, no doubt. She lets out a single laugh, and at that moment the camera CLICKS, with the grande dame smiling and the heiress frowning at her phone.

*What the fuck? How did? Where in God's name?
Oh God.*

Carolina opens her eyes wide as the faint light of dusk flickers like a candle in the tiny bedroom. She feels the softness of the slate-colored tattered quilt that barely covers her body against her warm skin. The room smells like a mixture of Armani perfume, rum, cigarettes, sweat, and sex.

*Damn mojitos!*

In her forty years, Carolina has woken up in a total of three strange beds. The first was David, a Cuban playboy, whom she met after a long night of drinking mojitos on Lincoln Road in South Beach. She was way too embarrassed to do the walk of shame in the daylight hours, so she walked all the way down Collins Avenue at two thirty in the morning to the Delano Hotel. The second, Eli, an Israeli financier visiting from London, was another product of too many mojitos. And once again to avoid the awkward conversation that often followed drunken sex, Carolina fled in the middle of the night like the character in *The Shawshank Redemption*.

She scans the room and is unnerved by the complete disorder that surrounds her. She feels the compulsion to clean and organize. Had she not noticed it before? She spots dirty plates with half-eaten Chinese food—dried brown sauce glued to the side. On the floor a can of Diet Coke is tipped over, a wet spot forging a trail on the beige carpet. She feels a shiver run down her spine. She must locate a bottle of Purell immediately. She can hear the tiny legs of cockroaches marching their way toward the plate. *Rats! I bet there are rats. There's open food. This is New York. Twelve rats to every one person.* Carolina read in the *Times* once that a single female rat could produce as many as 297 brand-new rats within a month's time. She must stop considering this. Her purse is currently MIA—otherwise, she'd have popped a Xanax or a Klonopin by now. Instead, she takes a deep breath and decides to give Anna's new mantra a go.

*Breathe.*

*What do you mean breathe? I'm already breathing.* She pulls at her hair.

*This is fucking stupid. Anna's a moron.*

Despite this judgment, she continues to take deep breaths. On the last inhale she notices a strangely familiar and comforting scent. Spicy berries and sandalwood.

*Wait a second. Oh God. It is.*

Carolina knows the scent. From 1985. Drakkar Noir.

She follows the familiar scent, and turns her head to the left. Lying next to her, completely naked, is Jack Vaughn, the first boy she ever fell in love with.

The events from earlier in the day rush back to her, as her massive headache goes into overdrive.

Several hours earlier, Carolina had parked her car on Eightieth Street just a few blocks from Metropolitan Avenue in Middle Village, Queens. As she walked back to her car from St. John's cemetery, she had heard a familiar voice calling her name.

"CAROLINA IMPRESARIO!" he shouted for the third time. Carolina knew the voice all too well, a vestige from her fast and fierce days at Forest Hills High School. Infallible as she might appear to everyone in New York social circles, Jack Vaughn could still make her unapologetically dizzy. She was unsure whether or not she should turn around and face him head-on or if she should just make an all-out sprint for her car. Looking down at her new orange Marc Jacobs patent leather pumps, she decided she'd better just turn around.

"Jack. Hi," she said with a smirk.

"Hello, stranger," Jack said. Jack stood with that same shit-eating grin that he'd had since high school. He'd aged perfectly. His wavy hair was close-cropped and manly without looking trendy. His deep-set blue eyes were just as beautiful as she'd remembered. The only signs that he'd aged at all were the tiny fine lines that were etched in his forehead—something that Carolina found even more alluring as most of the men in her circles had fallen victim to Botox.

"I was just visiting my dad's grave. I come here once a month to tidy up, then I realized I forgot the flowers in the car so I was running back here to get them and—" Carolina stopped. "Oh God. I sound pathetic. Hi, Jack. It's nice to see you," she said with a nervous smile.

"Not pathetic at all. You're adorable as ever," he said,

staring into her eyes. "You still look like a model!" Normally, a description like "adorable" would send Carolina right over the edge, and being told she looked like a model was something she heard from men on the street visiting from Boise as a bad pickup line. But at that moment she didn't care. She beamed.

"Thanks, I think," she said. She noticed Jack looking at his watch. Her defenses went back up instantly. "Goodbye, Jack."

Jack squinted his eyes, perplexed. "Huh? Oh," he said, realizing. "I'm sorry—I was on my way to this bar that I'm about to rehab, and I just realized I'm going to be late."

"No, it's fine. I understand. It was nice to see you," she said flatly.

"Listen, don't get an attitude with me. I saw you walking down the hill from up the block, double-parked my car, and came chasing after you—even though you ignored me," he said. Carolina was surprised by his confession.

"I wasn't ignoring you . . . much," she said.

"Follow me there. I'll do a five-minute walk-through, we'll stay and have a drink, and you'll be back in the city before supper," he said point-blank.

" 'Supper'? Did you really just say supper? Who says *that* anymore?"

"I do," he said with a smile.

"Apparently," she said, letting up. "Thank you, but I've got a huge deal I'm trying to close. I don't think I should.

I've already taken a half-day at work today. Give me your number. I'll call you, and we'll go for lunch the next time you're in the city."

"No we won't."

"What do you mean?" she asked, though she knew exactly what he meant.

Jack stared at her in silence, making Carolina even more uncomfortable.

"Okay, fine." Carolina was surprised at how quickly she conceded, but such was the power of Jack. "One drink."

"One drink," he repeated.

"And I need to be back by *supper*," she said, smirking.

Back in Jack's bedroom, Carolina suddenly remembers where the Chinese food came from—it was supper. None of the food had actually been eaten, as Jack had ended up being Carolina's main course. It was as if she was in high school all over again.

*Fucking mojitos!*

Carolina places one foot on the floor and slides down to the soda-stained carpet. With her teeth clenched, she crawls on the floor picking up her various articles of clothing along the way—by the time she reaches the door, she's fully dressed and holding her Marc Jacobs shoes in her left hand and her purse in her other. Jack doesn't move a muscle. It would be another perfect exit to yet another regrettable mojito-infused adventure. As she stands at the door she takes one last look at Jack as if to remember it for the rest of her life. Suddenly, her BlackBerry begins to vibrate. Carolina quickly rummages through her purse to silence it before waking Jack.

The caller ID reads "Ron." She quickly hits the ignore button and flees Jack's bedroom. Safely outside, she begins the long walk back to Eightieth Street, not exactly certain where she is. Rain begins to fall. She doesn't care, doesn't stop. If she has to, she'll call a car service to drive her back to her parked car. Right now, she needs this time to think, to clear her head, to process what happened.

*A model?* How could she have fallen for that line? He was so transparent. *I'm a model all right—a model idiot.* But it doesn't matter. She'll never see him again. It will be painless.

But one thought troubles her. Even more than the rain that is drenching her, or the fact she'd so easily fallen into bed with a man she hadn't seen in fifteen years. That one thought was this: Of all the emotions running through her mind at that moment, not a single one was guilt.

# rise and shine

t's seven thirty in the morning and Clinton Street is by all
accounts desolate save a lone busboy scrubbing down the
sidewalk with soapy water. The residents that populate
the quiet street off East Houston are primarily artists,
writers, designers, and musicians. For this particular Lower
East Side set, half past seven is an hour that is more commonly associated with their second hour of sleep. Nine-to-
fivers are as scarce as a doorman building on Avenue B. But
on this quiet street, on this quiet morning, seated inside a
tiny Chinese restaurant, three sisters wait unenthusiastically for their breakfast.

Since Anna started at the salon, Sofia has regularly scheduled breakfasts or lunches, depending on their schedules,
so the three siblings can reconnect. She thought it would be
good for Anna especially, considering everything that was
on her plate. Unfortunately for her two older sisters, Sofia

declared that Hunan Café was one of New York's best-kept secrets—according to *Daily Candy*. This was the latest in a long line of unusual meals that Sofia arranged: an early-morning Ethiopian breakfast of injera at Queen of Sheba, doughnuts for lunch at Kitchenette, and a Southern breakfast of fried chicken and eggs at The Pink Tea Cup. Carolina and Anna both winced at the idea of eating Chinese food for breakfast, but to indulge their kid sister, they had acquiesced.

Carolina's motivation for trekking this far downtown isn't for the dumplings. She needs to stop by the Canal Street market to buy a Marc Jacobs Catherine Clutch. There's a little five-by-five-square-foot box on the corner of Canal and Lafayette that has the best knockoffs in the entire bazaar. Sometimes, Carolina convinces herself the bags are actually real and had just been stolen off a truck, an urban legend that many a Manhattan lady believed. The bag is a gift for Bethany Evans, the wife of Ron's coworker, Luke. Carolina would place the bag in a Marc Jacobs box that had previously held her own *authentic* patchwork clutch and pass it off as the real deal to Bethany. No one would ever suspect, nor would they dare to question its authenticity. In fact, Carolina is certain that this practice was more common than anyone cares to admit. Carolina is sure the Louis Vuitton bag she'd received as a gift, from the wife of another one of Ron's coworkers, isn't worth more than the canvas bag it came in, and probably less.

Thirty-five dollars is as much as she will spend on dear

Bethany, who had so poetically said to Ron after a night of too many glasses of Veuve that she thought it was so sweet he was dating "outside of the box." Carolina was forced to hold her acid tongue since Luke was a member of Ron's firm. As trivial as it may seem, the idea of giving Bethany a designer imposter fills Carolina with sheer and absolute delight.

Carolina stares at Sofia's crinkled copy of *Time Out* that rests on the tiny table. She lets herself wonder for a moment whether or not it would be a good idea to tell Anna and Sofia about her indiscretion with Jack. For the last few weeks, Carolina attended every social event with Ron. She was swamped at the salon, but her sense of duty forced her to be on his arm. But those feelings were soon replaced by resentment. *Haven't I done enough penance?* Carolina never considered herself to be an adulterer. But she wasn't exactly married. *People have casual sex all the time. What he doesn't know won't hurt him.* She felt she was reciting lines from a *Cheating for Dummies* handbook in her head.

She lifts her eyes from the magazine and focuses on Anna and Sofia, who are now in the midst of conversation. *I'm a horrible human being. I cheated on a man who loves me unconditionally. They would never understand.* She tries to put the idea of a confession out of her mind. She has a great life: her own company, an amazing boyfriend, and two sisters who, despite everything, respect her entirely. But Jack is in her thoughts. Not at the forefront. But like a toothache that can't quite be pinpointed, he's there. Lingering, throbbing.

"I can see why they kept this place a secret. I certainly

wouldn't tell anyone I've eaten here," Anna says, and laughs, bringing Carolina back into the present.

Sofia grimaces and looks around the tiny room, then up at the office-style ceiling tiles only a few feet above her head. *There must be asbestos in here.* She turns her attention to the floor. The deep brown linoleum is severely worn, and the pattern resembles the color of feces that had been set afire and stamped out. The walls are plain but look freshly painted.

"I honestly think we just beat the morning rush. *Daily Candy* raved about it," Sofia says, trying to sound more certain than she really is.

"I hate to point out the obvious, but it's clearly not one of New York's best-kept secrets anymore if you read about it in *Daily Candy*, now is it?" Carolina quips.

Sofia's face falls. She looks down at her wonton soup, feeling somewhat defeated. It had never occurred to her that the other 8 million people living and eating in New York had also been let in on the "secret" thanks to the daily e-mail. Suddenly, her cherished new discovery has become as murky as the greasy film floating on the top of the soup.

"Furthermore, why are you trusting *Daily Candy*? Do you know the type of people that work at *Daily Candy*?" Carolina continues.

Sofia and Anna shake their heads.

"Bookish intellectuals who have an axe to grind because their chick-lit book treatment got turned down for the eleventh time by every publishing house in New York,"

Carolina vents. "Ugh. I need a cigarette." She clearly hasn't gotten over the crass way the Web site described Impresarios as "the place society women went to get rid of their mangy lady beards."

"Okay, I get it. So it's not Sarabeth's," Sofia says. "And a cigarette? It's not even eight o'clock."

The Upper East Side brunch institution that is known for exceptional homemade fare—especially their chocolate-chip scones—Sarabeth's had once been a regular spot for the girls. But even Carolina and Sofia had stopped going after Anna received numerous icy stares from parents because of Ariel, who during that time still looked like a boy wearing girl's clothes. Carolina wasn't particularly upset about the discrimination that her young niece had received; she was more peeved that she no longer had any children to accompany her to the restaurant. To fit in with the Sarabeth's brunch set, you either needed to bring your kids or rent your neighbors' offspring.

"Rough night?" Sofia says, noticing Anna's frequent yawns.

"I was on Skype with Lunetta last night. She was showing me what she learned in Pilates last week," Anna says.

"And?" Carolina asks.

"I had to make her stop. The combination of her short shorts and her legs being stretched abnormally wide was too much for me. I could practically see her ovaries," Anna says.

"OMELETS?" The host appears and screams in a thunderous voice, startling Anna.

"I think I just lost my appetite," Anna says.

"Why is he asking? We're the only people in the restaurant, of course they're for us," Carolina says, not caring that the small Chinese man is standing less than a foot away from her. He sets the three giant omelets on the table and walks away.

"*Bon Appetit!*" Sofia says with a smile. Sofia looks down at her plate and, out of the corner of her eye, notices Anna rubbing her left leg. "Oh my God!" she yells.

"What?" Anna asks, petrified.

"Your leg!" Sofia says, pointing at the round pale calf.

"I know. I need a touch of self-tanner. But honestly, cut me a little slack? I'm a mother, Sofia, I don't have time."

"Don't play the *mom* card," Sofia says. "Please."

"I'm just shocked you're not wearing pants," Carolina tosses in.

"I wasn't talking about self-tanner." Sofia pauses. "What exactly is that on your leg?" Sofia says, her face crunched, utterly grossed out.

Anna looks down at her calf and notices a thin layer of schmutz. Summer in New York also meant no socks or hose—and thus no protection from the elements, no buffer between one's skin and the mysterious rainbow-colored puddles, various pieces of garbage, and unidentified floating objects that clung to any piece of exposed flesh.

"What is that?" Sofia gasps.

"I don't know! I stepped in a puddle on my way out of

the subway station. What do you want me to do? I wiped it off as best as I could."

"I think we have disinfectant wipes in the supply room on the—"

"Third shelf. I know. I stocked that supply closet for a week with Kiki," Anna says.

"I hope you don't show up to work on clients like that," Carolina says.

"I'm not a *pig*, Carolina. I don't like to roll around in mud and shit all day, if that's what you're implying."

Sofia smiles, then after a momentary delay, Carolina smirks.

"Oink. Oink," Anna says. The three women burst into laughter at the absolute absurdity not only of the farm animal noises but of the entire morning. For each of them, the laughter was a welcome relief to the chaos that was their lives, particularly of late.

"What time are you seeing *her* today?" Carolina asks.

"Right after this," Anna says, taking a bite of her scallion omelet that smells oddly more like Kung Pao Chicken than eggs.

After the photo shoot, JJ began sporadically booking house calls with Anna. Each time Candace snickered that JJ had made yet another appointment, it left Anna and several staff members to wonder what JJ could possibly have left to wax. No one was quite sure what to make of it. But thanks to these frequent visits, JJ was in effect paying for

Stagedoor Manor, a summer theater camp in the Catskills that Fabiana had begged to attend. Until recently, Stage-door Manor wasn't a remote possibility. But thanks to JJ's generous tips, Fabiana left in less than six weeks. There was no doubt that Anna made money; she just didn't make enough money to pay her half of the mortgage, plus bills, and the day-to-day expenses of three kids. Then there were the doctor's bills for Ariel: medical and psychological.

"She must be like one of those hairless cats—what are they called?" Sofia asks.

"Sphynx," Anna replies.

Anna wasn't about to tell anyone that JJ often had her wax the most obscure areas, a few stray hairs on top of her knuckle, her underarm, her right middle toe. She was working her way up, she'd often say playfully, and a bikini wax was the top.

"The sphynx called me personally," Carolina says. "She's paying double the rate so there wasn't any way I could turn her down. It wouldn't make financial sense. Plus, even I know better than to tell her no," she says, unconsciously lining up her fork and spoon for the twenty-third time.

*Does anyone ever to tell the rich no?* Anna thought. Since she'd met JJ, Anna had heard on more than one occasion from several different people that no one dared answer JJ in the negative.

"I think it's sweet. Maybe she just wants some company," Sofia interrupts. When Sofia first learned of the sphynx and her sister's frequent visits, it terrified her, primarily because, despite having never met the woman, she secretly felt a strange kinship to JJ. Sofia knew what it was like to live practically alone, and was afraid that when she was JJ's age, she would make up reasons for someone to come visit. Except in Sofia's case, it wouldn't be her bikini waxer; it would be the guy who delivered vanilla cupcakes from Billy's Bakery.

"Company? Is that what you have with your new gay boyfriend?" Anna asks, reaching across Carolina for the salt.

Sofia swallows hard, embarrassed by the insinuation of anything . . . *inappropriate*. "He's not my 'gay boyfriend.' He's simply someone to hang out with."

Carolina looks at Anna, then back at Sofia. "And what the hell are we?"

"Don't even try it," Sofia says, and smiles. "You're always working, and Anna's with her kids all the time. It's nothing but harmless fun; we literally had one drink and had brunch the following weekend."

"Sounds like a gay boyfriend to me," Anna goads.

"Can you pass me the soy sauce?" Sofia asks.

"That's something I thought I'd never hear before noon," Carolina says.

Sofia takes a sip of her green tea and gets lost in thoughts of her time with Dennis. Her trip to the "Garden of Ono" party at the Hotel Gansevoort a few weeks earlier was the most fun she'd had in a long time. The attention she received from the throngs of gay men was just the right amount of a healthy ego boost that she'd been craving for the last six months. The crowd was decidedly downtown: a smattering of men in bright-colored fedoras, and though a few emo gays donned eyeliner, for the most part the bar was filled with lots of beautiful men with gargantuan biceps and perfect pecs, and surprisingly a lot more men in T-shirts and jeans than Sofia had expected. Apparently the gay fabulosity had traded in their Dior for denim.

Expecting to find Dennis in some great shirt by Tom Ford or at the very least John Varvatos, Sofia was aghast when she saw him walking toward her in a tight-fitting tattered gray tee that read I SHAVED MY BALLS FOR THIS?

Dennis saw the astonishment written all over Sofia's face as he reached her. "I wore it for you," he said, and flashed a mischievous grin. "I looked everywhere for an 'I *waxed* my balls for this,' shirt but sadly none exists. Impresarios should consider starting a line."

"You've got some jokes up your sleeve, I see," she teased. "Been saving up all day?"

"I'd say I have a lot more up my sleeve than jokes, but we both know you already know that," he said. "Acai margarita?"

"I don't know what you just asked me, but I understood the margarita part, so yes."

"It's a margarita with crushed acai berries. They're these wonder berries from the Amazon that have a shitload of antioxidants in them. So the way I look at it, the berries cancel out the toxins in the alcohol, so it's a wash."

"Meaning?" Sofia asked.

"Let's get drunk!" Dennis said, ushering Sofia to the bar.

And drunk they got.

Three acai margaritas later, Sofia found herself at a banquette surrounded by a group of twentysomething men discussing home décor and remodeling—her favorite subjects. She compared the merits of a trusty dishwasher like GE instead of going for the obvious flashier Viking brand. Scott wanted the Viking, but Sofia insisted on the tried-and-true GE model, she told her new friends. The table was made up of a cross section of occupations, from a marketing director for Sony Music to a snarky celebrity blogger who had just scored a six-figure book deal. Sofia was fascinated to meet such innovators and creative types.

Sofia had found a certain security and kinship among her new gaggle of gays. *This feels nice.* She couldn't remember the last night she was out with someone other than Scott, or her sisters. It felt fresh. She could be anyone she wanted to be.

But old habits died hard, and as she looked down at her phone to find a text message from Scott, her face lit up, and she longed for home.

*"Hey. Just got home. Feels weird when you're not here. Hope you're havin fun. Luv u. xoxo, S."*

Dennis returned from sneaking a cigarette and a phone call and saddled up next to Sofia. He turned to no one in particular, and asked, "Isn't she the best?"

"Love her!" a fair-skinned blond with a Southern accent declared.

"No, you don't understand," Dennis slurred slightly.

"This girl rocks. And I can say that because she's seen parts of me up close that only the select few have seen."

"Okay, on that note we're going to the bar," said a husky voice from the corner. His name was Billy, and his New York Giants T-shirt showed off his perfectly sculpted body. He was by far the sexiest guy at the table, Sofia thought. "You want?" he said, looking her dead in the eye.

*I want you not to be gay and for me not to be married*, Sofia buzzed in her head.

"Sofia?" Dennis nudged.

"Oh. No thanks," she said, smiling. Dennis nodded, and the rest of the flock left the banquette and followed behind him.

"Finally, a moment alone," Dennis sighed.

"Thank you."

"For what?" Dennis asked.

"For breaking me out of my rut," Sofia said. "I get so caught up with work and home that it's easy to forget about me, and what I like," she confessed.

Dennis nodded but remained silent.

"I was hoping to get to meet your other half tonight," Sofia said. "Is he as gorgeous as you are?" she said, leaning into his chest.

"He's out of my league," he said, staring blankly into the crowd.

"No one is out of your league. But that's sweet. I have to meet this guy."

"You will. I promise. He's not really one for bars. Besides, I told him I wanted to hang out with my friends tonight and not have to worry about entertaining him."

"Excuse me, Miss Independent!" Sofia said with a sassy tone.

"Did you really just reference a Kelly Clarkson song in conversation?" Dennis asked, aghast.

"I did."

"Go. Get out of my sight. We can't be friends anymore," he said, straight-faced for only a moment before bursting into laughter. "Are you ready to head over to Hiro for a little dancing? I was thinking we'd stop by Marquee first—mix it up with *your* kind for a bit before dancing with the gays."

"Dancing with the gays? Is that a show on Bravo?" Sofia said.

"I LOVE you! I think we were separated at birth!" Dennis said, beaming.

"I'm going to go home. I think I'm feeling more of the margarita and less of the acai." Though she had a great buzz and could have stayed for another two hours, she had, before leaving her apartment, made a single rule for herself: She would only venture to gay establishments. Nowhere else. Any other place would make Scott worry and could only be harmful. She was happily married, after all, so what good could come from being drunk in a club full of horny straight men? Sofia scooted out of the banquette, kissed Dennis on the cheek, and thanked him for a great night.

Walking slowly in her heels from Ninth Avenue up to Eighth to catch a taxi uptown, she began to sweat through her new sundress. She couldn't tell if it was the alcohol or the sheer excitement of being out, but despite the heat and her aching feet, Sofia felt invigorated. While life with Scott was all that she'd dreamed of as a girl . . . there was something aching. Perhaps this was the problem: *My life is the dream of a young girl.* Something in her felt as though Dennis had lifted her out of herself. Something deep within had been awakened. And once you've had an awakening, there's no turning back. Even she'd read Chopin.

The next morning, a Monday, like a young woman after a really great date, Sofia anxiously waited for him to call her, constantly checking her BlackBerry in between—and a few times during—appointments with clients. Awaiting a text, an e-mail, a call from Dennis. Then at two thirty, while she was sculpting a lightning bolt on a young nineteen-year-old cosmetic heiress, he called.

"Sofia?" Carolina nudges.

Back at Hunan Café, Sofia finishes sipping her green tea, and says with a glint in her eye, "Okay, fine. Maybe, he's my gay boyfriend."

"Ya think?" Anna says. "You just had an out-of-body or something."

The waiter places the check on the table, along with a lone fortune cookie for the three of them. He disappears into the kitchen before anyone can say a word.

"What kind of a Chinese restaurant asks customers to split a fortune cookie?" Anna asks.

"I'm e-mailing *New York* magazine later to tell them that

this place should be on their 'best of the worst list,'" Carolina says.

"Oh, let's just see what our fortune is and get out of here. It's bad luck if you don't," Sofia says. Carolina throws two twenty-dollar bills on the table, covering breakfast and the tip.

"And none of us need that," Anna says.

Carolina grabs the cookie, tears off the plastic, and neatly places the wrapper under the saltshaker. She reaches for the small serving plate that was unused and cracks the cookie with her fist. She hands each sister a piece.

"Read the fortune!" Sofia says excitedly.

Carolina pulls out the tiny piece of paper, and reads aloud, *"A bold adventure is in your future."*

The three sisters avoid eye contact with one another as they gather their things, each thinking more than the others could know. Their minds already elsewhere, one by one they file out through the tiny door and onto Clinton Street, leaving the cookie on the table, and imagining the adventure that lay ahead.

# Seven

## you send me flying

Pacing outside of JJ's town house, Tim, JJ's fetching young attorney, yammers the obligatory "uh-huh" and "yes" every half a second into his BlackBerry, incognizant of anything around him. He pauses momentarily in front of JJ's stoop and faces the door, wondering when Her Highness will be making her entrance.

As he stares at the cracked black paint on the trim around the door, Tim detects a distinct yet familiar lemony smell. He tries as best as he can to concentrate on his call but can't place the scent, and it's driving him crazy. He puts his one free hand into his heather gray pin-striped pants pocket and closes his eyes. Tim inhales deeply, hoping he'll be able solve the riddle. This time, the lemon has been replaced by traces of vanilla and jasmine, and he's still unsure of its origin. Then like a neon sign emerging out of a black, desert night, it hits him.

Tim whips around in a flurry to find Anna standing behind him, holding a cup of coffee. In his haste, he knocks the hot coffee onto his pin-striped pants.

"DAMN! THAT'S HOT!" Tim shouts.

"Oh my God! I'm so sorry! Oh my God!" Anna says frantically.

Tim covers the phone with his hand. "It's okay. It's my fault."

"I didn't want to interrupt your call, so I was just going to sneak past you and go into JJ's, I, well, I'm so sor—"

"Really, it's fine," Tim says, and looks down at his thigh, now sopping wet. Despite the discomfort, he somehow manages a smile.

"Yes, I'm here," Tim says into the phone, recomposing himself. "I had the contracts sent by messenger to Patricia yesterday." He turns the phone away from his mouth. "Don't worry about it. These pants are really old." He teeters between bursting into laughter and shouting from the pain, but suppresses both urges, and speaks lucidly into the cell. "Yes, I said I'm here."

Judging by their pristine condition, Anna surmises the pants can't be more than a week old. She stares, thoroughly mortified, at the large wet stain on Tim's thigh, and begins searching her bag for something to absorb the coffee. She finally finds a small packet of citrus-scented antibacterial Wet Ones, sits down on the step, and without so much as a second thought, begins to blot the top of his thigh.

As consumed by her task as Tim is by his conversation, neither she nor he hear the door to JJ's town house open. As Anna dries Tim's pant leg, JJ stands peering down at the both of them.

"Jesus Christ! At least let him buy you dinner, girly!" JJ caws from the top of the steps. JJ had taken to referring to Anna as "girly" over the last several weeks.

Anna's head snaps up, and Tim spins around, his pants darkened from the coffee.

*No. She. Didn't,* Anna thinks. *Could this be more embarrassing?*

JJ slowly descends in bright pink, loose-fitting, lululemon drawstring pants and a black long sleeve T-shirt, a slim grin desperately trying to emerge from her tight lips. "With what his firm charges, I thought I was the only one getting screwed around here!"

Anna flashes a nervous smile as her face turns a deeper crimson.

Tim looks down, slightly embarrassed, and grins at Anna. *God,* she thinks, *I could live in those dimples.*

"It was just . . . I spilled my cof—" she begins, then cuts herself off. "Nothing I could say at this moment could possibly make you stop, could it?"

JJ is enormously pleased with her comedic timing and laughs so hard she has to steady herself against the wrought-iron railing.

"Not a word," JJ says.

Anna fixates on JJ, not sure whether she should push her

down the steps or join in her laughter. As she contemplates her choices, Tim sneezes repeatedly.

"Luke, I-I'm going to have to call you back," Tim says into his phone just before he sneezes once more. This gives JJ a reason to continue to guffaw. She's now seated on the third step with teardrops splattering her cheeks.

"Are you okay?" Anna asks.

"It's the perfume in the wipes. I'm highly sensitive to smells," he says before beginning yet another round of sneezes.

*I must have killed my entire family in a past life to deserve this.*

Tim pulls a handkerchief out of his back pocket.

"I'm so sorry," Anna repeats.

"Really, it's fine. Don't worry about it. I should've been paying more attention," Tim says.

"Did you bring the papers?" JJ shouts from the stoop.

"Yes—" *Sneeze.* "Yes, ma'am," Tim calls back.

Anna's brow crinkles. "What's going on?"

"Don't make an old lady walk down there," JJ chides. "Can't you two sons of bitches come to me? Don't let the sweatpants fool you. I'm old, and I'm lazy."

Anna looks at Tim and shrugs. Being the well-mannered gentleman that he is, Tim lets Anna go first, then follows a step behind. Anna sits down next to JJ on the stoop while Tim stands in front of them. He is dashing in his two-button charcoal suit, the image of professional perfection, save the awkward damp spot.

*His eyes practically sparkle against that purple button-down shirt.* Anna is lost in the moment, staring at Tim. She hears nothing else but the breeze ruffling through the street's perfectly pruned trees.

"Hello? Are you listening, girly?" JJ says, and nudges Anna's arm.

"What? I'm sorry. I guess I'm a bit out of it today," Anna says.

"Think maybe those sweatpants are cutting off the circulation to your brain?" JJ teases.

"Speaking of, why did you ask that I wear them?" Anna says, before turning to face JJ. "I had a heckuva time explaining—"

"Well, girly, if you'd been listening, you'd know why. It's the fuck-it list."

"The fu—" Anna starts, then stops, embarrassed to say the word in its entirety in front of Tim. "You were serious about that?"

"There's one thing you should've learned by now. I hate bullshit. I'm allergic to it. Makes me sneeze. Metaphorically speaking. I will not eat it, and I will not feed it."

Anna turns to Tim, whose eyes meet hers for a moment. She quickly averts hers.

"It's true. She hates bullshit," Tim confirms. Opening his Jack Spade messenger bag, he withdraws a stack of papers and hands them to Anna.

"What's this?" Anna asks, flipping through the pages.

"It's a contract, genius," JJ chimes in.

"I can see that, but what does it have to do with me?" Anna says, and cocks her head.

"This agreement basically has granted us, I mean JJ, your exclusive services for the next eight weeks," Tim explains.

Anna's eyes bulge, and her mouth opens widely.

"Now that's not a face I'd do too often if I were you, girly. Really not your best look," JJ says.

Anna quickly closes her mouth and collects herself. "Eight weeks? My services? But there's not a hair on you left to wax!" Anna says, turning to JJ again. "Well, except—"

"Easy there, bushwhacker, you're not going to be waxing me or my lady bits. You're going to be helping me with my fu—" Tim furrows his brow at JJ. "Oh, God, I'm surrounded by prudes. Fine, my 'eff-it list,'" JJ says daintily.

"But Carolina will—" Anna argues.

"Ms. Impresario was sent a sizable check that more than covers the hourly rate that you'd typically receive for a full day of clients over the course of the next eight weeks," Tim adds. *A full day of clients?* Anna thinks. She'd yet to book the entire day, but they didn't know that.

"So how much?" Anna asks with a hint of defiance in her tone.

"I'm sorry?" Tim asks.

"How much did my sister sell me out for?"

"I don't think that really is important . . ." Tim begins.

"Fifty K," JJ blurts out.

"OH MY GOD!" Anna can't help but scream. She quickly covers her mouth like a child who's just been scolded.

"Really. We must work on your subtlety," JJ says in blasé fashion.

Anna's strategically placed hand conceals the fullness of her grin, but the evidence is apparent in her sparkling eyes. The sisterly part of Anna wants to be furious at Carolina for pimping her out before consulting her. *Does she think I have no integrity?* But her ego quashes that argument before it begins. *Integrity is a luxury only the rich can afford!*

Anna removes her hand from her mouth. "Do I need to sign some sort of paperwork or something?" Anna asks no one in particular.

"Oh, no. Ms. Impresario signed the paperwork. Since she's your employer, we contracted you through her, and she assured us that you'd have no problem with the arrangement," Tim says, shifting his weight from left to right.

"I bet she did," Anna says under her breath.

"But there is this one thing we *do* need you to sign," Tim says, his tone slightly higher.

"It's a release form," Tim explains. "It basically removes any personal liability to JJ in the case of an injury or death."

"INJURY? DEATH?" Anna yells, standing up from the step. "I don't know what you have planned, but I'm a mother, Mrs. Powers!" Anna quickly corrects herself. "JJ. And I cannot do anything that could leave my children without their mother. They've been through too much already. I'm sorry, but you'll just have to pay someone else at the salon to complete your list with you." Anna is quick with her words, and her reaction is visceral, almost as if she's rehearsed a similar speech before. She walks down the steps and onto the sidewalk, silently walking toward the corner.

JJ shakes her head in dismay. She looks at Tim, who shrugs. "I told you we didn't need any stupid waiver. Now go get her. I'm too old to be running up the street. And I'm lazy. Plus your pants need drying—they could use the wind."

Tim doesn't hesitate, hurrying down the tree-lined block.

"Anna!" Tim shouts.

*I like the way he says it*, she thinks, but continues walking. She's overreacted, she knows, but can't quite figure out how to backtrack.

"Anna, wait!"

She stops and turns. "Stop chasing me, Tim," she says, completely aware of how little she means it.

"Thank you. You're too kind. This way you don't have to witness just how painfully out of shape I truly am. The brilliance of this suit is that it hides a lot of imperfections," Tim says.

Anna laughs. "Sorry. I just . . ." She pauses to collect her thoughts. "It's just that my kids are the most important things in my life, and I want to protect them from as much pain as possible." Anna leans against a redbrick building and feels its sandy texture, slightly warm from the mid-morning sun.

"It's okay. I get it. And I don't want you to do anything you don't want to do. You can walk away from this at any time. Neither JJ nor I, especially me, would never want anything to happen to you," Tim says, leaning gently against the side of the building.

*Especially me?*

"No, I'm sorry, it's fine. I'm being a baby. Just what does this lady want to do that could possibly get her and *me* killed?"

"Nothing. Trust me, I wouldn't even let her do half of that stuff on that damn list from *New York*. Everything is very tame. Trust me." Tim leans in closer. "I just have to protect her. I *want* to protect her. She's like family to me, you know? You could be some crazy litigious nutjob. A very sweet nutjob, but a nutjob nonetheless. I just want to make sure that while you're on whatever adventure with JJ that if you break a nail or an arm that you won't turn around and try to take everything this woman has. Do you hear what I'm saying?"

"God, you're a tough negotiator. Playing the sentimental card. I'll sign the friggin' thing," Anna says, straightening herself and leading Tim back down East Sixty-third.

"I do try," he says.

"So where are JJ and I going today?"

"Antigravity class," Tim deadpans.

Anna stops. "Antigravity? Those people that hang from what looks like bedsheets from the rafters of extremely high ceilings?"

Tim nods, a smile on his lips.

"Whatever happened to 'Everything is very tame, Anna,' 'Nothing to worry about Anna'?"

"You'll be fine," he says, touching her shoulder. A rush of warmth runs to her face. "You'll have the nets to catch you while you're suspended above the ground doing your hanging backbends, handstands, and aerial somersaults."

Antigravity was fine today. She already felt like she was floating.

"I really, really don't like you," Anna says, completely aware of how little she means it.

Back on solid ground, Impresarios is as frenzied as a blender on "liquefy." The reception area buzzes with the sounds of women, and a few men, shouting into their cell phones, the chimes of text messages, and the dings of BBMs. The reception staff attempts to conduct this technological orchestra while maintaining smiles.

A few hundred feet away, Carolina methodically straightens up a recently converted treatment room in anticipation of her next client. Even under the camouflage of the standard beige robe, Carolina is still decidedly striking. Her hair is blown straight, and her eyes are smoldering behind her dark eye makeup. She's runway ready, except unlike most models, Carolina is not dead in the eyes. In fact, Carolina's eyes dance in excitement. With the imminent release of her hair-removal creams for Sephora, Carolina had begun taking appointments again in order to test out her new product.

As Carolina lights a candle under her aromatherapy oils, she hears a subtle knock on the door. Her rule at the salon is to keep the treatment areas quiet and peaceful. Impresarios may not be a spa complete with massages and seaweed wraps, but she wants to maintain the integrity of a salon environment.

"I have your twelve thirty here," Candace says softly through the door.

Carolina finishes smoothing out the creases in the sheet on top of the treatment table. She casually walks to the door and before reaching for the handle, as if on cue, she plants a half smile on her face to greet her next client. She slowly opens the door and begins to say "Hel—" when she abruptly stops and gasps. Standing next to Candace, with a yet another shit-eating grin, is Jack.

"Oh, you scared me!" Carolina says, trying to cover her surprise.

"But I just told you he was here," Candace says, puzzled.

"Mr. McLeery?" Carolina says, glaring at Jack, who nods appropriately but is obviously amused. "Thank you, Candace," says Carolina, calmly ushering Jack into the treatment room and quickly closing the door behind him.

"What are you doing Jack?" Carolina asks.

"What?" Jack says innocently. "I'm getting a wax, babe!" He quickly peels off his shirt to reveal his taut, muscular body. His perfect chest and the smattering of hair swirling between his pecs momentarily diverts Carolina's attention.

"But how did you know I was taking clients again?" Carolina asks, averting her eyes, with much difficulty, from his skin. His unclothed body in front of her is like a bottle of Grey Goose in front of an alcoholic. *God, he smells good*, she thinks.

"I took a shot," he says, shrugging, and hops onto the cushy table.

"McLeery? Where'd that name come from? Sounds like you're straight off the boat from Ireland."

"I knew you wouldn't take the appointment if you knew it was me." He lies down on the table, as if it were his couch. "Do you need me to take off my pants, too? Because, you know, I'm happy to do so." He smiles cockily. Normally, Carolina would have found his arrogance intolerable. However, with Jack it was painfully adorable.

"Don't be cute. Since there's not a bottle of tequila in sight, nothing's going to happen."

Jack's face falls. He appears genuinely stunned and more than a little bit hurt.

"Are you going to wax me, or am I going to have to leave a negative review of the salon on Citysearch and Yelp? I'd hate to ruin your perfect five stars."

Carolina is taken aback, flattered that Jack took the time to read about her business. She feels herself weakening and tries to cut it off with a tone far less warm than her skin. "What are you doing here, Jack?"

"Well, I thought I was getting a wax. Do you prefer me smooth or with some hair?"

"Neither," she says coldly, pretending to look at something urgent on the laptop she brought from her office. She furrows her brow for dramatic effect. "Why are you here?"

"What did you expect to me to do? You won't return my phone calls or my texts. I wanted to see you. Is that such a horrible thing?" he asks, turning on his side to face Carolina.

*Stay strong. God, stay strong.*

"And what if someone saw you?"

"No one knows who I am except your sisters—and I haven't seen them since we were teenagers."

"This is a salon. When a hot man walks in, *everyone* talks about it," Carolina retorts.

"Hot, huh?" he says cockily, and turns onto his back again. "I'll take it." He rolls his head back and forth and practically beams.

"What?"

"Nothing," Jack says maintaining his shit-eating grin. Carolina cocks her head and stares him down. "It's nice to know I still got it, that's all. Hot is not something usually connected to a guy my age. A guy in his twenties, maybe early thirties, but not at for—" he says, then suddenly stops. "It's really cool is all that I'm saying."

"Okay, Mr. Hot, you want a wax? A wax is what you'll get." Carolina knows that the best way to resolve the current dilemma is to get Jack out of her salon as quickly as possible. Jack stretches out full plume on Carolina's table as if he were posing for *Playgirl*.

"Take off your pants," she says, sounding like a clinician rather than someone who'd shared a bed with him. Jack is taken off guard. He hadn't actually expected Carolina to wax him. He'd come for dinner and a movie, not hair removal and a rash.

"Oh, I get it." He sits up, a bit nervously. "This is all just a ploy, a plan to see me naked."

"Been there, drank the tequila, and made that mistake," Carolina says, without facing him. She opens an unmarked white jar. "Take 'em off, cowboy."

Jack reluctantly unbuttons his jeans, slowly, one button at a time. He rubs each button, feeling the texture underneath his fingertips. Jack notices Carolina stealing glances as she prepares her cart and takes extra time with the two bottom ones, seductively caressing them before finally unhinging his pants.

Carolina's mouth goes dry. She tries to swallow, but can't. She quickly reaches for her cup of water and brings it to her mouth, her hand trembling.

*Don't look. Do not. He's not superhuman. STOP LOOKING! Oh my God. What is he doing?*

Jack runs his thumb under the waistband of his jeans and slowly pulls them down. He goes a little too far, pulling his boxers down slightly.

*Give me strength*, she prays, but the strength is not given. When Jack looks down, she stares at his boxers.

"What in the hell is *that*?" Carolina says, pointing. "What is that you're wearing?"

"What do you mean?" he asks. Carolina points at him again. "They're called boxer shorts," Jack says flatly.

Carolina takes a step closer and looks down at his dark eggplant-colored boxers. "Are those what I think they are?"

"Airplanes," Jack says proudly, grinning like a twelve-year-old.

"Airplanes? I'm sorry, I didn't know they make Underoos for adults." The sultriness of Jack's ministriptease had gone as quickly as it had come.

"They're J.Crew, funny girl. And what's wrong with airplanes?" Jack says in a faux huff.

"Nothing," she says, looking down at him. "If you're eight."

"Hmm," he says, looking down at his boxers. "I've never actually measured, so I can't tell you for sure that it's eight. Maybe seven and half?"

"You're beyond incorrigible!" Carolina says, and slaps him in the stomach.

"Ouch!" Jack yells.

"Seriously, look into some sort of shock therapy."

Carolina would never have admitted it, but Jack looked adorable. The way he smiled, how he furrowed his brow when he was frustrated, the way he held her eyes. She wasn't going to get into the game of comparing Jack and Ron; that was pointless and dangerous. But she knew Jack always made eye contact when speaking to her. In fact, when they were in the same room together, he never took his eyes off her.

"Why didn't we ever . . . ?" Jack begins.

"Oh God, is this the part where you're going to get sentimental because if it is, I might have to jump out a window to my death," Carolina says and moves the canister to the table.

"I'm serious. I remember we had sparks, but I was the one trying my hardest to fan the flame. You had to go and ruin everything by wanting out of Queens," he says, and smiles. Before waiting for Carolina's response, Jack looks at the unlabeled jar, and says, "Wait, are you sure this stuff is okay to put on me?"

"You're in luck, my friend. Today you are my very own lab rat," Carolina says, pointing over to a small box containing several similar jars. "The manufacturer sent these samples over today." Jack nervously bites the side of his cheek, a habit he's had since they were freshmen in high school. *The man of steel is nervous.* Carolina revels in the fact that she has the upper hand on Jack. He's vulnerable, and she likes it.

"I have to try it on someone—you don't think I'm going to send this to Sephora without testing it out on an actual client, do you?" Carolina says.

"If it helps you make a hundred million, then burn me, baby," he says. "Anything for you." He watches her scoop the lotion out of the jar and stares back at her face. "Why didn't we ever make another run at it? You know me, unequivocally. You're the only person I have ever completely opened up to."

"First, you're stalling. Second, you opened up quite *literally* to what was her name? Sasha? Olga? Claudia? I know it's something Russian," Carolina says flippantly. "By the way, did you save your receipts from the time you spent with her? I think in some states you can write off a hooker on your taxes."

"Don't be cute. I was a stupid kid back then, and you were ready to move on and get out of the neighborhood." He turns his attention away from Carolina's eyes, wounded by her quick dismissal. CNN plays on the ceiling television, installed to distract the clients from the pain of the wax; for most of Impresarios' customers it took only a little Anderson Cooper to help them forgot where they were.

"My apologies," she says halfheartedly. She realizes that Jack's still silent and that she may have actually hurt his feelings. She finally offers, "Thank you. I appreciate the gesture."

"Now that you mention it, what *was* her name? I should look her up again," he says, and laughs.

"Maybe she'd give you a discount for return customers. And I'm sure she must need a green card by now," Carolina says, with a snicker.

"That's the thing I've always loved about you."

"My startling wit?"

"That the clothes may change, the bank statements may grow exponentially, but at the heart of it—you're still just a tough girl from Queens," he says, and sighs.

Even though he meant it as a compliment, hearing Jack reduce her to a "tough girl from Queens" feels like a punch in the gut. She instantly snaps back to business-owner mode. "So are we going to do this or not? I'm booked solid and don't have time for this."

"I'd hoped you'd forgotten," he says, flashing that trademark grin.

"Lie back," Carolina says. Jack leans back on the table and stares at the miniflatscreen placed on the ceiling, wondering why Anderson Cooper's eyes are so small. He closes his eyes and clenches his face, panic-stricken by the idea of the little hair he had on his chest and stomach being removed with a mystery cream. He lies waiting for something to happen . . . but nothing does.

Carolina stares down at Jack, her eyes move up his legs, past the airplanes, to his stomach and chest and bite-sized nipples. *What the hell am I doing?* she thinks. *Ron is a good man. And I—I'm not that woman.* Carolina ponders this, a multitude of questions distracting her from the task at hand.

Through clenched teeth and with closed eyes, Jack speaks. "If you're going to do it, do it now before I change my mind."

Before he could utter another word, a soft pair of wet lips presses against his own.

Soon, the little airplanes were off and flying, crash-diving onto the floor.

Where are you?" Scott asks into the phone.

"I'm leaving this restaurant in NoLita called Delicatessen. It's really cool—we have to come here," Sofia says loudly, shouting over Euro-lounge music that sounds to Scott like something off one of his Hotel Costes CDs.

"We have a delicatessen around the corner from our house. Why do we need to go all the way down to NoLita?" Scott says, toying with her.

"Funny," she says, sounding more irritated than she meant to.

"So you're on your way home?" he asks.

"Well, actually that's what I was calling you about. Would you be upset if I stayed out a little longer? Dennis really wants me to go with him to this party, but I promise it won't be a late night," she says.

"Oh, well . . ." He pauses. "I guess I'll have to eat these chocolate-chip cookies I just took out of the oven all by myself."

"WHAT? You didn't!" The one and only meal Scott knew how to make was dessert in the form of the premade roll of chocolate-chip cookies he got from D'Agostino's. Even he couldn't screw up slicing them and putting them in the oven for twelve minutes. He was inordinately proud of them.

"I did," he says, and laughs loudly like a child. "I even got the roll with the M&M's in them. Your mom told me they're your favorite."

"You spoke to Lunetta?" Sofia says.

"Briefly. She called me to see if we were still alive since she said you hadn't returned her last three calls."

Sofia sighs loudly but attempts to remain upbeat. "Why

didn't you tell me you were doing dessert night? We haven't done that in months!"

"Because you weren't expecting it, that's why. That is—I mean, that *was*—the fun of it," Scott says, his voice trailing off. "But now . . ."

Despite the loud electronic beats blaring at Delicatessen, Sofia hears something strangely familiar. "What are you doing?" she asks.

"What do you mean?"

"Are you trying to make me cry?" Sofia says, her voice cracking. "Billie Myers?"

Billie Myers had provided the soundtrack for a weekend in Key West a few years ago that Scott and Sofia relished. They checked into a picturesque bed-and-breakfast just a few blocks from famed Duval Street. Unfortunately, the couple arrived the second week of August, which, as any Floridian will attest, is high hurricane season. Sofia had been looking forward to feeling the warm sand under her feet and a cool, plush terry-cloth towel against her skin. It wasn't mean to be: The rain started to fall within thirty minutes of their arrival, and it didn't stop. Scott refused to let it ruin their trip, however, and he had a surprise waiting for Sofia when she returned from getting coffee. With the help of the inn's owner, Scott had lit more than thirty tea lights that he had strategically placed around the large bedroom. He had borrowed table linens from the kitchen and set the small coffee table for a romantic dinner. Sofia, still soaked from the tropical storm, walked into the room and let out a gasp so loud it made Scott nearly lose his balance. Dressed in the wrinkled suit that he'd brought with him, Scott pressed play on the CD alarm clock, containing the only CD in the hotel—one accidentally left by the room's last occupants. It was Billie Myers's *Growing Pains*, and the song was "You Send Me Flying." Sofia wept while it played, and Scott took his hand in hers, then placed her arms around his neck as Billie sang the chorus: "You send me flying, flying over the moon for joy." He grabbed her waist, and as they danced, Scott did what seemed like the unthinkable. He proposed.

The song still makes Sofia emotional, and she's sensitive to it in a way she is with no other song. She can recognize it by two of its notes, and she recognizes it now, currently playing in the background of their apartment. "Oh!" he said. "I didn't even realize. I just put my iPod on shuffle."

"Uh-huh," Sofia huffs.

"What? I'm serious," Scott says. "What did you have for dinner?"

"Cheeseburger spring rolls," she says in a contemplative tone.

"Cheeseburger what? That sounds . . . nice, I suppose."

"Maybe I'll come home," Sofia says.

"I'm not going to tell you what to do. But . . ." Scott teases. "But what?"

"I've got freshly baked cookies, Billie Myers, and a healthy appetite for something other than Toll House," he says, punctuating the request with a voice of pure sex.

"Well, in that case . . ." Sofia begins. At that moment, Dennis returns to the table with his friend Miles. "One second, babe," Sofia says into the phone. She unconsciously covers the phone so Scott can't hear her conversation.

"You ready?" Dennis asks devilishly.

"Well, I'm not sure . . ." she starts.

"Come on! You wanted to go five minutes ago. What happened?" Dennis interrupts. He looks down at Sofia's phone. "Ah, I see. Your husband. When are you going to have some fun? I'm sure he won't mind. Here, let me talk to him," he says, reaching out his hand for the phone.

Sofia contemplates letting Dennis speak to Scott, but quickly decides against it. *I'm a grown woman. I can tell my husband that I'm going to have a night out without him.* "No, I can do it. You're right. What's one night?" she says, and smiles.

Dennis turns to Miles. "Do you not *love* her?"

"Love," Miles concurs.

Sofia takes her hand away from the phone. "Babe?" she says.

"I'm here," Scott replies cheerily.

"I'm going to go out with the boys only for a bit. But I won't be late," Sofia says, desperately, trying to assert her independence. "I promise."

"Oh. Okay, then. No worries. Have fun."

"Thanks," Sofia says, standing up and following 'the boys' through the bustling crowd to the exit.

"I love you," Scott adds.

"What?" Sofia shouts, straining to hear over the noise from the nearby bar.

"I love you," he repeats.

"Babe, I'm losing you. I'll see you when I get home. Bye!" Sofia puts her phone back in her bag and heads out onto Prince Street, where Miles and Dennis are waiting.

Still uneasy about declining Scott's invitation, Sofia feigns a smile, then asks, "Ready, boys?"

"Wait!" Dennis exclaims and stops walking. "Do you still have that bottle of water in your purse from the deli?" he asks Sofia.

"Yeah, but it's lukewarm at best, and there's like three sips left. Why?"

Dennis runs ahead of Miles and Sofia and ducks into a vestibule. Sofia and Miles catch up to him.

"What was that about?" she asks.

"I think I know where this is going," Miles interjects. Dennis smiles like the Cheshire cat. He digs into his pocket and returns with a closed fist.

"Open," Dennis says, and stares at Sofia's hand. She opens it and he drops a small white pill in her palm. He repeats the favor with Miles.

"Oh, God. Really? What are we, nineteen? Ecstasy's not my thing. Actually, no drugs are." She hands the pill back to Dennis.

"Are you sober?" Miles asks.

"What? No. I just never had an interest," Sofia explains.

"Please—just this once," Dennis pleads. "I swear to you,

you'll be fine. I'll be with you the entire time. It's going to be incredible!"

"I don't know. It's just not me," she argues.

"I don't think you really know who 'me' is," Dennis retorts. "So why don't you give this version a try?"

"Just how many versions of you are there?" she asks and smiles. Dennis flashes her his best little-boy-lost look. Sofia lets out a loud sigh, and asks, "Where are we going?"

"It's this really amazing loft party. Fabulous straight girls like you, and lots of gays obviously, and I heard Marc Jacobs is supposed to be there—Come on!" He can see her weakening. "I think it could be a really great bonding experience for us. Take our friendship to the next level."

"I wonder if this is how Alice was convinced to go down the rabbit hole," she says, and slowly holds out her hand. Dennis grabs it excitedly.

"I think she was high as a kite! Open your mouth!" he says, giggling.

She complies and he drops the white pill on her tongue. She takes the bottle, sips, and swallows. What girl this was, she did not know.

Three hours later, Dennis and Sofia are in the middle of a makeshift dance floor in an enormous Chelsea loft. Thundering dance music blares from the speakers and a well-known DJ is in command of the turntables. A hundred or so beautiful gay boys, models, and downtown scenesters decorate the industrial-loft space. No Marc Jacobs sighting yet, but Sofia and Dennis don't care. They haven't stopped dancing since their Ecstasy kicked in hours ago. Dennis was right: Sofia hasn't ever felt closer to him than she does at this moment.

"I'm so glad we met!" Dennis says, as genuine as he can be while off his face.

"Oh my God! Me, too!" Sofia says and hugs Dennis tightly. Miles had disappeared a few hours earlier with a young Brazilian visiting from São Paulo. "You've brought me back to life!" Sofia says, still gripping Dennis.

"I love you," Dennis says, and squeezes Sofia back. "You're amazing!" He breaks away from her hug and sways to the cavalcade of beats, disappearing into a crowd of shirtless boys.

*I love you, too.*

Sofia grabs a bottle of water and sits down near the huge floor-to-ceiling window overlooking the Hudson. The bright light from the moon bounces off the water, and the music suddenly seems far away. She looks up at the moon, and closes her eyes.

She was flying, over the moon.

## Eight

# keeping up appearances

Anna's Banana Republic pants are hot and clingy, and she deeply regrets the choice. When she got dressed this morning, she'd thought Pier Sixty-Two would at least offer a few degrees of relief; it is directly on the Hudson River, after all. But not today. Not a chance.

Anna didn't understand why they couldn't do this on a much cooler day, and more importantly on a *weekday*. But JJ had insisted. When she called this morning and said that today was *the* day for "the screamer," the fact that it was Anna's day off didn't seem to matter. *New York* magazine had proclaimed the Chelsea Screamer, a speedboat that "splashed and dashed" around Manhattan, the best solution for cooling down when the thermometer reached over eighty-five degrees. *Fucking New York* magazine, Anna thought. She'd have canceled her subscription in protest, but she didn't actually subscribe to any magazines.

Anna would like nothing more than to be home right now in a pair of baggy shorts, a loose-fitting T-shirt, the air conditioner on full blast, sprawled out on the couch watching a *Real Housewives* marathon on Bravo with a box of SnackWells. Hell, at this point she'd even prefer to be at the salon, putting up with insults from Kiki.

"Why do people go outside in this sort of weather?" JJ shouts to Anna from a bench under a nearby awning. Anna, waiting in line to purchase tickets, pretends not to hear her. It's too hot to listen to complaints. "Hello, girly! I know you can hear me!"

Anna's patience is decreasing in direct relation to the rising temperature. She whips her head around, ready to spew fire and venom, but quickly reconsiders. "I'll be over in a minute. I'm almost to the front." The line moves Anna out of earshot.

The ticket-booth cashier, a girl no more than a few years older than Fabiana, text messages on her phone without acknowledging Anna. Anna coughs loudly enough for the young woman to finally look up from her phone, annoyed of course.

"Two please."

"Twenty-two," the ticket taker says with as little energy as possible.

Anna's cell phone rings before she can hand over the money. She rarely receives calls on her cell, and her first thoughts run to the object of greatest concern: Ariel. *Something happened to Ariel at school. Oh God.*

Anna will never forget the day that Fabiana brought

Anna's youngest home from a nearby park, covered in blood. Anna had not yet allowed her son, Matt, to dress as a girl. However, that didn't stop him from rubber banding one of Anna's old, grimy dish towels around his head to pretend it was his long hair. This, coupled with his constant playing with all of Fabiana's old dolls vexed both Anna and Christopher. Every time Christopher hid the dolls, not only did Matt's emotional state change, but physically he turned gray, devoid of any life. Anna persuaded Christopher to come up with a compromise until they figured everything out. Matt was forbidden to wear the rag outside of the house, and his father demanded that he never play with Fabiana's dolls again in public. While Fabiana was off talking with a girl-friend, Matt took out the two Barbie dolls that he had hid in his backpack and began playing with them openly. He was sitting on the end of a seesaw with his toys lined up in a row when three twelve-year-old boys started calling him a "girl" and a "faggot," a word Matt was too young to know the meaning of but old enough to sense the immense anger behind it. Within seconds, the boys threw him off the seesaw and onto the rocky pavement splitting his forehead wide open. Then they kicked him. He was four years old. Fabiana screamed at the boys and sprinted toward Matt, but by the time she reached him it was too late, and the boys had fled. Fabiana had been unable to forgive herself ever since, and Anna never got over his bloodied image. When the phone rang, and Ariel was not in her line of vision, the panic returned.

Anna rapidly digs through her purse. The caller ID reads: JJ. *What the hell?* Anna cranes her neck to see JJ on her cell phone.

"Oh, Jesus, it's you. Hello?" Anna answers, befuddled but relieved.

"See if they have seats in row seven. Row seven is said to be the best," JJ says, reading from her prized copy of *New York*.

"Row seven. Got it." Anna balances the phone between her shoulder and her ear, and plucks the cash from her wallet. "Do you have anything available in row seven?" Anna asks the girl behind the window.

"It's first come, first served."

Anna speaks into her phone. "Sorry. It's first come, first served. Is that okay?"

"Come on, girly! That's the best you got? A five-year-old negotiates better than you," JJ taunts. "I would've never have made a splash onstage if I'd had your resolve."

"Onstage?" Anna asks.

It was long rumored yet never actually confirmed, until now, that the legendary JJ Powers was once a New York City showgirl. If Anna only knew the kernel of gossip that had just been revealed, she could have made an extra five hundred bucks with one quick phone call to Cindy Adams.

"It was a lifetime ago," JJ says. "And that's all I'll say." Anna knows it's in her best interest not to follow up in this instance.

Anna puts the twenty-two dollars on the counter. "Isn't

there something you could do?" she says pulling out an additional twenty-dollar bill.

"Hey, lady! Are you going to buy a ticket or talk on your friggin' cell phone?" a man with a distinctive Long Island accent yells out behind Anna.

"Mind your business!" Anna shouts without turning around. She may be polite, but she won't be pushed around by random strangers. Anna looks at the ticket-booth girl, and says, "So, can you help me out?"

"Twenty bucks? Really?" the girl goes back to her cell phone.

Anna sighs and pulls out another twenty. *If you were my daughter, I'd take that cell phone and smash it up in front of you.* "This is my final offer. I know for a fact this job can't pay more than six-fifty an hour and these extra forty bucks could buy you forty more applications for that phone of yours." The young girl looks up, her interest piqued. *Bingo. Who knew that arguing with Fabiana over cell-phone charges would actually pay off?*

"Row seven?"

"Row seven," Anna says.

"I'll tape two reserved signs on the boat. Sit there," the cashier says. She hands Anna two tickets, and Anna throws them in her purse along with her cell phone, and returns to JJ.

"Forty bucks?" JJ asks. "Are you friggin' kidding me? Why didn't you just give her the keys to your house?"

"Next time, *you* can stand in line and do the negotiation."

"Next time, *you* shouldn't listen to an old lady," JJ says, and shakes her head.

"I thought you wanted to sit in those seats," Anna says, exasperated.

"Yes, but money isn't going to solve the world's problems, girly. That's the problem with this country."

*Says the woman with an estimated worth of 70 million dollars*, Anna thinks.

"You could've told the little bitch I was dying, and you were fulfilling my last wish. You could've said you were going to be fired if you didn't get those seats. You could've said you had lice, and we could've had the whole row to ourselves," JJ continues.

"I'll keep that in mind next time," Anna says through gritted teeth. She wipes her brow and turns her back to JJ for a brief respite. Anna looks toward the Hudson River Greenway, a stretch of pavement along the Hudson filled with bicyclists, Rollerbladers, and joggers. *I'd kill to be walking with the kids on that pathway right now, like we did when Christopher . . .*

"What in God's name?" Anna says.

"What?" JJ says. "Is the boat leaving without us?"

"No," Anna says, flummoxed. "My daughters are here."

"Your daughters?" JJ says with surprise.

With JJ standing next to her, Anna watches her girls from under the awning in total disbelief. Fabiana, dressed in short shorts and a white tank top, dodges Rollerbladers and bikers that zoom by at breakneck speeds. Ariel, who stands nearly to Fabiana's waist, wears a pair of Anna's old Anne Klein sunglasses that nearly cover her entire forehead. Ariel looks like a miniaturized Anna—*Anna Wintour*, that is. Ariel pulls up the strap on her pink tank top and adjusts her silver ballerina skirt as if she were about to be photographed for *Vogue*. She stands proudly beside her older sister, watching and mimicking her every move. She places one hand in Fabiana's and the other on her doll. To the casual observer, she looked the quintessential little sister tagging along with her annoyed big sister.

"What happened? Is someone hurt? Where's Michael?" Anna shouts.

"Mommy!" Ariel runs over to her mother and hugs her leg. Anna rubs the top of Ariel's head.

"Hi, sweetie!" Anna says to Ariel, feigning a smile to give off a calm front. Then she turns to the hellcat. "Fabiana, I'm waiting."

Fabiana rolls her eyes and looks back at her mom. "He's at his baseball game with Daddy. Don't you remember?"

"Is something else wrong? What are you not telling me?"

"No, Mom. God. Everything's FINE, all right?" Fabiana says.

JJ abruptly stands up. "I am JJ Powers, and I'm the only bitch around here. You want my title, you'll have to wait until I croak." Fabiana, made speechless by JJ's brashness, simply stares. Anna's anger lessens, and the terror threat of red is lowered to orange thanks to JJ's sharp tongue.

"JJ, my daughters, Fabiana and Ariel," Anna says.

"I like your necklace," Ariel says, pointing to JJ's Van Cleef necklace, worn daily as though it were costume jewelry.

"Well, you can't have it," JJ says sternly, without cracking a smile. Ariel's eyes widen.

"Fabiana." Anna nudges her eldest.

"Hi," Fabiana says flatly.

"Hi," JJ says, mirroring her exact tone.

"Is that goddamn boat ever boarding?" JJ complains before sitting back down on the bench.

Anna turns her focus back to Fabiana. "If everything is fine, then why are the two of you here?" Anna asks, her anger growing again. Fabiana shrugs.

"You had better start talking. And now. Because not only am I angry that you came into the city without permission, but you also brought your little sister. Do you know what could've happened? Do you know how many sick people are out there? People who could want to hurt you or your sister?" Horrific thoughts flood Anna's mind as she begins to pace back and forth. Anna imagines an amber alert with both girls names emblazoned on it. "I hope you have a good answer."

Fabiana is resigned in her silence.

"Well?" Anna asks again.

"Mother," Fabiana hisses. "I told you before, I'm meeting Joelle and Blaire at the movies later."

"Oh, this one's got an attitude. Charming," JJ chimes in from the bench.

"Fabiana!" Anna says, raising her voice. Anna looks around

at the throngs of people walking in and around Chelsea
Piers. She's not one for a scene, especially in front of JJ.
Anna looks down at Ariel who's holding her Bratz doll,
then shifts her eyes to JJ.

"Would you mind sitting with Ariel for a minute while I
speak to Fabiana privately?" Anna asks. After she asks, Anna
feels a pang in her stomach. She wonders if JJ will realize
that Ariel was born male. What would she think? Will she
call Carolina and request someone else? *No. There's no need
to get worked up.* For all intents and purposes, Ariel *is* a girl.
*Surely, JJ has kids of her own, probably even grandkids.* Anna
quickly looks at JJ on the bench to reassure herself. *I'm sure
JJ is good with kids.*

"I suppose, but you should know I don't particularly like
children," JJ says.

*Or not.*

"Thanks, I'll keep that in mind," Anna says, and grabs Fabiana by the arm and pulls her a few feet away near the dock.

"OW!" Fabiana yelps, more for melodrama than actual
pain. "What, are you going to throw me in the river now?"
Fabiana huffs.

"Way too many witnesses," Anna barks. Fabiana turns
her back on Anna and looks out at the Hudson. *I am even-
tempered and emotionally stable. I am one with the universe.*
"What is going on with you? I ask you to watch your sister
for one afternoon, and you can't do it?"

"It's not fair. It's Saturday. All my friends are hanging
out, and I'm—"

"Do you think I want to work on Saturday? I'd rather be having drinks with your aunt Sofia right about now, but I'm here working." The truth was as of late her weekend brunch drinks with Sofia had all but disappeared. In fact, Anna barely had seen either of her sisters lately.

"Oh, get over it, Mother," Fabiana says. Anna takes a step forward so she can look her daughter in the eyes. Fabiana instantly looks away. She quietly mumbles, "Lately I've been working just as hard if not harder than you."

"I don't know what you even mean by that," Anna says with calm control. "And I don't know what is going on with you, but you need to get over it, and you need to get over it real quick, miss," she continues.

"What's gotten into *me*? I have a 4.0 GPA and have not missed one day of school. Have you already forgotten what you and Daddy nicknamed me when I was in the seventh grade?"

"Of course not." Christopher and Anna christened Fabiana with the moniker "four-point" after her first semester of junior high. The running family joke was that she was "their little nerderella," a self-effacing nickname that Fabiana herself had created.

"I don't cut gym or snort Adderall in the bathroom stalls, I don't flash my boobs in my MySpace photos, and I'm not giving blow jobs during PE like Lanie Youngman. So I would say, for the most part, you're pretty goddamned lucky that I am only occasionally bitchy considering you've been a nonparent the last eight months." Fabiana folds her arms and shakes her head. She's so mad that she's afraid, fearful of what may come out of her mouth next.

*Note to self: Tell Lanie Youngman's nosy mother, Joann, this tidbit the next time I run into her at Target.*

"You want to talk about nonparent? Where's your dad? *That's* a parent to you? Let me remind you that I've been working at Impresarios so that *you* can go to theater arts camp upstate, so *you* can have a cell phone, so *you* can have spending money . . ." Anna takes a step closer to Fabiana, and leans into her face. She's close enough to smell the sour-cream-and-onion chips on her daughter's breath.

"I'm not talking about working for Aunt Carolina. I just wouldn't consider going on a boat ride around Manhattan a 'job,'" Fabiana says, and takes a step to the left—perhaps to maintain some physical distance, perhaps to dodge a potential smack across the mouth. Even though Anna has only spanked Fabiana once in her entire life, Fabiana knows she was treading on dangerous ground. "I'm talking about the months before you started work," Fabiana continues. "Who do you think got Ariel ready for school when you didn't want to get out of bed after Daddy left? Who do you think signed permission slips for Michael when all you did was sleep? Who do you think lied to Grandma every time she called from Florida? ME."

Anna attempts to form a sentence, but her mind won't form the words.

Fabiana persists. "Do you know how many mornings I'd come into your room before school and ask you if I looked all right, and without even lifting your head off the pillow, you'd say, 'you look fine'?"

"Because I know you're a beautiful girl, Fabiana. You could wear a Glad bag and look incredible. It's not because I didn't care or don't love you."

"It would've been nice to hear *that* at least once before school," Fabiana fires back. "But I guess your 'medi- cine . . .'"—Fabiana makes air quotes—". . . made you too tired to speak."

"My what?" Anna's insides felt like they were imploding at the very suggestion that she was some kind of drug ad- dict. She would never classify herself as a pill popper. So she leaned on a few antidepressants during a particularly dark two months. Was that a crime? And so on two occasions she "leaned" quite heavily. It didn't make her a bad mother. *Did it?*

Fabiana ignores her. "Ariel is not your only child, you know. Did you ever stop to ask Michael and I how *we* were doing?"

"That's not fair. I asked! Of course I asked!" Anna searches her mind. *Did I ask?* She was certain she asked daily. *Did I ask enough?*

Fabiana smirks. "You really have no idea."

"Then give me an idea," Anna argues.

"How do you think it feels to walk down the hallway at school and hear kids refer to your family as a bunch of freaks?"

There it was. It had been confirmed. Anna's deepest fears were a reality. Sofia and Carolina had warned her about these kinds of scenarios, and even of the threat of physical violence with other children, but she had refused to hear it. Anna thought her older kids could take care of themselves in the off chance that problems arose. It was Ariel that concerned her—the mental and physical well-being of Ariel, a loving environment for Ariel, a safe world for Ariel.

"Then there's Brian Pellicani," Fabiana says, continuing with her rant.

"From the neighborhood? Little Brian?" Anna says.

"Megan and Kate told me to wait in the cafeteria after lunch because they heard Brian was going to ask me out. I couldn't believe that, after all this time—seeing him at birthday parties, at the bus stop, and summer barbecues—he was into me." Fabiana momentarily smiles.

"Fabi . . ." Anna begins.

"I waited in the empty lunchroom, and after five minutes I was sure he wasn't coming. I was pissed. But when I grabbed my books to go to fifth period, Brian walked up. I seriously thought I was going to, like, throw up. Do you want to know what he said to me?"

Anna did nothing. It was not really a question. She shook her head slightly. "No."

"Brian Pellicani asked me if I was an 'it' too. He and Frankie Gravali had a bet going, and I was the only one who could settle it for them. He said maybe my mom had let me be a girl, too, when I was Ariel's age, and that I really had a dick under my skirt."

"Stop!" Anna gasps, waving her hand in front of her face. "I can't hear any more! Fabiana, I—"

"Then he stretched out his arm and reached up my skirt," Fabiana says.

"No . . ." Anna says, biting her lip.

"He stuck his hand in between my legs. My body was as stiff as a stick, I felt like I'd break if I moved. He stopped for a minute, like he wasn't sure what he might find, but just to be sure he stuck his finger in me. Right in the middle of the cafeteria. I wanted to scream, but who was going to believe *me*? Everyone already thinks I come from an insane family, and they'd think I was making it up."

"Why didn't you tell me?" Anna says softly.

Fabiana ignores her. "Before he ran off to class, he said, 'I guess I win the bet.'"

"Fabiana—" Anna reaches out to hug her.

"Don't," she says, pushing her away. "If I want to go see a movie and escape the fucked-up thing called my life for a few hours with Joelle and Blaire, I'm going to do it." She stares at her mother for one long second, a moment of silence to punctuate the soliloquy. And then she walks away.

"Fabi," Anna calls quietly, without anger or authority, too softly for her daughter to hear. She doesn't try to stop her, and within a few moments she has disappeared into the crowd. Anna stands at the railing in silence.

"They're boarding the screamer," JJ says from her spot on the bench. "We better go." JJ holds Ariel's hand as if Ariel was her own, but the sweetness of the moment is lost on Anna. Her head is with Fabiana, even though her body stands on the pier. The unusual trio walks toward the boat without speaking.

Anna reads a sign on the cashier's window. "I don't know that I'm up for this anymore, JJ. And anyway, we only have two tickets and the sign says it's sold out."

"If you've learned one thing about me in this time we've spent together," JJ says, "it should have been this: Nobody tells me no."

Too broken to argue, Anna follows JJ and Ariel onto the boat, to the two seats reserved in row seven. Ariel immediately sits on JJ's lap and studies her emerald-and-gold necklace with a great deal of intensity. Seconds later, the uniformed employee asks for their tickets and JJ hands over the two stubs. The man looks down at the three, then catches JJ's eye. He moves on casually to the next row. Anna, still reeling from her collision with Fabiana, did not notice the hundred-dollar bill folded between the two tickets.

Money isn't going to solve the world's problems, but there are moments when it's magic.

Ariel inspects every last piece of jewelry on JJ. Feeling like she has to say something about Ariel, Anna leans over to JJ. "I should tell . . ."

"She's a very well behaved young lady," JJ says, and winks.

*She couldn't possibly* . . . Anna says nothing else. The boat pulls away from the pier, and the engine roars, the thundering noise strangely calming to Anna. Had the events of this day happened eight months ago, Anna would have reached for one of her prescription pills. Not today. Today she had her own version of Xanax: the sun on the Hudson, Ariel happy, and the company of a friend.

"You take the good with the bad, girly, you should know that by now," JJ opines, as the warm breeze begins to hit her face. " 'The web of life is a mingled yarn, good and ill together.' " JJ pauses and straightens her sunglasses. "That's Shakespeare, girly. I couldn't agree with him more."

"Were the two of you childhood friends?" Anna says, and finally breaks a smile. JJ cackles, the wind carrying her laughter across to the Jersey shore. Manhattan's buildings look small and plastic, the city's complications a continent away. As the boat gains speed, and the water laps the sides of the boat, she closes her eyes.

*Faster. Go Faster.*

Dell'anima, the West Village's hottest Italian restaurant, is filled with New York's usual suspects: waiflike models and the Wall Street men who adore them, hipster socialites who dress as if they are homeless and in desperate need of a hot bath, and a smattering of fabulous gay men. It's loud. It's chaotic. It's perfect.

Carolina needed a place where she and Ron could double-date with Sofia and Scott, and where conversation could be kept to an absolute minimum. After forty-five minutes of making grueling small talk at the bar, the couples, led by Carolina, walk to the small outdoor seating area and, as per usual, all eyes in the room turn their focus toward Carolina as she saunters through the crowded eatery.

"You know your hot spots, Carol," Ron says as he pulls out Carolina's chair. *Carol? Are we really doing this tonight? Stop—don't be such a bitch. You're the one cheating.* In an embarrassing and stereotypical Italian accent, Ron continues, "*Dell' anima*," that means 'of the soul' in Italian." *There's a bitch slap from irony. God, I am the worst human being on the fucking planet.*

"I've been wanting to try it for a while since it's so close to the salon. I wish they'd relax the smoking laws in this city," Carolina says. She takes in her fashionable surroundings. "It's no big deal really. Its just a little neighborhood trattoria," Carolina says, unconsciously aligning her silverware and water glass.

Normally, Sofia would pick up on her sister's shaky voice and trite explanation. But Sofia's mind is not presently at the dinner table, but on her new gaggle of gays—especially the gaggle's ringleader, Dennis. She only catches the last bit of Carolina's answer and responds in kind.

"Calling this place a neighborhood restaurant is like calling Barneys a place to buy socks," Sofia says, looking out onto Jane Street and Eighth Avenue. Dell'anima's bustling bar scene overflows nearly onto the street.

"Yeah, our diner uptown doesn't serve quail," Scott says, and laughs. "You're just too fancy for our blood, Carolina," he taunts. Carolina rolls her eyes. Carolina and Scott's relationship had been unpredictable and contemptuous since the first time Sofia introduced them. But that wasn't a bad thing. Their tête-à-têtes were actually a welcome relief to Carolina, and if there was one thing she could rely on to keep the evening interesting, it would be Scott's backhanded compliments.

As Sofia sips her acai margarita, her new drink of choice as of late, she remembers the first time Scott and Carolina met. He came to the salon to pick up Sofia. However, thanks to a seventeen-year-old perfectionist that demanded her boyfriend's initials be symmetrical on her vagina, Sofia was running twenty minutes late. A regular desk job this was not.

Scott had waited patiently in the lobby and aimlessly flipped through old copies of *People*. He overheard the receptionist refer to the woman with whom she spoke as Carolina. He remembered the name from prior conversations with Sofia and thought it would be the perfect opportunity for an introduction.

"Carolina?" he said.

"Hi. Yes?" she said, smiling politely as if he were a client of the salon.

"I'm Scott Carnahan. I'm a friend of your sister's, or rather, I guess she wouldn't mind if I told you, we're dating," he said, and smiled.

Carolina's facial expression dramatically changed. She looked as if Scott had just burped in her mouth. Whereas most would've been put off by Carolina's reaction, Scott didn't give a shit. In fact, Scott pretty much held his own with anybody.

"So what's your story?" Carolina asked him, while giving him the once-over.

"My story?" Scott replied with surprise and a tinge of annoyance. "Hmm . . ."

"Okay, if it's going to take you this long, I don't need and or want to know your answer," Carolina snipped.

"Actually, I'd like to think of myself as a great book. Each chapter gets more and more interesting the more you get to know me," he cockily explained.

"I'd stop here then and skip those chapters," Carolina said, and exited to the treatment rooms.

Thinking Carolina was out of earshot, Scott uttered, "What a bitch!" and looked at Candace, who pretended to be booking an appointment.

"I heard that," Carolina called from behind the frosted-glass door.

Always quick on his feet, Scott replied with, "And I meant you to!" A few minutes later, Sofia appeared.

Ever since that day, Sofia has found herself somewhere in the middle of a continuous stream of snarky comments volleying between her husband and her big sister. Essentially, both Scott and Carolina agree on one thing, that the other is too controlling of Sofia.

Tonight, Scott and Carolina are on par. But as Sofia sets

her drink on the slick tabletop, a realization dawns on her: Something, she thinks, is definitely off. She looks at Carolina, then at Ron.

*What the hell is going on? Carolina never invites both Scott and me to dinner. And with Ron? This must be major.*

Sofia reaches for the iPhone in her Marc Jacobs hobo bag and sets it on the table. As she's about to start typing on her keypad, Scott puts his hand on top of hers, subtly letting her know that she shouldn't be texting at the dinner table. Their eyes meet, Scott makes the most miniscule shake of the head, and Sofia takes her hand away from the phone. However, nothing goes unnoticed when Carolina is present.

"I don't mind," Carolina says, and looks at Sofia.

"What? Oh," Sofia says, a little bit embarrassed. "This thing is seriously addictive, I don't even realize that I'm doing it."

A second later, Sofia's phone rings. A rush of adrenaline washes over her at the thought of Dennis breaking her out of an awkward dinner. She glances down at her phone. LUNETTA. She hits ignore and rejoins the conversation as if the phone never rang.

"You know, there're studies that show checking your BlackBerry or iPhone is as addictive as alcohol, drugs, or sex," Ron interjects.

"But far more boring. I can't drink, snort, or fuck my phone," Scott says. "At least not the version I have," he adds. This gets a laugh from the table, even from Carolina. "Sof e-mails and text messages constantly. She texts when we're on the couch watching TV, she e-mails at the dinner table, she even sleeps with her iPhone in bed. Do you know how many times after it's fallen to the floor that I've almost squashed that friggin' thing in the middle of the night when I have to take a piss?"

"Scott!" Sofia says, embarrassed.

"Oh God, there's a visual I don't need," Carolina says.

"Anyway, she's always talking to someone, and something tells me I have you and Anna to blame," he says, looking directly at Carolina.

*What in the hell is this putz talking about?* Carolina thinks. *I think we've texted three times in my entire life, and Anna wouldn't know how to text if she had a gun pressed against her skull. What is going on here? Could the young suddenly have gotten restless?*

"Sisters always like to be in touch," Carolina says cryptically. "Ladies' room?" Carolina says, looking at Sofia, getting straight to the point. Sofia nods, and both women get up from the table and exit toward the back of the restaurant.

"You realize they're going to be in there talking about us, don't you?" Ron says.

"Oh, I'm hoping so," Scott answers.

At the back of the restaurant, Carolina and Sofia stand in a narrow hall and wait for the bathroom. Carolina leans against the wall, holding her Stoli on the rocks.

"You brought your drink with you to the bathroom?" Sofia asks, and arches an eyebrow.

"What?" Carolina asks, daring Sofia to comment.

"It's a bit weird is all, and borderline crazy."

"I look at it as being efficient," Carolina says, nodding at the bathroom door. She also knows that she needs a strong drink if she's going to make an even stronger confession.

Neither of them says a word; they'd prefer to grill one another behind the comfort of a locked door. The smoke from the open kitchen escapes in plumes and leaves the two with a new perfume: grilled sea bass. When finally the bathroom door opens, the ladies dart inside.

"God, at least she could've used the spray," Sofia says, grimacing and reaching for the air freshener.

"Don't. I'm already skeeved-out to be inside a public bathroom," Carolina says.

"What do you mean?" Sofia asks incredulously.

"I can count on one hand the number of times I've actually used public facilities in my adult life," Carolina explains.

"I never knew this about you," Sofia says, gobsmacked. *Explains the private bathroom in her office!* "I know you have your tics or twitches or whatever they're called. But no public bathrooms? Ever?" Carolina doesn't say a word.

Sofia squats on the toilet without another thought.

"All right. Go," Carolina says.

"Carolina, you can't order me to pee," Sofia protests. "And could you at least turn the other way. It's menacing."

"I don't mean pee. I mean talk. And don't play coy. I know when something's up."

"That's funny. I was just about to say the same thing to you. But only after I was finished peeing."

"Fine. I'm turning around," Carolina says, pivoting slowly and taking another swig of her chilled vodka.

"I just don't understand why you let him control you the way you do. Frankly, it's embarrassing," Carolina says.

"Controlling? Leave it to you to pick apart the sweetest man in Manhattan."

"I just hate to see you, you know, *shrink* when you're around him," Carolina says. If Sofia were being completely honest with herself, she would recognize that Carolina was partially right. She did shrink around him, but that was what she thought she *should* do. She'd seen the mistakes of both of her sisters in their prior relationships, and if being in a more traditional and supportive role to her husband made the relationship work, then Sofia was willing to play that role. Or she *had* been willing. Until lately.

"I don't 'shrink.' I just don't lead my husband around like a dominatrix, like you do with Ron."

Carolina is momentarily oblivious, staring at a photograph on the wall. The picture is of a vibrant pink living room marvelously decorated without a single person in it. Even an amateur art connoisseur would surmise the photo was there to represent the emptiness of material possessions if no one is present with whom to share. At least that was what Sofia sees when she glances at it briefly while trying to focus on her flow. Carolina, on the other hand, has a different take. *Olivia Wilder. It's clearly and unquestionably a room that Olivia designed. Is she coming in next week or is it at the end of this month?* Olivia Wilder is one of the world's most-sought-after interior designers. To those in the know, she's reached legendary status, often being compared to their Queen Mother of all things haute, Sarah Jessica Parker. But to Carolina, Olivia was a slight landing strip. Simple, clean, elegant. Like the rooms she decorated.

The flush of a toilet and the flow of a faucet's water snap Carolina back to the conversation. "Uh-huh," she says absently.

"So?" Sophia asks. "Why don't you just tell me what's going on with you? You never invite me *and* Scott to dinner—and you never bring Ron. So what's up?"

"You first: Who're you texting at all hours?"

Sofia laughs. "You make it sound as though I'm doing something below board." Carolina holds her stare on her sister. "What? It's nothing. A friend. Dennis."

"Uh-huh. Was that him calling a few minutes ago?"

"No, it was Lunetta," Sofia says dimly.

"Oh, she called me in the taxi on the way over. I haven't listened to the message yet. I'm sure Anna will be next on her hit list. Let her handle Lunetta," she says. "Now, back to your boy toy."

"He's *gay*," Sofia explains, drying her hands. "So that's that. Now, what's *your* story?" Sofia asks to avoid any follow-up questions.

Carolina takes another sip of her drink.

"Well?" Sofia asks again. "Is it Mom? Anna? The salon?"

Carolina takes a deep breath in and exhales loudly.

"I see you've picked up a few of Anna's breathing techniques when she wasn't looking," Sofia says.

"Stop talking," Carolina says softly.

"What?"

"If I'm going to do this, I need you to be quiet. Please, Sofia, just give me a minute," Carolina says as she paces in the tiny bathroom.

Sofia is genuinely worried. *She's dying. She's got cancer just like Daddy had and is afraid to tell me. Oh Jesus. I need some air. What are we going to do? We'll get through this.* "Carolina?" Sofia says gently.

"I-I can't believe I'm about to . . ."

BANG! BANG! BANG! on the wooden door. Both women simultaneously jump and squeal. The remnants of Carolina's drink flows through a maze of ceramic tiles on the floor before coming to a halt at the toe of Sofia's Stella McCartney knee boots.

"Hello? Is there anyone in there? There're people waiting out here!" a female voice calls out from behind the door.

"In a minute!" Sofia angrily shouts back. She stands with her back pressing against the bathroom door, and looks at her sister with worry. "Whatever it is you're going to tell me, you probably better do it now because I don't know how much longer I can hold off the pee police."

"I don't know if I should," Carolina begins. Then she folds her arms across her chest. "I might as well. It's so ironic that I should be telling you this here, in the toilet, when my personal life seems to be headed in that direction," she says.

"Come on!" the woman from behind the door shouts. Sofia stands motionless, waiting.

"I cheated on Ron," Carolina finally confesses. She walks to the sink, turns on the faucet, lathers her hands with lavender soap, and holds them under the faucet. She scrubs her fingers hard.

"You WHAT?" Sofia exclaims. "YOU? I can't even . . ."

"What about you? You made out with someone after you and Scott started dating. Don't think I've forgotten about Subway Guy," Carolina argues, fully aware of the weakness of her argument.

"So you're telling me all you did was make out with this guy?" Sofia asks.

Carolina focuses on her thumbnail and sees a speck of dirt underneath it, and maniacally soaps her thumb. "No." The lather is dense and spectacular. "We slept together." The speck of dirt disappears. "More than once."

"Unbelievable." Sofia fidgets. "This—this isn't you, especially with our family history. It feels too . . . what's the word I'm looking for?"

"Messy." The mirror steams up from the hot water.

"I was thinking low-class and cheap. But messy definitely fits."

Unwavering when it comes to infidelity, Sofia's loyalty was formed early, and by a demonstration of its opposite. She was the first to discover that their mother was cheating on their father—on a Monday afternoon, during a surprise visit to her parents' house in Queens to pick up some earrings and a faux-diamond necklace she had bought at her mother's jewelry party the previous weekend. Lunetta, the girls' mother, was always hosting some type of party—be it purses, makeup, or jewelry—to make a quick buck. Lunetta was as industrious as she was a free spirit. In Italian, her name literally translated to "moon goddess," and the title seemed to give her license to do everything but howl at the moon. People in the neighborhood often referred to her as "Lunetta the lunatic." Needless to say, her entire existence was an utter humiliation to Carolina. On that Monday, when she walked up the front steps and saw the man leaving through the front door, Sofia knew immediately. Her mother stood in the doorway in her robe. Sofia broke down instantly, weeping in the middle of their front porch at three in the afternoon. Eventually, after several hours, Lunetta confessed. Hours after that, Sofia broke the news to Carolina and Anna. Carolina made her sisters promise not to tell their dad. There was no need. He had just begun chemo, and that would have sent him to the grave even faster.

"I don't know. I got caught up," Carolina says, still scrubbing her hands.

"Caught up? You get 'caught up' at the gym. You get 'caught up' at Saks. You don't get caught up with some man's penis inside of you."

"He makes me feel different, appreciated," Carolina says, as much to herself as to her sister.

"Makes? As in present tense? Oh, this is rich. I don't want to hear any more because I'm already starting to feel like an accessory to your lies," Sofia says wildly. The lump in Sofia's throat grows. She feels as though she's spewing everything she ever wanted to say to her mother, but lacked the courage to. It wasn't Carolina's fault per se, but Sofia couldn't help the way she felt. "Do you know what kind of position you're putting me in? Knowing about all of your bullshit? It makes me feel as guilty as you should be feeling."

Carolina can't face her sister. She stares at herself in the mirror and speaks almost as if she's having a conversation with her conscious. "Ron isn't your family," Carolina says.

"Don't justify your deceit. Lies are lies, Carolina, plain and simple. And I'm not sure I can cover them up for you. I've done that once before in my life, and I can't do it again. So don't ask me to!"

"Sofia, stop! I didn't choose to have an affair. It happened. It's not like I'm married."

"Thank God for that!" Sofia shouts.

Another BANG! on the door. "Jesus Christ! There are people in pain out here!" the same woman yells from outside the bathroom.

Sofia opens the bathroom door and quickly marches past a tall brunette standing an inch away from the door. Carolina finally shuts off the water faucet and follows behind her.

"Oh my God!" the brunette gasps, staring at Carolina.

Carolina looks down at her hands. A deep magenta color, they're raw, scalded from the boiling-hot water.

"Are you okay? Do you want me to call someone?" the woman, suddenly concerned, asks.

"I don't feel a thing," Carolina says robotically.

The rest of dinner the boys did most of the talking, with Carolina and Sofia only interacting through their significant others. Any woman would have immediately picked up on the iciness, but the two unassuming men were more interested in debating the value of Alex Rodriguez to the New York Yankees to notice.

During the cab ride home from dinner, Carolina is lost in a wave of thought. *What am I doing? Ron is a good man. I'm not in high school anymore. Can't I ever be happy with what I have? How do I know Ron's not cheating on me? No. He wouldn't. He couldn't. He thinks more than he feels. I, on the other hand, feel more than I think—at least lately.*

"Carol?" Ron asks.

Carolina leans her head against the glass window of the taxi—something that, had she been in her right mind, she wouldn't have gone near without a gargantuan bottle of disinfectant.

"Hey," Ron nudges.

"What? Sorry," she says quietly.

"Is everything okay? You barely said a word at dinner— even to Sofia."

"I'm fine. A little stressed-out with work and the product

launch. I don't want to bore you. It's always the same with me, you know?" Carolina says and looks at Ron. *He is painfully adorable. His eyes are as sweet as they come.*

"Come here," he says, and lifts his arm.

Carolina nestles herself under Ron's arm and places her head on his chest. His pressed shirt smells of a mixture of sweat and Reve en Cuir cologne. As the cab continues on Eighth Avenue, a single tear falls from her eye. She holds back the flood that could follow it. The show must go on.

Shirtless, Scott lies in bed, his loose shorts draping his legs, his hands holding Paul Auster's *Man in the Dark*. Sofia shuffles around the bed nervously, looking for her phone. She spots it on the chair, where it fell out when she was unzipping her boots. She picks it up, notices she has a text message, and clicks the phone. It's from Dennis. "Miss you! ☺ Drinks tomorrow? XO DEN S."

Sofia feels a rush of adrenaline; she can't wait to see him again. She quickly types back: "Miss you too. Tomorrow sounds perfect. SOAPIA." Dennis had christened her with the name because of the soapy scent of the CLEAN perfume she wore.

Sofia looks furtively at Scott and places the phone back on the charger. She jumps onto the mattress, and Scott looks over at her and smiles for a moment, adoration in his eyes, before returning to the novel. Within seconds, the joy of Dennis's text is gone, replaced by Sofia's anger. She wants to say so many things, to tell her husband about Carolina, how it brought everything with her mom and dad barreling back. But she says nothing. She will keep Carolina's secret. She will be silent for fear of what might be said if she makes even a sound. So she kisses Scott on the lips and turns on her side and shuts her eyes.

An hour later, Sofia continues to toss in bed, her thoughts bubbling over, her speeches to Carolina growing longer and more pointed. But no matter how many insults she hypothetically hurls at Carolina, she is unable to break the mirror that Carolina held up to her. Sofia's anger isn't about Carolina or even their mom. Sofia is angry at herself, angry at her own guilt over her feelings for Dennis. She could tell herself it didn't matter, that because Dennis was clearly gay there was no threat. But there was more. A spotlight had been shone, and her own feelings of living an unfulfilled life revealed. Gay or not, Dennis makes her feel alive. And this fact terrifies her.

In the darkness Sofia moves over to Scott, cuddles into him, and eventually drifts to sleep. In her dreams, she sees her mother's house, a figure standing on the porch. It is her mother, but . . . not. It is Carolina, a glass of vodka in her red hands. A man walks out the front door. When Sofia wakes up a few hours later, she can barely remember, but is almost certain the man was Dennis.

## Nine

# shaken not stirred

Fall in New York is many things. It's strolling through Central Park in wonderment at trees so beautiful and colors so vibrant—the most potent of mushrooms couldn't produce a trip nearly as poetic. Fall is buying tickets to the New Yorker Festival, waking up early to cheer on runners in the New York City Marathon, and digging an old sweater out of the back of the closet to meet friends for brunch at Paris Commune. Fall is pumpkin spice lattes, gray Saturday mornings, and Diana Krall "Live in Paris" playing on repeat. But most of all, fall in New York is all about change.

Fall at the salon means a brief repose. Between the hell of bikini season and the mania of the holidays, the salon takes a deep breath and relaxes. Somewhat. Manhattan's finest still flock to Impresarios (where else would they go?), and the regulars come no matter what. But for the women who prefer that their vaginas take a trip to Brazil only during the summer, they tuck their passports away until next season.

Peering over a giant Mac flat-screen monitor, Candace is working the phones when Anna arrives. The receptionist's face is hidden behind the computer, but from what Anna can see, Candace looks alarmingly older.

"Impresarios, please hold," Candace says unenthusiastically into the phone. The feeling at the salon is akin to that of an apartment after an insane all-night party: Everyone moves a few steps slower, voices are gravelly, and headaches are rampant.

"Hi, Candace," Anna says, relaxed, almost breezy.

Anna had barely set foot in the salon over the last few months. JJ had occupied the majority of her time to complete "the list," and it had been an adventure thus far, to say the least. They traveled to Bristol, Connecticut, to ride a terrifying roller coaster built into the side of a mountain, did a round of speed dating in the East Village—to the horror of the young emo men—and bought their way into an illegal poker game on the Lower East Side. To date, though, Anna's personal favorite was the punk-rock pillow fight in Brooklyn. Two civilized women: a seventysomething and thirtysomething fighting amid tattooed and mohawked men and women on old mattresses. It was a sight to behold. Anna was initially petrified that she might crack a septuagenarian's bones, but true to form, JJ immediately nailed Anna in the face. And not with a grungy thrift-store pillow like the rest of the pillow fighters in the dingy Brooklyn basement. No, JJ brought her own pillow outfitted in Charlotte Thomas' Bespoke linens, the world's most expensive at twelve hundred dollars for a single pillowcase. To her credit, JJ scrapped with the best of them, and if it hadn't been for a hefty Asian woman, JJ might have been the last woman standing.

"Um, hi?" Candace is taken aback by Anna's casualness, a stark contrast to her normal popping knuckles, cracking voice, and awkward laugh. Candace places the phone on hold, suspicious of Anna's new energy. She gawks at Anna from her head to her waist—all Candace could see from her desk.

"I'm a little surprised," Candace says. "But, you know, in a good way."

Since working with JJ, Anna's style has improved tenfold. As an added perk to taking pillows in the face, Anna was on the receiving end of visiting *New York*'s best hair salons, private gyms, and nearly every specialized boutique known to women. Physically, Anna hadn't lost a lot of weight, maybe five pounds, but what she gained was more important: self-confidence.

"What do you mean?" Anna says, wanting to hear her say it.

"You look—dare I say it—*great*," Candace says begrudgingly.

"And that surprises you because . . ."

"You just strike me as one of those people who is destined to have some sort of tragic ending."

Anna feels her joints go rigid. *Tragic ending? What the hell is that supposed to mean?* She knew she was a bit scattered, but she never thought she came off as doomed to fail. *I express myself with great ease. With great ease . . .*

"Oh to hell with it, I don't need 'em anymore," Anna says aloud, referring her to her daily motivational chants.

Candace crinkles her forehead in confusion.

Anna quickly recovers and takes a deep breath, and says with a confident smile, "Maybe I'll just put that ending on pause for a while."

Anna rounds the corner of Candace's desk and places her hand on the door that leads to the waxing studio, allowing Candace to see her fall wardrobe from head to toe. A long cocoa-colored tweed skirt is paired with taupe Manolo Blahnik booties, which Anna had chosen mainly for Sofia's benefit, as she was the fashionista in the family. More importantly, they weren't even secondhand. She couldn't wait to show them to her because she had already decided to give them to Sofia. The shoes were a gift from JJ, who told Anna she needed to start "dressing more *Desperate Housewives*, instead of plain old desperate," especially if she planned to attract someone of the opposite sex. Unfortunately, Candace doesn't notice the ankle boots.

"Oh my God. Is that?" Candace says, her tongue frozen in admiration of Anna's cream tie-neck top.

"What?" Anna smiles.

"That's not a Stella . . ." Candace begins.

"McCartney?" Anna finishes. "Yup," she says, and pushes the glass door open. "Even tragic endings can look pretty."

Anna disappears down the corridor toward the staff

room. Before she is able to stuff her purse into her locker, she hears a familiar voice call out from the corner, "Why aren't you working with the crypt keeper today?"

Anna hears a few giggles from the other side of the locker door. The staff room is half-empty, but full enough for Kiki to know she has an audience. Anna takes a deep breath and quietly exhales before responding.

"Hello, Kiki," she says calmly. Anna had almost forgotten Kiki's cynicism. Between Candace's passive-aggressive stares and Kiki's snide remarks, Anna remembers why she didn't miss walking through the salon door every morning.

"So?" Kiki asks, popping her head around the locker door. "Why aren't you with her? Did she get sick of you? Come on. Tell us." Anna feels like she's standing before every bully she's withered in front of since she was a child.

"Not that it's any of your business, but Mrs. Powers has meetings all week, so I'll be working here," Anna says, a slight pang emerging in her belly.

The truth was that JJ had been feeling tired the last few weeks—*abnormally* tired. She had attempted to blame it on their trip to RollerJam in Staten Island, New York City's only existing roller rink. Somehow JJ talked her way into a practice for the Staten Island Spankers, a female roller derby team. Anna, of course, was forced to join them, but barely made it around the rink once without falling, the tough ladies knocking her down shortly after she began lap two. That was the end of her roller-skating experience. But to everyone's surprise, JJ managed to keep up with the team as they dashed around the circle. Anna sat on an old wooden stool and watched from the sidelines. As JJ passed her, Anna delighted in the enormous smile that came from JJ's face. Her face exuded a combination of exhilaration, adrenaline, and freedom. Anna's eyes moistened, but she refused to shed a single tear until after JJ sped by. At the end of practice, the Spankers presented JJ with a team jersey and named her an honorary member. Despite JJ's faux protests, Anna insisted on taking a team photo for posterity. During the car ride home, JJ's adrenaline surged, and she spoke in rapid sentences, almost haiku. Anna laughed at her excitement—it reminded her of when her children tried something for the first time. At day's end, JJ was emphatic that Anna give the team jersey to Ariel to sleep in.

Dancing around on roller skates would make anyone exhausted, let alone a seventy-nine-year-old woman, but JJ's tiredness was due to something else. And Anna knew it. True to form, JJ blamed her old age for her fatigue, but both Anna and Tim demanded JJ immediately see her doctor. Even though Anna knew JJ's condition was terminal from the get-go, the very thought of JJ becoming ill made Anna shiver and invited a thousand painful family memories to haunt her days. There was nothing worse, she knew, than watching someone you love wilt slowly like a flower, then crumble before you.

"Well, lucky us," Kiki says, reapplying her MAC lipstick, puffing herself up in front of the other hens.

The ornate bright orange tube catches Anna's eye. The

shade of bright pink was named "Girl About Town." *Fitting for a Queen Bee*, Anna thinks. A few of the employees pretend to be getting ready for their next appointment, desperately trying to go unnoticed, while others overtly stand waiting for Kiki's next move. Kiki feels the warmth of the spotlight on her.

"I hope you brought some magazines to read because it's slowed down since you were last here. I mean, I'm busy, but I'm sure *you're* going to be spending most of your day at reception catching up on gossip with Candace," Kiki jibes. A few of her cronies snicker.

Anna grabs the beige robe out of her locker and places it over her new outfit. "Oh, I have clients."

"Wait," Kiki says, then pauses dramatically. "The old lady is coming into the salon to get her cobwebbed business waxed so you'll look busy, right?"

*You're the reason parents force their kids to eat soap.* "No, actually I'm pretty booked today. And I'd appreciate it if you'd stop speaking so disrespectfully about my friend," Anna says.

"What do you mean you're *booked* today?" Kiki hisses.

"Booked," Anna says plainly.

"You're lying," Kiki says.

Anna looks at herself in the mirror, and, without looking at Kiki, says, "Michaela Goodman, Serena Von Bercy, and Ivy something or other."

Kiki almost swallows her lip gloss. "Lane?" she asks. "Ivy Lane?"

"Yes, that's it."

"How do *you* know Ivy Lane? Or any of those girls? Or did you just read a society blog this morning? Maybe memorize some boldface names from Page Six today? That's not your crowd."

"I met Ivy at a photo shoot a few months ago and the others are the granddaughters of—what do you call her again?—the crypt keeper?" Anna says, smiling at herself in the mirror. Kiki is visibly flustered.

"Fine. So you got a couple of rich bitches," she says flippantly. "But I don't know what room you're gonna use. We don't have any available space." Kiki rolls her eyes. The other girls, now undecided who wields the power, are quiet.

That is until, Emily, a salon newbie dares to speaks up. "You can double up with me, I seem to have a manageable level of crazy today."

Kiki quickly shifts her eyes to Emily, and narrows them, making them even more razor-sharp.

"Thanks, Em," Anna says without taking her eyes off Kiki. "But Carolina asked that Kiki and I share a treatment room. Apparently Kiki's not that busy after all."

"WHAT?" Kiki gasps, slamming her locker shut. "Hell no."

"Is there a problem?" Anna says sweetly.

"I have clients!"

"As do I. How about that?" Anna's voice is as smooth as Kiki's face is red. "Candace was told to stagger our appointments so that we could accommodate everyone."

"You've got to be friggin' kidding me," Kiki says.

"No, I'm not. I'm off to see Carolina, you know—my sister and *our* boss." Anna opens the door and looks back at a speechless Kiki.

Carolina sits at her desk, staring at her computer. A black Tom Ford cape rests on her shoulders, and her hair is pulled back into a long ponytail, a rarity for her. Her eyes are slightly puffy, something that only Carolina and her dermatologist would notice. The October chill crept its way into her office and was there to greet her when she walked into Impresarios at 6:30 A.M. She came into work early to get a handle on her life. Her nonfat soy latte from Starbucks is within reach—on a coaster, naturally. Next to her latte sits an unopened box of Marlboro Lights. Cesária Évora plays on her tiny Bose iPod speakers on her shelf. When Carolina needed to think, she always turned on music that she didn't know the words to or didn't understand. Today is that kind of day.

On her twenty-four-inch computer screen she had composed two columns. At the top of one RON; at the top of the other JACK. She was going old school.

Under Ron's name she lists the following attributes: insanely smart, loyal, gentle, caring, successful, attentive, organized, affable. She stares at the last entry again.

*Affable? That's a reason to stay with someone? Bank tellers are affable.*

She deletes the last adjective and replaces it with handsome.

Jack's descriptors are decidedly different in nature: pure sex, hysterical, straightforward, self-starter, kind, spontaneous, romantic, giving, hot.

Carolina glances at her sunburst wall clock and lets out a frustrated exhale.

*Three hours, and this is it? Fucking pathetic. These are my options? At my age?*

Her eyes turn back to her list, wondering why she loves one man until she finds a reason to utterly despise him, and yet hates the other until she scans farther down her columns only to find a reason to love him. *God, this is so fucked.*

Last night during a quiet dinner with Ron at Alias on the Lower East Side, Carolina said that she had to call it an early night in order to prepare for a huge marketing meeting with the Sephora executives. No such meeting existed. The truth was she needed to be alone, a necessity that had become increasingly prevalent while juggling two men. Carolina's guilt had forced her away from everything that had previously given her comfort.

Ron was quietly disappointed that he wouldn't be spending the night with Carolina, but he understood; business came first with her, something that she never attempted to conceal. He kissed her sweetly on the lips as he always did when they said good-bye. It was the kind of kiss that said, "I'm always here—available to you whenever you need me to be." It was a sentiment that made Carolina want to both run and stay still at the same time, a feeling that seemed to be overwhelming her for the last few months.

As she stepped out of the cab, she heard Jack calling her name. She spun toward the voice, and there he was, seated in a black, shiny, beautiful Mercedes C300. Carolina stood motionless as the wind billowed her black-chiffon blouse.

"Jack?" she said, and stared at the shiny black metallic paint.

"Get in," he said, smiling. Carolina examined the brand-new sedan for a moment before grinning and hopping in, only a few feet away from her front door, a few minutes from Ron's embrace.

"What happened to the truck?" Carolina asked, surprised.

"I thought it was time for an upgrade," he said proudly. "Do you like it? It's pretty sweet, right?" Carolina sensed that the car was more for her benefit than his.

"I don't know. I kinda liked the truck," she said. Jack's face fell, and Carolina quickly noticed that he was biting the side of his cheek. He was utterly flummoxed.

She looked at him more closely. He wore a light gray blazer with a black-and-white gingham shirt complete with a black bow tie. It appeared as though he'd even had his eyebrows waxed.

"What?" Jack asked her nervously as he caught her staring.

"Nothing," Carolina said, snapping out of the stare. "Anyway, what are you doing here?" Carolina asked. "It's ten thirty on a Wednesday night." She noticed a familiar smell but couldn't place her finger on it; the smell of the new car overpowered everything else.

"I wanted to show you the new car," he said. Carolina sensed there was something more and gave him a look that said as much. "Check this out," Jack said, and pressed a round button in the center of the car. A small television screen opened up smoothly, just as Carolina had guessed. Ron had an S-class sedan that was roughly seventy thousand dollars more than the car they sat in.

"Nice," she said. "Should I be impressed?"

"Oh, shut up. You don't know what I'm doing," he said. Jack fidgeted around with a few buttons until finally pressing PLAY.

"I'm much too old for a mix tape."

A few seconds later, the title credits of Fellini's *Nights of Cabiria* appeared on the tiny screen. Ironic, considering the central character searches for love only to encounter heartbreak after heartbreak. It was Carolina's favorite movie, a seemingly minor detail, but a piece of information that Jack had bothered to remember, nonetheless. *This is why I stay.* Sofia and Anna never understood how Carolina could love a movie that on the surface was about heartbreak and despair. Carolina, for her part, thought the film served as a valuable lesson about the dangers of attachment. But what all three sisters refused to see was that the movie was actually about eternal optimism: Love, it said, was possible.

Carolina was silent, trying to figure out why Jack had driven in from Queens to play the opening sequence of the movie.

"I know it's your favorite movie," he said, breaking the silence. "And I also know that you strictly forbade any date nights in your apartment, as you're an attached and respectable woman. Or at least so you said," Jack said, and smiled. "The 'respectable' part is debatable." Carolina playfully socked him in the shoulder.

"And?" Carolina said.

"I thought we could still rent a movie and have a date night. Since my place grosses you out, here I am," he said, and shrugged. Then he reached behind Carolina's seat and grabbed a Tupperware bowl, and set it on her lap. "Open it," he said with a certain twinkle in his eye.

Carolina opened the pale green plastic dish and found a heaping mound of popcorn. *This explains the smell.* As she opened her mouth to speak, Jack's lips pressed against hers, then his tongue was in her mouth.

He pulled back and smiled. "So what do you think?" he asked with a familiar arrogance. He was certain that he'd hit it out of the park.

"I'm thinking you just raped my face," she said, and wiped a bit of spittle off the side of her lips. She laughed, not because her response was particularly funny but because it finally burst the emotional wall she'd been holding up. "It was very sweet. Thank you."

Jack grabbed the back of Carolina's hand. She ignored it and instead focused on the television screen as Cabiria lamented that the man she loved had attempted to drown her in the river for forty thousand lire. She'd given him everything and couldn't understand why. The screen was filled with the beautiful cinematography of Fellini, but all Jack saw was Carolina.

Carolina dug at her thumb cuticle with her ring finger so hard that the skin around her thumb was bright pink and near bleeding. She shifted in her leather seat. She peeled back one layer too many and her thumb started to bleed and she instantly placed it in her mouth. She looked like an overgrown child sucking her thumb as she watched the screen. Carolina didn't need the English subtitles; her Italian was nearly perfect, and she'd seen the movie enough times that she had the dialogue practically memorized.

Finally, she took her thumb out of her mouth, and shouted at the miniscreen. "*Ma quella comm'é stupida!*"

"My Italian is a little rusty, but who are you calling stupid?" Jack asked, grabbing a handful of popcorn.

"Her," Carolina said, and pointed at the screen. "Me."

"Am I missing something here?" Jack asked. "What's going on with you?"

"Nothing. I have to go. It's late, and I have a huge meeting tomorrow. Thanks for the popcorn," Carolina said, breaking the grip Jack had on her hand. *Get out of the car. He's not the one. You knew that a long time ago.* She opened the door and placed a foot on the curb.

"Carolina? Wait a second. Talk to me. Is it too much? What did I do?" Jack asked, flabbergasted.

"You are forcing me to remember all these memories from twenty years ago that I've long forgotten, when all I want . . ."

"All you want is what?" Jack asked, and looked at her with the all hope and courage he could muster.

"All I want," she said wearily, "is to forget you."

Jack's face looked as if he'd just been pushed off a narrow ledge.

"I mean, what are we doing here, Jack? Sneaking around? Hooking up in random locations around the city, cheating on a good and decent man, and the lying—I just can't stand myself anymore."

"You could . . ." Jack began.

"Don't even!" Carolina said angrily. "How dare you suggest that I leave everything I have! And for what? For Queens? For a filthy apartment? To play house? No, I can't do that," Carolina said, and shook her head. "I *won't* do that."

"I never asked you to give up anything," Jack said. "I guess I should've been asking you to *grow* up," he said.

"Fuck you, Jack," Carolina said as she got out of the sedan. She slammed the car door shut and darted inside her building.

She plopped down on the corner of her long sofa, embarrassed at what she considered to be such trite conflicts. Out of the corner of her eye she caught the top of the *New York Times* on the lower shelf of the coffee table. She must have read the piece a hundred times. The *New York Times* Business Section, not Sunday Styles, but the Business Section, profiled her. Carolina owned one of the most success-ful beauty businesses in Manhattan. She'd given the keynote address at the National Association of Women Business

Owners last year. Yet somehow it all came down to this, which one will she choose? And that more than anything was what she found the most unnerving thing about the mess she'd created. She was disappointed in herself yet couldn't seem to escape it. Her life had never been about men or belonging to someone.

"Ugh, I feel like I'm being swallowed up by all of this!" she shouted, throwing up her arms in her empty apartment.

Back in her office, in the comfort of Starbucks and Césaria, Carolina holds her BlackBerry in her hands and scrolls down to Lunetta's name. She stares at the name and contemplates calling her mom. Suddenly, she throws the phone back on her desk and buries her head in her hands. She hears a knock on the door.

"Fuck off," Carolina calls out.

The door opens, and Anna walks confidently into Carolina's office. "And good morning to you!" Anna says in a chipper tone bordering on annoying. Carolina momentarily looks up and stares at Anna before gazing back at her computer.

*Couldn't she at least have noticed the highlights? The shoes?*

Anna maneuvers herself flawlessly onto the egg chair in front of Carolina's desk. Her practice had paid off. As she waits for Carolina to acknowledge her, Anna looks around the office. It's unmistakably changed. It smells odd, the usual Armani White not drifting in the air.

"Oh my God," Anna says, and surveys the room.

The bright white office is even more blinding than ever.

The room's impeccable cleanliness has gone into overdrive, manically so. Anna felt like she'd walked into a cloud. She notices a small can of Behr Pure White Paint and a small paintbrush.

"I thought I smelled paint," Anna says.

"There were spots," Carolina says robotically.

"Spots? Carolina, there's not even so much as a scuff mark on one wall."

"You don't see them. I do."

"Okay, 'Crazy, party of one? Crazy, party of one, your table is ready,'" Anna says. "Honestly, Carolina, you need to pull it together. Whoever thought I would have it more together than you?" Anna asks cockily, before rising from the egg. She bends down to examine one baseboard where the paint is still wet, but she's unable to see anything besides shining white. She turns her head away and heads back to the chair, but her vision temporarily goes white from staring at the paint. When Anna tries to remount the egg chair, she fails miserably, resulting in a large *thud*.

"You were saying?" Carolina says.

"No really, I'm fine," Anna says, picking herself off the ground, using her hand to steady herself on Carolina's desk.

"I hope you didn't leave a mark," Carolina says, her eyes not leaving the screen.

"Honestly, what the hell kind of chairs are these?" Anna says and debates whether or not to attempt to sit once again.

Carolina, focused on her list, doesn't bother to comment.

"Oh come on, not even a 'it's a good thing I have extra

padding' comment from you?" Carolina remains quiet. "Carolina?" Nothing. Finally, Anna says loudly, "Carol."

She immediately looks up from her computer. "Do not call me Carol. I hate it. Do not fucking do it again," she says.

Anna can't see Carolina's face since it's buried behind the large monitor. *What is it with this salon and gargantuan monitors?* "Then answer me. I've been calling your name."

"Huh?"

"What's going on? Out with it. Something's up. Tell me. Oh shit!" Anna looks horrified. "Did the Sephora deal fall through?"

"No, Sephora is fine. Great actually," Carolina mumbles.

"Then what is it?"

Carolina pushes her chair back from the computer and spins to face the window. Looking out on Fourteenth Street, her back to her sister, she says into the glass, "I'm pregnant."

"OH MY GOD! That's so great—"

"What? It's not great. How is it great?"

"Oh honey. You're nervous. You're not sure whether you're capable of being a good mother," Anna blurts.

Carolina whips her chair around to face her sister. Carolina's eyes are red and swollen. She looks like shit. "No, Anna, I'm not actually worried about whether or not I could be mother of the fucking year. But thank you for the confidence." Carolina rotates her chair back around, giving Anna only a view of the black chair and her dark roots.

"I'm sorry. I didn't mean . . ." Suddenly Anna's shoes and highlights seem rather insignificant. "It's just that—"

"I don't know who the father is," Carolina confesses.

Anna awkwardly dismounts from her egg, and walks around Carolina's large Saarinen table, bumping it slightly. Her sister's proximity sends Carolina flying out of her chair. Too mentally drained to fight, Carolina's flight response kicks in.

"No," Carolina says, and waves off her sister. She backs away from Anna as if she were a knife-wielding mugger. Anna is unyielding and moves closer to Carolina, who begins to sob.

"No!" Carolina shouts.

Anna finally reaches Carolina and throws her arms around her. "I'm here," Anna says and rubs Carolina's back. Carolina's tears reach fever pitch.

"What is happening to me?" Carolina begs. "What is happening?" she repeats, her voice still cracking. Anna is terrified, having never seen Carolina show so much emotion. She reaches out to steady her weeping sister and inadvertently upends Carolina's latte, coffee spilling across the white desk and splattering the white walls, a few drops reaching as far as the white shelves. The deep brown stain is undeniable in the pristine room. The artifice has finally cracked.

As Anna squeezes Carolina tighter, she, too, begins to cry. She's not exactly sure why or who her tears are for. Maybe they're for Carolina. For JJ. For Fabiana. Yet out of everyone, Anna never stops for a moment to wonder if the tears could, in fact, be for herself.

———

A few hours later, Sofia breezes into Impresarios, her chocolate hair slicked back into a tight ponytail, her body covered by a long black coat, her eyes by dark aviators. She skips saying hello to Candace, much to Candace's surprise, and heads straight back to the employee locker room and slips into her robe. She's tired. Her head is thumping like the dance music that blared last night at Hiro. Digging into her purse for an Advil, her hands begin shaking and only after an intense effort does she steady them to open the bottle. She quickly puts two pills into her mouth. She lets her hand fall on the bench and notices how cool it feels against her palms. She looks around the vacant locker room and slowly lies down on her side, pressing her cheek against the cold wooden bench. *Oh my God. This is heaven. If only the room would stop spinning.*

Sofia feels as bad as the morning after her twenty-first birthday, when Carolina had treated Sofia and Anna to dinner at Nobu. Before dinner the three sisters each downed a Matsuhisa Martini, a mammoth cocktail named after the restaurant's owner and chef, a mix of vodka, sake, and ginger, with a few cucumbers thrown in for good measure. By the time their shrimp tempura and Japanese eel sushi roll arrived, Sofia could barely hold her head up. Whereas most rational human beings would have gone home after the obligatory dessert with a candle jammed in the center, Anna was determined to take her baby sister out. When they arrived at the door of Bar Seventeen, Sofia puked all over the doorman's shoes.

"Welcome to twenty-one," Anna had said, laughing as Sofia gripped the stanchion that held the velvet ropes.

"You can take the girl out of Queens . . ." Carolina had said, and finally laughed, while the doorman frowned. Afterward, Anna went back to Brooklyn to crawl into bed with Christopher while Carolina took Sofia back to her place, where she was on puke patrol. Considering her obsessive-compulsive order and need for immaculate cleanliness and order, Carolina was surprisingly genteel the next morning. She cleaned up vomit from the floor without saying a word, and when Sofia apologized profusely Carolina stopped her before she could finish her sentence. She'd handed her a cup of hot coffee and two Advil and told her to lie on the couch for as long as she needed. Those were the moments that Sofia loved the most about Carolina and what she missed. They'd barely spoken since the blow up at Dell'anima.

With her eyes closed and the memory of her twenty-first birthday fading, Sofia focuses on the hum of the halogen lights above her. She'd never heard it before, and didn't know halogen lights produced sound. She imagines that the bench she's on is a massage table at Bliss Spa. She feels her muscles relax and within a few minutes she's so fast asleep in the middle of the staff room she doesn't hear the door fly open behind her.

"Why don't you answer your goddamn phone?" Carolina shouts, sending Sofia flying off the bench, causing her to hit her head on the locker. "Jesus Christ, Sofia! I was about to call Scott to see if you were dead. And I'd rather pull out my fingernails with a pair of rusty pliers than call *him*."

"Oh my God, stop shouting," Sofia begs, holding her head and pulling herself to the bench. "That was cruel even by your standards," she says, and rubs her head. *I guess the Get Out of Jail Free card is only valid the day after your twenty-first birthday.* She stands up, tightens her Impresarios uniform and checks herself in the mirror. Her headache comes barreling back.

"Well?" Carolina asks tapping her foot. As much as her head tells her to relax, her emotions won't allow it.

"Well, what?" Sofia says.

"Where the hell have you been? You're two hours late, and Kiki had to cover your first two clients, which, let me tell you, went over *great*." Sofia rolls her eyes, but Carolina is too busy venting to notice. She fastens one hand on her hip like most people do when in the midst of an argument, but when Carolina does it, it looks like a work of art for a cover shoot for French *Vogue*. "She's already threatening to quit because she and Anna have to share a treatment room this week. And now this?"

"So let her quit," Sofia says flippantly.

"That's not the point." She sits down on the bench and stares at Sofia while she touches up her makeup. This wasn't the conversation that she'd imagined having.

Anna and Carolina had decided it was best not to mention any of it to Sofia, especially until Carolina made a decision about the baby. Carolina had cried on Anna's shoulder and said that she couldn't bear to see the kind of disappointment in Sofia's eyes as she did the night at the restaurant.

Carolina continues to look at her beautiful younger sister. There was just so much to say: I love you. I'm sorry. She inhales deeply to collect her thoughts, ready to open up to Sofia, then the odor hits her: a mixture of cigarettes and hairspray with a heaping amount of vodka seeping through Sofia's pores. Carolina gags.

"What?" Sofia says, irritated.

"It fucking reeks in here—like a turd with perfume sprayed on it," Carolina says. She gets up from the bench and grabs a clean towel and places it over her nose. She inhales the basil fabric softener, a welcome relief. "Did you bathe in Belvedere? I hope Scott is more worse for the wear than you—that will at least give me some comfort."

"Give him a break," Sofia says sternly.

"Why should I? These last few weeks you've been showing up late to work, falling asleep during your lunch break, and Candace told me she found you asleep in your treatment room," Carolina barks.

"Candace has a big mouth."

"It's obvious you're trying to punish me because of the affair. Grow up. I'm not Mom and life is not perfect."

"How do you fit your ego through the door each morning? It's really unbelievable. My going out has NOTHING to do with you," Sofia says.

"Look, I get it. I know that feeling of wanting to jump out

of your skin. You could be with the most amazing man and still get antsy, and feel like there's something more out there." Sofia is silent, and this irritates Carolina even more. "I get that, and trust me, sister, it's a gene you've clearly inherited."

Sofia momentarily pauses. Perhaps Carolina is more on point than she realized. However, she's not about to give in so easily.

"For once in my life, I'm enjoying myself. I'm not taking orders from Mother, Scott, Anna, or, least of all, *you.*"

"You will take orders from me when you're at this salon," Carolina says.

"If you've got a problem with my behavior, then fire me. Otherwise, stay out of my life. You of all people have no right to judge me."

Sofia storms out of the staff room at the exact moment Kiki walks in. Carolina sits alone in stunned silence on the bench.

"Since when did we start casting for the new season of *The Real Housewives of New York City?*" Kiki asks, and shakes her head.

## Ten

## TWEEDle dee

nna stands in a walk-in closet the size of Fabiana and Michael's bedrooms combined. The giant fitting room smells of lavender and basil—no doubt the result of the nearly sixty satin sachets that line the drawers and hangers. Despite the large amount of fragrance, the smell does not overpower. The scent makes its presence known, but doesn't overwhelm. The closet is stockpiled with tweed: tweed suits, tweed pants, tweed coats, tweed skirts. The Italians have also made their presence known in JJ's wardrobe: Gucci, Valentino, Armani—but JJ's favorite is Parisian: Chanel. On anyone else, so much tweed would run the risk of appearing affectedly quaint, but not on JJ. Anna periodically has to remind herself that she's not standing in a studio apartment but an actual room that houses only clothes. No matter how many times she's been in the house, Anna is still awestruck by its grandeur.

A few months back, during lunch at Impresarios, Carolina told Anna that many years ago at one of JJ's legendary charity lunches, a middle-aged woman with a trailerful of brand-new money turned to the lady next to her and remarked loudly that JJ's town house was "perfect for a husband and wife who never wanted to see each other." JJ stopped her conversation with another guest in midsentence and turned to the entire table, and declared, "Oh my dear, you don't need my house never to see your husband. His time is already spent with the Korean call girls downtown. Besides, my house, unlike everything of yours, is not for lease."

When JJ's late husband Miles was still alive, JJ wouldn't have bothered to address such a remark. Perhaps that was why JJ and Miles loved the place so much: Everyone just assumed the pair couldn't stand one another even though the reality was quite the opposite. Carolina told Anna that the couple had almost no friends primarily because they wanted to spend any and all of their free time with each other. *That explains her social skills*, Anna thought. Miles had passed away from a massive heart attack years ago, and JJ had been dying of heartbreak every day since. Therefore, to speak of JJ's relationship with her late husband with such flippancy was blasphemous, punishable by social death. The executioner was JJ herself.

Anna watches as JJ scrutinizes every last garment on the racks.

"Honestly, it's like I'm in freakin' Bergdorf's," Anna says, shaking her head and taking it all in. "That one is gorgeous."

Anna points to a salmon-colored tweed jacket with yellow and orange accents.

"Which? The Lacroix?" JJ says as if an acrid aroma is seeping from Anna's skin.

"What?"

"Nothing. It's just so . . . gauche."

"Gauche? You bought it, not me," Anna argues.

"Meh," JJ huffs, and rolls her eyes. "It was a different time, and I didn't mind dropping twenty-six hundred on a blazer. JJ reaches for the jacket. "Try it on."

"I couldn't," Anna says.

"Okay, can we skip this part? It bores me. Just try on the friggin' jacket," she says, holding the jacket open for Anna.

Anna excitedly puts her arms through the holes in the jacket and slides it on. Before she even looks in the mirror, she feels she's entered a new stratosphere. She buttons the top two ceramic-button closures. The slight flare of the jacket at the bottom gives it a little extra pizzazz.

"It fits perfectly," Anna says excitedly as she runs her hands along the sleeves, then along the side of her hips.

"I was a bit heftier when I bought it."

Anna ignores the jab, walks to the mirror, and takes a deep breath, enjoying all twenty-six hundred dollars of the jacket. She studies the lemon yellows, mixed with the tangerine oranges that are all swirled into a salmon-colored pink. Finally, she exhales.

"God," she says. "It's hideous."

"I tried telling you," JJ offers.

"But it looked so good on the hanger . . ."

"That's what I said. But when I brought it home I looked like a scoop of Neapolitan ice cream," JJ explains.

"So why didn't you return it?"

"You never met Mr. Powers. He would've died of embarrassment. Worried that the people at the store would think we couldn't afford it. So no matter how ugly or ill-fitting, I never returned a single article of clothing. You can sure as hell bet that I made certain that everything looked exquisite after that fashion disaster." JJ stares at the jacket, lost in time and the memory of seeing Miles's face when she tried the jacket on for him. His hearty laugh, and the way his eyes would squint when he bellowed. She missed him enormously.

Anna begins to take off the jacket. "What are you doing?" JJ says, snapping out of it.

"I'm hanging the jacket back up," she says.

"Keep it," JJ says.

"Thank you, but I couldn't. It's too much," Anna says politely. JJ shoots her a knowing look. "Okay. I'd rather light myself on fire than wear it."

"Give it to that daughter of yours. The older one," JJ quickly clarifies.

"Oh it's too sophisticated and expensive for her. What girl her age has a jacket worth this kind of money? Wait, what am I talking about? What woman my age that I know has a jacket worth this kind of money?" Anna says and laughs.

"Give it to her." When JJ is persistent, there is no denying her. "Let her get creative with it. You never know."

Fabiana was still barely speaking to Anna. No matter how hard Anna tried, she continued to pull away. But Anna was determined to persevere, because that's what mothers do. "Okay, I'll tell her it's a gift from . . . what was it you told her to call you? 'That mean old bitch'?" JJ nods in glee. "Anyway, aren't we supposed to be looking for something for you to wear to the ballet?"

"Among other things," JJ responds. "But let's take care of you first."

"Me?"

"Yes, you don't think I'm going to the kick off of the American Ballet Theatre's season by myself, do you? You're going as my date. But don't get any lesbo ideas."

Anna is stunned and scrambles to find the right words to politely decline. "JJ, I so appreciate you wanting to invite me to such a grand event, but that's not really my thing. Galas are more . . . Carolina than me."

"Have you ever been?" JJ asks.

"No," Anna mumbles.

"Then how do you know it's not your thing," JJ barks. "Nonsense."

"And I have nothing to wear!"

"Open the last door, Cinderella," JJ says, nodding at a large hanging closet door.

Anna looks down the rows of shoes, clothes, and accessories to three long white doors with silver handles. "Oh for

God's sake," JJ says, and walks to the last door. JJ opens it and grabs a large wardrobe box with both hands. She struggles to move it and looks back at Anna. "You could help me, you know. I may look like a butch lesbian with this scarf around my head, but I'm not. Get your ass over here."

Last month, JJ had begun chemo again, and the little of the crew-cut hair she had left was beginning to fall out. In response, she'd taken to her "cancer chic" wardrobe. She adorned her head with everything from pricey Hermès scarves to do-rags that were typically worn by motorcyclists. This was fitting since JJ could glide in and out of either group with ease. When Anna would ask her questions about her health, JJ only answered in some sort of a quick retort that had little to do with how she actually felt. Even though they'd spent nearly every day together, JJ still hadn't let Anna all the way in.

"Sorry!" Anna says, and scurries to help JJ. Anna stretches her arms around the massive black cardboard container and feels a flurry of emotion. It feels like Christmas morning, and she has the biggest present under the tree. She carefully sets the heavy package down on the carpeted floor and momentarily stares at it. *What in the hell could it be? What if it's horrible-looking? She'll see right through me.*

"Jesus, girly—I don't have much time left on this earth. Would you hurry up and open it already?" JJ says.

"You're just awful," Anna says, and shakes her head, but she can't pretend to be even the slightest bit upset. Anna's face begins to beam before she even reaches for the box.

Finally, she sits down on the plush floor and feels the smooth surface. *It feels expensive. It smells perfumey. It smells like Barneys.* She places her fingers under the lid and lifts, revealing pristine black tissue. She carefully pulls back the delicate paper. There, precisely folded, is the most gorgeous black dress Anna has ever seen. She lifts the sleeveless, jet-black dress from the box and marvels at it, its ombré pattern perfectly aligned with the ballerina neckline and banded jeweled waist. The dress is simply exquisite.

"I-I-I can't believe. Oh my God!" Anna says, rushing to her feet to squeeze JJ. "Nobody has ever given me a gift like this before—not even my own mother," Anna whispers softly, on the verge of tears.

"Don't squoosh the dress, dear. I don't think Mr. de la Renta would be happy to know that you're dribbling all over his frock."

"I don't know what to say. How? Why?" Anna says.

"Let's just say I had to go to a master tailor because Oscar doesn't make dresses in a size fourteen—at least none that I've seen."

*Not exactly what I meant when I asked how.*

"But why?" Anna repeats.

"I don't know. Every girl should go to opening night of the ballet at least once in her life. Didn't we all dream of being a ballerina at one point?" JJ secretly delights in Anna's excitement. "Don't answer that," JJ cackles.

She stops laughing long enough to grab a smaller box. She hands the shoe box to Anna. This time Anna doesn't bother to go slow; she tears open the box to find a pair of simple black heels with signature red soles. *Unbelievable*.

"I'm—I'm at a loss," Anna says.

"Christmas came early," JJ says.

Anna finally comes down from the excitement, and reality suddenly sets in. *The kids*. "JJ, I'd love to but . . ."

"I called the salon and persuaded your sister to babysit," JJ informs her.

"Carolina?!"

"No, the younger one. Carolina was in a meeting and wouldn't take my urgent call for *your* babysitting needs. Imagine the likelihood. So I asked to speak to the other sister, and she happily obliged my request," JJ explains.

"You're joking."

"I have cancer. I do not joke," JJ says in a stern voice, before breaking out into laughter.

"You'll play that cancer card whenever you can," Anna says, and shakes her head. "You're going straight to hell." Anna catches a glimpse of herself in the mirror and focuses on her strawlike hair and the enormous zit right above her chin. "I've got to go home and get ready! Look at me."

"Paulette from Fekkai is coming over here to give you a blowout and Janelle from MAC is doing our makeup," JJ interrupts.

"You've thought of everything. Let me guess—they're the 'best in New York.'"

"Nice to see you are finally catching on after five months,"

JJ snips. She walks back to the opposite end of the closet and pushes through the racks of hanging clothes—predominantly tweed. She furrows her brow in frustration. "I know it's here somewhere. It's never been worn," JJ says, and places her hand on her hip.

"Why don't you tell me what you're looking for, and maybe I can help?" Anna says and walks toward JJ.

JJ ignores her and looks underneath every box, dry cleaning bag, and jacket. She takes a step back to survey the grandiose room. Then, suddenly, she marches to the middle of the tweed heap and reaches deep into the closet. She pulls out a beautiful skirt suit—a mix of beige, navy, and cream. The jacket has an intricate beaded band around the waist with a grosgrain ribbon tie. "There you are."

"Wow—that's gorgeous," Anna says admiring the petit day dress.

"Do you like?" JJ coos.

"I love it. But I have to tell you—if that's what you're wearing to the ballet, I'm way overdressed. I'm going to look like a whore in church," Anna says, staring at the detail in the jacket. JJ laughs.

"It's true," Anna says.

"That's not why I'm laughing. I would never wear this to the ballet. I'm wearing that crimson number over there. Miles gave it to me. It was his favorite dress on me," JJ says, and nods at a long deep red dress with Swarovski crystals around the neck.

"Okay, so what's this for?" Anna asks, and tugs at the tweed suit.

"This is the suit that I want you to bury me in."

Despite the creepy record by Merle Haggard combined with Liv Tyler's screams of terror, *The Strangers* has not upset the blasé mood in Anna's living room. Neither Sofia, who sits at one end of the long, cushy couch flipping through a copy of *People*, nor Fabiana, who is at the other end making a cross-knot friendship bracelet, pays much attention to the gruesome flick. Michael begged his favorite aunt to watch the R-rated film, and after a great deal of negotiating, Sofia finally caved under the condition he not mention a word about it to his mother. After the first fifteen minutes, however, Michael was too scared to watch and retreated to the safety of the latest Grand Theft Auto on his PlayStation 3. Hookers, guns, and threats from a Russian gangster apparently soothed even the jitteriest of tween nerves. As for Sofia and Fabiana, maybe it is the soothing aroma of the peppermint-eucalyptus incense filling the air, but neither is in the least bit afraid.

"How do they know this is a true story?" Fabiana asks without looking up at the TV.

"There's probably point nine, nine, nine, nine, nine percent truth in it. That's how they get away with saying the movie was inspired by true events," Sofia explains.

"Good to know."

Sofia smiles and turns the page in her magazine. "Something tells me the next time you tell your mom you're going to a study group, *that* will be inspired by true events," Sofia says, and chuckles.

Sofia is a combination of exhaustion and calm, and the citrus chamomile tea is making her increasingly tired. Curled up on the couch, Sofia wears jeans and one of Scott's New York Giants sweatshirts over her tiny frame. Her hair is pulled back into a ponytail, and she's not wearing a bit of makeup. Still she radiates. This is Sofia's uniform for a typical "log-cabin night." Scott and Sofia coined the phrase during a particularly chilly fall evening years ago, when neither one of them felt like leaving the house. Instead, they put on their sweats, grabbed a throw blanket, and cuddled on the sofa, popped popcorn on the stove instead of the microwave, sipped hot chocolate, and watched movies till two in the morning as if they were in a log cabin in the middle of nowhere. She misses him now. He was supposed to be watching the kids with her, but he got called to a business dinner thirty minutes before they were about to leave.

Sofia continues, "At least that's what I would do. 'Inspired by true events'," she ponders. "I like that."

The notion of true events abruptly pummels Sofia like a punch to the head. As of late, the majority of her conversations with Scott and even Carolina, while they may have been inspired, lacked the true events part of the equation. *What does Carolina know about truth?*

Fabiana laughs. "And why aren't *you* my mother?"

Sofia doesn't respond as she's still lost in thoughts of Carolina's adultery, Scott's long hours, and, of course, Dennis. Fabiana's sentence hangs in the air, and the longer it does, the guiltier she feels.

"I mean, I love her and everything—but you're just so much more . . ." she begins. Fabiana chooses her words carefully because she doesn't want to completely disparage her mom. ". . . I don't know, simply more, I guess." Sofia is silent. Fabiana glances up and sees Sofia obliviously staring at her magazine.

"Hello? Aunt Sofia?" Fabiana says.

"What? Oh, sorry, honey. I was just zoning out," Sofia explains.

"It's okay. It wasn't important," Fabiana says, and goes back to her friendship bracelet.

"Of course it is," Sofia says. "What were you saying?"

"Nothing," Fabiana says annoyed.

"Fabi, please. Don't be dramatic. What did you say?" Sofia says, and nudges Fabiana with her foot.

"Ew!" Fabiana shouts. "You know I hate feet!" Sofia grins and places both of her feet on Fabiana's arm. "And those socks—gross!"

"What's wrong with my socks?" Sofia looks down at her vintage Pac Man–emblazoned socks.

"Nothing . . . if you're eight years old," Fabiana quips. Sofia studies them. "If those were on a guy your age, I'd say he was a definite pedophile."

"My age?" Sofia gasps. Fabiana giggles. In retaliation,

Sofia takes off her left sock and whips it at Fabiana's face.

"GROSS! Oh my God!"

Sofia laughs and looks down at the ball of string in Fabiana's lap. "That's gorgeous!" Sofia says, staring at the half-finished string bracelet. "God, I used to make these when I was your age. We called them friendship bracelets," Sofia says.

"Well, I had friends until I was grounded by *your* sister," Fabiana hisses.

"Oh yeah. That. I was just thinking, shouldn't you be MySpacing or text messaging at the very least?" Sofia says and smiles.

"I prefer real life," Fabiana says. "Before you try and psychoanalyze me and drag me out of my state of apocalyptic doom by aiming your faux happiness at me like a guided laser, just save it please. Let me wallow in my melancholy," she continues.

"My God. Are you fifteen or forty-three? Psychoanalyze? Melancholy? I had never even heard or seen the word 'melancholy' until I saw it on the cover of a Smashing Pumpkins CD. I think I get why your mom calls you four-point now."

"The Smashing Pumpkins?" Fabiana asks.

"I was trying to prove a point," Sofia says, and laughs.

Sofia glances at the television as one of the killers bangs on the front door of the house. Liv Tyler frantically runs around desperately looking for a sharp object. As the banging gets louder, Sofia and Fabiana finally become engaged.

Bang after terrifying bang, the killer's intensity grows. Sofia wraps her arms around her knees and huddles in nervousness, while Fabiana bites her pale pink painted fingernail.

Then suddenly, *BANG! BANG! BANG!* Both of them scream in terror at the movie, then laugh nervously.

*BANG! BANG! BANG! BANG!* the noise repeats.

"Wait," Sofia says paralyzed with fear. She looks at the TV, then at Fabiana and finally at the door.

"W-W-Was that here?" Sofia asks nervously.

"I don't know. Was it? Oh my God. I'm calling 911," Fabiana says, and reaches for her cell phone, but it's not there. It's in her bedroom.

*BANG! BANG!* The thunderous knocks on the front door come rumbling back.

Sofia slinks off the couch and slowly inches her way toward the door.

"Aunt Sofia!" Fabiana says in a hushed voice. She reaches for something off the floor and throws it to Sofia.

Sofia looks at it momentarily. "What the hell?" She looks at it closer. "Is this a nunchuck?" Fabiana nods. "For a Wii!" Sofia says in a loud whisper. "What am I supposed to do with this?"

*BANG! BANG! BANG!* Sofia and Fabiana jump and quickly cover their mouths. Sofia looks out of the corner of the window but doesn't see anyone. She sees her phone on the dining-room table and quickly grabs it. She puts her ear against the door.

"Who is it?" Sofia says shakily.

"It's me. Let me in," a man's voice says so quietly that Sofia can barely hear him. The doorknob jerks from side to side, and the banging begins again just as it is on the television.

"LET ME IN!" The voice gets louder. Sofia dials nine and then abruptly stops.

"Who's there?" Sofia repeats.

"OPEN THE GODDAMN DOOR!" he shouts.

Then, silence.

"Dad?" Fabiana says, standing on top of the couch. She takes a step down and walks toward Sofia.

Sofia cautiously opens the door with the nunchuck in her hand.

"Oh. It's you. I thought you were Anna," a tall and beefy man dressed in faded blue jeans and a New York Rangers jersey says.

"Couldn't you have simply said, 'It's Christopher'? I nearly wet myself," Sofia says, and opens the door.

Christopher ignores Sofia and gives Fabiana a hug. "Hey, princess," he says, and squeezes her.

"Hi, Dad!" she says, instantly smiling. "What are you doing here?"

"I came to talk to your mother. Where is she?" Christopher asks. He scans the living room, then cocks his head to look behind the sofa.

"She's not hiding behind the couch," Sofia says smugly.

"Cute. I was looking for Greta. Where's my dog?"

"She's in bed with Ariel. They fell asleep together while Ariel was watching *The Little Mermaid* for the umpteenth time," Fabiana interjects.

Sofia studies Christopher's reaction. She looks for something in Christopher's dazzling green eyes at the mention of Ariel. *Nothing.* Sofia studies the crevices in his large forehead. He's handsome, but not nearly what he once was. Christopher's good looks are now weathered, and he's become slightly bloated. He looks like a president who completed his first term in office; gray hairs have sprouted, and deep worry lines track across his face. As far as Sofia knows, Christopher still hasn't accepted the fact that his son is living as a female.

"Where's Mikey?" he asks.

"Where do you think?" Fabiana answers.

"Grand Theft Auto?" Christopher asks. Fabiana nods.

Christopher smirks and pulls out a chair from the dining-room table. He studies the grain in the wood. He remembers buying the table with Anna in Albany ten years ago. They had gone upstate for the weekend for the wedding of one of Christopher's buddies. On their way home, they'd spotted the table at a yard sale—and Anna had begged Christopher to buy it, insisting it would be perfect for their growing family. It felt like a lifetime ago.

"Is everything okay, Christopher?" Sofia asks.

"Yeah," he says, snapping out of the memory. "Anyway, where's Anna? It's a Wednesday night. Why isn't she home?"

"She went out," Sofia says mysteriously.

"Out?" Christopher asks. Sofia nods. "As in, out on a date?"

Before Sofia can respond Fabiana quickly interjects, "No, she's with Mrs. Powers. JJ, I mean."

"The old lady?" Christopher says, and slightly tilts his head to the side. "At this hour? What the hell does she have your mom doing now?"

"She's not working. JJ asked her to go to the ballet as a surprise. And JJ called me to hang out with the gang," Sofia says, and smiles at Fabiana. She knew better than to use the word "babysit."

"The ballet? Anna doesn't like the ballet," Christopher says, and shakes his head, then flashes an indignant smile. "Come on. Where is she?"

Sofia and Fabiana exchange glances. "She's at the ballet. It's opening night of the fall season," Fabiana explains. "It's kind of a big deal."

"I'll wait," he says. "I'm sure she'll be home soon."

"No really, it might be hours until she gets home. You know how these things are," Sofia says, reaching for an answer. *I don't even know how these things are, what am I talking about?*

"You can go, Sof, I'll stay with the kids," Christopher says blankly.

"I'm sorry, what?" Sofia asks.

"I'll stay with the kids. You can go home," Christopher repeats.

"No, it's fine. Fabiana and I are having a good time.

Besides, I promised JJ I'd stay," Sofia says, doing her best to come up with a reason to stay with kids. She can only imagine what Anna's reaction would be if she came home to find Christopher sitting in her living room.

"You promised some old lady you don't even know," Christopher replies, "that you'd stay with my children?"

"Yes," she says. "You don't know JJ, but when she asks, you obey."

"Go home, Sofia. Really," Christopher says.

"But—" Sofia begins.

"But what? They're my kids," Christopher argues.

"Come on, Aunt Sofia, please," Fabiana interrupts. Sofia glares at Christopher, then turns her attention to Fabiana.

"Can you give us a minute, Fabi?" Sofia says politely. Fabiana lets out a deep sigh and retreats to her room, leaving the door open a crack so she won't miss a single word.

"Christopher, I wasn't suggesting you're not capable of watching your own kids, but I don't think my sister would take too kindly to finding her ex-husband sitting on her couch watching TV when she got home."

Christopher gets up from the table and looks out the front window. "Fine. Then call her. Tell her I'm here."

"I think that's a good idea, actually," Sofia says. She dials Anna while Christopher walks around the living room, looking to see if Anna has changed anything since he left. To his relief, the rooms are untouched. He pauses at a picture of Fabiana, Michael, and Ariel.

"Voice mail," Sofia says from the dining room.

"Huh?" Christopher says, still lost in thought.

"I'm sure she's shut her phone off because of the ballet—" Sofia abruptly stops and then speaks into the phone. "Hey, it's me. Give me a call when you get this. The kids are fine. I wanted to . . ." She hesitates, and decides that a mention of Christopher is best saved for a conversation. "Just call me as soon as you get this."

"There you go. You're absolved," Christopher says, and sits on the couch.

Sofia isn't about to go anywhere. "Let me send her a text."

Christopher shakes his head. "You never change, Sofia."

Sofia goes to the text menu and is about to text Anna when she notices she has a message in her text in-box. It must have come during the commotion at the door.

She opens the message: COME OUT AND PLAY TONITE? MEET ME AT VLADA.

There it is, the slight tug Carolina preached about. *Dennis.* Sofia debates her next move. *Scott is with clients. Christopher's got the kids. It's one drink.*

She hits reply: SEE YOU IN AN HOUR.

"So you texted her?" Christopher asks.

"My bases are covered. They're all yours," Sofia says, and packs up her purse.

"Wow. That was easier than I thought."

Christopher puts his feet on the coffee table and exhales. Fabiana opens her bedroom door and comes darting out, hurtling toward the couch to land next to her Dad.

"Bye, Aunt Sofia. Thanks!" Fabiana says.

"Good night, honey," Sofia says, and smiles.

"Wait! I almost forgot," Fabiana says, getting up from the couch. She takes out the friendship bracelet she was making earlier and wraps it around Sofia's wrist.

"You don't have to give this to me," Sofia says.

"I want to," Fabiana insists. "You're my friend."

"That I am," Sofia says, and hugs her. Sofia looks at Christopher again and opens the door. There's no way in hell she should be leaving. But these days "should" doesn't mean what it used to. She knows deep down that had she not gotten a text from Dennis, she would have stayed. But she didn't, and that decision would change everything.

During the American Ballet Theatre's special performance at City Center, where Principal Dancers performed highlights from the fall season, JJ would intermittently wake up long enough to applaud a performance before nearly immediately falling back asleep. Anna nudged her a few times, as JJ's snores became a distraction to the nearby guests, but no one would dare tell JJ Powers to be quiet—such a move was social suicide. Anna tried as best as she could to keep an open mind, and it worked for the first twenty minutes. She reveled in the fact that she was wearing Oscar de la Renta and that she'd walked the red carpet with JJ and even had her picture taken. It was all very exhilarating for her, but once she was inside, she was utterly bored. She pinched herself periodically, and dug her fingernails into her arm to keep from falling asleep. It wasn't a big deal for JJ to fall asleep; she had been going through chemotherapy, after all. The only thing that Anna was in danger of dying from was boredom. She couldn't even text Carolina to see if she was also at the theatre since guests were required to turn off their cell phones once inside.

Ninety minutes later, when Anna and JJ finally returned to JJ's waiting town car, Anna was relieved to be going home.

"Thank you so much for everything, JJ. I had a great time," Anna says, as the car pulls away. JJ looks at Anna out of the corner of her eye and is silent. "If it's easier for me to just hop in a cab to Brooklyn, I'm happy to do it." JJ laughs. "What's so funny?" Anna asks.

"We're not going home, girly. Now's the most important part," JJ explains. Anna stares at JJ blankly. "The party! Hello?"

"Oh, I really don't have to go to a party. Go without me. I'm sure you know everyone there. I'll just be a downer."

"You're going. I'm not walking into this event alone," JJ barks. Anna is surprised at JJ's tone but chalks it up to her exhaustion.

"Okay, maybe I should just check in with Sofia," Anna says, and reaches for her phone.

"There's no time. We're here," JJ says, as a man clad in a tuxedo opens the car door. Anna glances out of the open door and notices that all of the guests from the ballet have descended on the Pierre Hotel. Anna lets go of her cell phone and drops it back in her bag.

"Okay, but I'm only staying for one drink, then I'm gone," Anna insists. JJ stands next to the car and waits for Anna to get out.

"Well, just look at you," JJ says.

"What? What's wrong?" Anna asks nervously.

"Nothing. You clean up nice, girly. You look exquisite," JJ says so sweetly that Anna is stunned. "From pussies to the Pierre, you've come a long way, my dear," JJ says, and bursts into laughter.

"I knew you couldn't just let it be," Anna says, and rolls her eyes.

"Of course not. Now let's do the step and repeat, and get inside. I'm starving," JJ says.

"The step and what?" Anna asks.

JJ shakes her head, annoyed. "You're going to have your picture taken again. Do you not understand English?" JJ locks arms with Anna and the two women walk toward the red carpet, each steadying the other for completely different reasons.

They work their way down the red carpet, and everyone from Patrick McMullan to Wire Images photographs JJ, the legend. Anna delights in seeing the shutterbugs give JJ her due. She's surprised that she doesn't care about walking the red carpet herself. The fun has worn off. *Good for JJ.* The sentiment continually runs through Anna's mind. The photographers constantly call for Anna to step out of the picture. However, just as she is about to do so, JJ clenches down on Anna's meaty forearm like a guillotine. The red carpet is small, and the strobes are so intense that Anna can barely see what's in front of her. Thankfully, a nearby publicist grabs Anna's arm and ushers the pair into the ballroom.

"Anna?" a familiar voice calls from behind her. Anna and JJ, still arm and arm, turn around in unison.

"Carolina! Hi!" Anna says excitedly.

Carolina is dressed in a stunning purple floor-length dress, a rare instance in which she has stepped out of her life in a black-and-white photo and opted for a splash of refined color. Instead of the usual bone-straight hairdo, her hair boasts a bit of her natural wave. She looks softer, almost ethereal, and every head in the room has turned. Ron stands beside her, dressed in a perfectly tailored black tuxedo.

"Oh great, a family reunion," JJ says, miffed.

"Hello, JJ," Carolina says. "You look beautiful."

"I look like death in a dress, but thanks for lying," JJ quips.

"You look amazing," Anna gasps at Carolina. "Have you been here long?"

"No, we were held back," Carolina says, irritated. "Some odd couple was walking the red carpet . . ."

JJ glances at Carolina's dress again. "Interesting," she says.

"What's that?" Carolina says.

"I thought green was the color of envy, not lilac." JJ snickers, without taking her eyes off Carolina's dress. Finally, JJ looks up and turns her attention to Ron. "You, cute guy."

Ron is taken aback. "Yes, you. Take this old lady to the bar, will you?"

Ever the consummate gentleman, Ron steps up and smiles at Anna and kisses her on the cheek hello. He then turns to JJ. "To the bar we shall go, beautiful lady."

"I might just have to keep this one. Watch out, Carolina," JJ says, as Ron offers JJ his arm. The two disappear across the ballroom and walk toward the bar, but are stopped nearly every step of the way by sycophants kissing up to JJ. For his part, Ron basks in the attention. He wasn't a starfucker per se, but he did enjoy being photographed.

"I have to say I'm surprised to see you here," Carolina says.

"I'm surprised myself. JJ sprang this on me at the last minute. You know me—ballet, black-tie parties, they're not my thing," Anna says.

"You don't say," Carolina says sarcastically.

"I'm going to ignore the fact that that was a bitchy thing to say and chalk it up to you being hormonal because of your condition," Anna hisses.

"Lower your voice!" Carolina says, flustered.

"Wow. You're going to make a great mom," Anna says, unable to resist.

"Unbelievable," Carolina says, shaking her head.

"Oh, Carolina, relax. If you can't laugh, what can you do?"

"Run into oncoming traffic?" Carolina says. Anna throws her arm around Carolina's shoulder.

"You're touching me. You know I don't like anyone touching me," Carolina says, her eyes wild.

"Carolina, no matter how hard you try to drive Sofia or me away, we're not leaving."

"You told her?" Carolina says with a look of horror.

"No. It's not my story to tell," Anna says.

"She barely speaks to me. She's going out nonstop. She's probably passed out drunk somewhere now."

"Relax, JJ got Sofia to babysit the kids," Anna explains.

Anna grabs Carolina's arm and guides her into the large ballroom.

"Where are we going?" Carolina asks.

"To the dance floor. We need to show them how it's done!" Anna insists.

"Um, yeah. I don't think so," Carolina says, and pulls away.

"It wasn't a request. Now let's go, preggers," Anna says.

Anna dances awkwardly, then Carolina finally joins in, loosening up with every beat of the drum. Within a few minutes both sisters get lost in the music dancing with one another. JJ looks on from the edge of the dance floor and smiles, remembering the countless number of evenings that Miles and she spent dancing, and the subsequent blisters the morning after.

The music changes to a more refined, sophisticated beat—a slow song. As Carolina and Anna make their exit from the dance floor, Ron snatches Carolina's hand and leads her back. Anna smiles and watches as a multitude of couples join them. Even though she is at an ultraexclusive soiree, it is pretty much the same as every other party she'd been to in Queens and Brooklyn: clumsy men trying to beguile their dates, patient women enduring bruised toes with a smile. All in the name of love. Anna watches Ron holding Carolina close to him as they seemingly glide across the dance floor. As Ron whispers into Carolina's ear, she momentarily smiles, but her face quickly returns to that of worry. Anna's happy for Carolina even if Carolina isn't happy for herself. *How nice to have two men head over heels for you.*

"It'd be nice to have one man," Anna says softly aloud.

"Anna?" a man's voice says from behind her.

"Oh God. Yes?" Anna says praying that no one has heard her. She turns her head. "Tim! Hi."

Tim is dashing in his tuxedo—instead of the usual bow tie, he has opted for a long, black, skinny tie that slips perfectly down his chest. His jet-black hair is flawlessly swept to the side, and his eyes are even more piercing than usual. And the dimples are making their appearance. *He's so beautiful. He makes Jon Hamm look average.*

"Hello," Tim says. Anna inhales and nearly passes out in ecstasy. He smells of amber and the type of clean freshness that you get at a barbershop. *I would drop my dress to the floor in front of all these people for this man.*

"What are you doing here?" Anna asks with surprise. "I mean, of course you come to these things all the time, why wouldn't you? You're . . . yeah . . . you are . . ." Anna stops. "I'm going to stop talking now."

"I will tell you what I'm doing here. I'm asking you to dance," Tim says, and faces Anna squarely.

"I'm sorry what? Could you repeat that, please?"

Tim laughs. "Anna, would you like to dance? And don't tell me you can't dance, I saw you out there not less than five minutes ago."

"I'd love to," Anna says excitedly.

Even though she'd imagined for the last two months what being this close to Tim was going to be like, it was still enough to cause a full-blown panic attack. As Tim leads her to the dance floor, Anna takes in the room. *I want to remember this.*

A portly man sings "Beyond the Sea," as Tim pulls Anna close to him. *Press PAUSE. I don't want to go beyond this moment.* As the pair sways to the music, Carolina notices Anna's look of terror. The two sisters lock eyes on the middle of the dance floor. Carolina purposely breathes in and exhales, relaxing into Ron, implying that Anna do the same. Anna inhales, hoping to be as breezily carefree as possible, but on the exhale she suddenly begins to cough. Carolina shakes her head from a distance and continues to dance with Ron.

"Sorry, I had a tickle in my throat," Anna says.

"No problem. Are you sure you're feeling okay? We can stop if you want to," Tim offers.

"NO!" Anna quickly snaps.

Tim smirks. "Good, because I really didn't want to look like the jerk on the middle of the dance floor by himself."

"You? A jerk? I don't think that could be possible," Anna says and smiles.

"At any rate, you let me know when you want to stop. I just want to make sure you're not coming down with something like our favorite senior citizen," he says.

"JJ? What's wrong with her?" Anna asks and momentarily stops dancing.

"What do you mean? She left about ten minutes ago saying she was tired. I'm escorting you home now. I thought you knew," Tim says confused.

*Damn, she's good. Today's manipulators could learn a few things from her.* "Oh. You don't have to take me home. I don't want to be a burden," Anna says, as the couple begins to move their feet again.

"Burden? A burden should be so lucky to look like you," he says. Anna smiles demurely.

"Honestly, I can take a taxi or ask my sister to drive me. She's right over there," Anna explains, and nods at Carolina and Ron.

"I don't think you understand," Tim interrupts.

"I don't?" Anna says.

"*I* asked JJ if I could take you home," Tim explains.

"Oh," Anna says, and continues dancing.

"Is that okay?" Tim asks.

"Um, yeah. It's great."

The chanteur finishes the last bars, and Anna feels a tingling in the pit of her stomach. She's disappointed that their first dance has ended. Tim smiles and claps for the singer. Then he grabs Anna's hand to lead her off the dance floor.

As they walk, Tim whispers, "I can't do fast ones. It's always good to know your limits. And I know mine," he says, and laughs.

Two mojitos and one waltz later, Anna asks, "Tim, would you mind taking me home?"

"It'd be my pleasure," he says, and offers his arm.

It's nearly twelve thirty in the morning when the town car pulls in front of Anna's house. The streets are nearly deserted except for a lone midnight jogger. Anna rolls down her window a crack to feel the cold October air. It's brisk yet refreshing. She notices the jogger up the street.

"Unbelievable," she says.

"Honestly, I think there's one in every city. Who jogs at this hour?"

"Serial killers and rapists," Anna says deadpan.

"It's a good thing I'm walking you to the door then," Tim says, and opens his door. He gets out of the car and shuts the door behind him. Anna feels the cool breeze hit her neck, sending a chill down her back. *Oh my God. He's walking me to my door. What if he tries to kiss me? Do I go in for the hug?*

"I can't believe how chilly it got," Anna says, leading the way to her modest home. "But I kind of love it." Without prompting, Tim takes off his jacket and drapes it around Anna's shoulders. They walk up the sidewalk to Anna's front door.

"I take it this is you," Tim says.

"It is," she says, looking him directly in the eye.

"I think I owe JJ a bouquet of flowers," Tim says, and grins.

"And why is that?" Anna asks, moving her face closer to his.

"Her scheming allowed me to spend most of the evening with you," he explains.

"Well, there *is* that . . ." she says. Tim moves in and places his hand on the small of her back and gently moves her to him. ". . . but don't send flowers just yet," Anna continues.

Now suddenly doubting his advance, Tim nervously asks, "Why not?"

"JJ hates flowers," Anna says, before pressing her lips against his.

Anna's eyes are barely closed when her front door flies open.

"ANNA?"

"Christopher?!" Anna screams in shock. "What are you doing here?"

Eleven

# into the cold night air

It's a quarter past twelve and the temperature has dropped at least fifteen degrees in the hour since Carolina and Ron left the Pierre. The brutal and frigid air is an exclamation point on the end of fall. As it tears through the Manhattan streets, the erratic wind stirs up everything in its path and gives the few pedestrians on the sidewalks an eerie sense of foreboding. The icy temperatures and tempestlike weather have kept the usual number of night owls off the streets. The chilled Midtown streets are almost deserted—like the financial district after six o'clock.

Inside a nondescript twenty-four-hour diner on the East Side, Carolina sits in a large banquette under shoddy fluorescent lighting outmatched in its kitschiness only by the gruff waitress. The server looks as happy to take an order as she is to have her unibrow waxed. Still dressed in her strapless lilac ball gown, Carolina sips a mint tea and listens to Ron pontificate about the decline of true New York culture. Despite the horrific lighting, Carolina is stunning: The dress fits her beautifully. As it spills across her seat, the five-thousand-dollar gown at a cheap diner is as classic as Sinatra playing on the crackling speaker system.

Carolina brushes a long strand of hair out of her eye and tucks it behind her ear. Her skin glows, in part due to self-tanner, and perhaps also because of her pregnancy. Her brown eyes radiate but don't yet betray her secret. Slouched in his tuxedo, Ron leans against the wall with one leg out-stretched onto the vinyl seat, a look of great discontent upon his face.

"Oh come on. It's not that bad," Carolina says impatiently.

"I think I'm confused. I don't know why you insisted on coming here. We have tea at both of our places, and we could've had your plate of chili french fries delivered. That is one of the perks of living in New York, after all," Ron says, and sighs.

"The fries get soggy in those plastic containers. And you know I like them crisp," Carolina says, and sips her tea.

As if on cue, a plate of crisp french fries drenched in chili and cheese is slung in front of Carolina. Normally, she'd be repulsed by such a sight and even obsess at the discolored diner plate. Instead, she breathes deeply, letting the smell of the chili and the deep fryer travel through her nose to her brain.

Ron studies the steaming-hot plate. "That looks so disgusting. Inedible, even," he says with a grimace.

"I'm going to pretend you didn't say that and proceed to enjoy every last artery-blocking bite, thank you," Carolina says, and grabs three chili-soaked fries and pops them into her mouth. Chewing slowly, she looks around the diner and flashes a peculiar smile.

"What?" Ron asks.

"Nothing. This is one of the reasons why I was drawn to Manhattan," she says, pondering.

"Shitty diner food?" Ron says dismissively.

"No, the ability to get shitty diner food at"—she looks down at her Rolex—"twelve twenty-two in the morning. I *love* that about Manhattan. I told myself when I moved here that I'd take advantage of it." She trails off for a moment. "And yet I don't."

"You're at every society event, you go to the best restaurants, we had an amazing summer in the Hamptons. And yet *this* is the ultimate New York experience?"

"I know, but I don't dance till daylight like Sofia," Carolina argues. "Or go roller skating in Staten Island like Anna."

"I'm going to do you a favor and break it down. A) You hate sweaty, crowded nightclubs. B) The last time you roller-skated, you called the skates, and I quote, 'a bone fracture with wheels.' And C) You're a grown woman," Ron says. Carolina frowns. "Are you having some sort of midlife thing I need to know about?"

"I still want the option, that's all," Carolina says, and stops herself before saying too much.

Without turning his head, Ron continues to stare at the waitress, who dumps coffee grounds out of a can into a filter. "Fine, you want to dance at gay bars like Sofia, I'll take you." He sighs. "I'd rather just dance at home, but I'll go," he says reluctantly. "And roller skating? That one is tough. I'm about as coordinated as Jell-O, but fine—we'll do it. Can we go home now?" he asks flippantly.

"You know what? I can't do this," Carolina says, flinging a french fry back on the plate. She isn't quite sure where the words are coming from, but the harsh lighting and strange environment have given her an edge. She shifts her eyes downward toward the table.

"That's a bit dramatic for a couple of fries, don't you think?" Ron says, then sees her face. "What?"

"The pretending. I just can't. I don't want to be in a relationship where life is a checklist to mark off. I want to be with someone who *wants* to do those things, not because he always fulfills obligations."

"Okay, Jesus Christ, we won't go to the fuckin' roller rink," Ron says loudly. "Can we get out of here? I have to be at the office early."

After several awkward seconds, Carolina looks up from the table, her eyes nearly drowning in tears. Months of contemplation and a year of silent unhappiness had led to this moment. The issue had risen to the surface, and it could no longer be pushed below by the salon, the product lines, or the social calendar. It demanded to be addressed.

"Carol?" Ron asks, suddenly compassionate. "Carol, what is it?"

Carolina shakes her head and presses her lips shut, embarrassed and disappointed by such a public display of emotion. "I can't do 'us' anymore," she finally mumbles. Her throat feels raw. It burns. She swallows hard. She had not planned to speak these things. The sentiments—*you should go and this should end*—were internal monologues, not meant for others' ears. To hear them now is both relieving and terrifying.

Ron reaches out his hand and places it on hers, still warm from gripping her tea. "Talk to me," he says softly.

Tears fall from Carolina's eyes, and she finds it difficult to speak. "I don't deserve to be with you," she says. "You're just so good."

He looks at her, and she remembers why she fell in love with him: his fresh wit, his big, beautiful eyes, tilted slightly to give him a constant countenance of worry, and of course his gentleness. *This* gentleness. It was easy to remember why and when she fell in love. But, sitting across from the man with the anxious eyes, she cannot pinpoint why and when she fell out of it.

"What are you talking about?" Ron says. "Of course we deserve each other. You're just tired. Let's go home. We'll get some rest. You'll wake up tomorrow and feel so much better, I promise."

"Ron," Carolina says, refusing his dismissal, "I think we've run our course."

Ron pauses, his eyes revealing shock and terror. "What—

what do you need from me? What am I not giving you? Tell me," he pleads.

She hesitates.

"We can go to therapy. We can do anything."

"We're like best friends. We talk about everything, movies to politics to business. But there's nothing sexual about our relationship—despite the occasional scheduled sex date. I can't stay with a man simply because he makes me feel safe. Life is about constantly seeking contrast, challenge. You and I . . ." She looks at him now, her eyes in his. "You and I have become terrifyingly boring."

"I didn't realize best friends was a bad thing," Ron says.

"It is when you rarely have sex. And if we are simply best friends, then why are we even in a relationship and not simply just that—friends?"

After eighteen months of wondering what she was doing wrong, of blaming herself for not loving Ron enough, clarity settles on Carolina.

"I'll do whatever you want," Ron says, his voice cracking. "I'll go to therapy, I'll role-play, we can spice it up. Just tell me what you want."

"I think," Carolina begins, "we're past that—"

"Have sex with someone else," Ron says suddenly. Emotionless.

"What?"

"Do it. Get it out of your system. The inevitable will happen. I don't care who it's with," he says, stone-faced. Carolina stares at him in stunned silence. "Because I know one thing for sure: The sex will ultimately turn tepid, then monotonous, and finally repulsive. You'll see. And then you'll realize just what a good thing we have here."

Carolina's emotions are in overdrive, and for a moment she considers telling Ron about Jack. One sentence. *I've been sleeping with Jack.* One sentence would do it. But she stays silent. She would have revealed the truth only to spar with Ron, to prove him wrong, to say that sex with another man was more passionate now than when it had begun. As quickly and as certain, Carolina's feelings for Jack build like a giant wave, powerful in their force and fury, but dissipating as they reach the shore. The emotional fluctuation combined with her pregnancy makes her dizzy, and she's forced to steady herself on the table.

"Are you okay?" Ron asks.

"I'm not sure," Carolina says, feeling a mix of shock and disgust. She takes a breath and squints her eyes. "I can't believe you're giving me permission to have an affair."

"I do so reluctantly—and only if it means saving our relationship," Ron explains. Carolina had read countless articles in *Cosmo* and *Vogue* about women turning a blind eye to their men's indiscretions if it meant salvaging a relationship. But she never expected for her boyfriend to offer the same.

"Where does this go? What's the endgame here, the goal?" Carolina asks.

"We have to have a goal?" Ron asks indignantly. "I guess I thought *my* goal was to share my life with someone; to have another human being bear witness to my life. Do you know how happy it makes me when I watch a silly video on YouTube or get an accolade at work that I have you to turn to and share it with? There's no one I'd rather do that with than you. Sure, could I meet someone else and go through the motions—you're goddamn right I could. But that's just it, Carol, I don't want to. I want you." Ron takes a sip of water and swallows hard.

"I didn't think I'd be back here again." She shakes her head in disbelief. "At least with Barrett I was still young. I had my whole life in front of me." Her eyes grow wider. "I can't believe I'm forty-three years old, and I'm starting this all over again."

"But you don't have—"

"Stop."

Carolina stares at him for a long while without saying a word. He reaches his other hand across the table and cups her hand in both of his. He sinks his head down and rests it on their hands. Carolina begins to silently cry again. She's never seen him so vulnerable, so utterly helpless. She places her hand on top of his head and gently strokes his hair. She detects the faint smell of his orange-scented shampoo. He's used it every day since Carolina gave it to him as a stocking stuffer for Christmas three years ago. She didn't tell him she'd gotten it in a gift bag. It didn't matter because he loved it just the same.

"I'm so sorry," Carolina says softly. The crotchety wait-ress passes by to check in and notices Ron's head cradled in Carolina's hands, and sees Carolina's swollen eyes. She rolls her eyes and retreats to the back of the restaurant to check on the only other customer. "But I can't be in this relationship just because I'm afraid of hurting you."

"Maybe," Ron says, and she can barely withstand the brokenness in his voice, ". . . maybe this is like before. Maybe you need space like before."

"Not this time." Carolina grabs the back of his hand and squeezes. "It's better this way. You need to be with someone you feel passion for, that you can't breathe without."

"I do feel that," he begins. "God, I hate this!" Ron says, slamming his fist against the table. Carolina flinches. "I feel like you're physically slipping away from me, like your arms are covered in oil, and I can't get a grip."

"Then maybe it's better to just let go."

Ron's shoulders sink. He stares blankly at nothing in particular, and says, "I'll be here for you while you take your time. And I don't care how long you take. I will still be here, waiting. If it takes my whole life. Our story . . . our story isn't over," Ron says, quickly wiping a tear from just below his eye. He stares at her for a moment, the strange light of the diner making his eyes look as brown as she's ever seen them. He sits up abruptly and steps out of the booth.

"Ron," Carolina begins.

"Since the day we met, I had this thought," he says to the floor. "I thought, what if she wished me away tomorrow? What would happen to me? What would I do? So I told myself to make sure every day with you was a day so special that you would never wish for anything else."

"You did—" Carolina begins.

"No!" Ron interrupts. "No, I got lazy. Goddamn it—I got lazy."

He turns his back on Carolina and takes a step toward the door.

"Ron, wait," Carolina says.

"No, I will not let you say it's your fault," Ron says softly. "I know whose fault it is."

"Ron, please!" Carolina says, and raises her voice as he takes another step. He walks through the diner's door, sending a burst of cold air shooting through the restaurant.

Carolina wipes the tears from her eyes and takes a deep breath. *What have I just done?* Why she chose this moment to run, why she kept Jack and her pregnancy an unspoken truth—these things she does not know. She stares into the now-cold plate of fries and lets her vision blur.

As she listens to the hum of fluorescents, the wind banging against the thin glass windows, she silently wonders if the real beauty of sitting at a diner at twelve thirty-six in the morning is that it allows one to strip away the frivolity of life and focus on what's right in front of you. Or in this case, what's no longer there.

As she huddles with Dennis in the corner of the modest apartment in Hells Kitchen, Sofia considers how it's far less glamorous than the loft party they'd gone to long ago. It's not that there wasn't an attempt at glamour—a feeble attempt perhaps, but an attempt nonetheless. A large, white, fake fur area rug anchors the room, and, judging by the various and unidentifiable stains, it has seen better days. A giant floor-to-ceiling mirror covers the back wall, looking more Florida timeshare than Manhattan chic. A white orb chandelier dangles in the center of the room like a disco ball as the tiny studio thunders with dance music. The blended smell of pot and cigarettes hangs in the air like smog in LA. For over an hour the two have been sitting on the hardwood floor, staring at the menagerie of people: drag queens, club kids, musclemen, a smattering of girls. And lots of cocaine. ("It's not only back," Dennis had told her, "but it's stronger than ever.") Dennis alternates between a highball glass of Stoli and a cup of water. After each sip, he hands the cup to Sofia for her to imbibe. Presently, they're watching a six-foot-two, African-American drag queen that could pass for Naomi Campbell's sister teach a five-foot-five, pudgy, stereotypical guido how to do a runway walk in the small walkway between the front door and the bedroom. Unfortunately, they're constantly dodging partygoers who need to use the bathroom, and the drag queen is not pleased.

"Move, bitches!" she shouts at two women in line for the bathroom.

As Dennis and Sofia stare wondrously at the scene before them, Dennis's phone chimes for the third time. He reaches for his phone, stares at it, and smiles.

"Is this your illustrious boyfriend again?" Sofia says, noticing Dennis's wide smile. His boyfriend had already texted twice while they were on the dance floor.

"Yes," he says simply.

"He's persistent!" Sofia says. "And up so late . . ."

"He's horny, that's all," Dennis says, and shrugs.

"He *is* your boyfriend. Is it such a bad thing that he wants to be with you? He loves you, right?" Sofia asks, taking the vodka from his hand.

Dennis hesitates. "Yeah, I suppose. Sure."

"God, that was tough," Sofia says, elbowing him gently. He is unusually quiet. "Uh-oh."

"What?" Dennis says coyly.

"Don't even try it. What's going on?" she asks.

He sighs. "I'm just"—he sips the vodka—"having my doubts. Maybe he's not the guy for me, that's all."

"Why not?" Sofia pries. "Does he treat you well?"

Dennis nods, and says flatly, "Like I'm the only guy in the world for him."

"You say it as if it's a bad thing," Sofia says. "Does he make you laugh?"

"He's got quite the twisted sense of humor."

"And despite not ever having seen him, I'm guessing he's brutally handsome," Sofia says, smiling. "You would never be with some slouch."

"He's the most beautiful man I've ever been with," Dennis says, trailing off. "I don't know. It's complicated. As much as I love him . . . it's probably best that I let him go."

Sofia stares hard at Dennis, who sighs deeply. "There's more to this story," she says.

"Can we change the subject?" Dennis shifts nervously.

"Okay, sure," Sofia says, touching his arm gently. "We'll come back to this at a later date, agreed?"

Dennis nods slowly. "I'm sure we will."

"But can I just say this one last thing?" Sofia begins.

"Oh God," Dennis says, annoyed.

"If Scott texted me for a booty call at this hour, I'd sprint out of this dump."

"It's not a dump. Dump*ish* maybe, but not a complete dump. Anyway, you make it sound like you never have sex with your husband."

"No, we have sex. We have great sex," she says, pausing to remember the hot shower they shared a few mornings ago.

"No offense, but I don't want to hear about your straight sex. It's gross and totally unnatural," Dennis says, and chuckles.

Sofia smacks Dennis's forearm and rests her head on his shoulder. "I meant Scott has probably been asleep for hours, and there is no way he'd be texting me at this hour."

"And he's okay with you being out with 'another man'?"

"Absolutely! I said I was going out with my gay husband, and I might not see him, my real husband, until tomorrow," Sofia explains with her eyes closed, feeling the wave of euphoria wash over her body in waves. Even though they'd taken the Ecstasy nearly four hours ago, hints of the drug still surfaced every now and then. Random images flood her mind: Scott lying in bed naked, his tan body on the white sheets; the two hundredth lightning bolt she created on a middle-aged mother's vagina; and sitting on the couch with Fabiana watching the scary movie earlier that night. It's as though she's floating somewhere between reality and a dream, and Dennis is her only anchor. Her thoughts jump: nonsequential, illogical. Fitting, she thinks, as there isn't anything logical about this night or about her life over these last six months.

A song with wailing vocals is blasting from the speakers and almost in unison the after-hours circus gets up from their chairs and dances wildly, arms waving, asses shaking, feet stomping. It jolts Sofia from her mind trip, momentarily jarring her senses. She stares at the group in amazement. The scene is like nothing she's ever seen: a hodgepodge of New York glitterati and gays.

"I wonder if the neighbors are pissed about the noise," Sofia says, dazed.

After a long silence, Dennis turns to her, and finally says, "Who the fuck cares?" and bursts into laughter.

"What?" she asks and grins.

"Even rolling on Ecstasy, you're still so good, so controlled. Worrying about the neighbors and shit. That's so adorable and so sad at the same time," Dennis says and kisses Sofia's cheek. His lips feel dry like a callus rubbing against her cold cheek. The magic little pill has heightened nearly every sensation.

"Why do you love me?" Sofia asks, fishing, practically begging for a compliment.

"Someone's feeling a bit needy, eh?" Dennis taunts. Sofia rolls her eyes.

"I love you because you have a style that has the sophistication of Padma Lakshmi and the spontaneity of Kelly Wearstler," Dennis says.

Sofia quickly interrupts. "I don't know whether to be horrified or delighted that your only touch points are personalities from reality competition shows on Bravo. But go on. What else?"

"I love you because you make a fantastic stunt 'boyfriend' when mine isn't around," Dennis says.

"Boyfriend? In spite of earlier questioning, I'm not sure he even exists. If he did, I'd have met him by now," Sofia says, blasé. Dennis cocks his head back. "So all you got is two superficial reasons? Wow. That says a lot, Hilding," Sofia continues.

"Oh God, you're more dramatic than any gay guy in this room," Dennis moans. "Okay, okay. Give me a minute."

Sofia looks at her watch and yawns. She intended to do it only to drive home her point, but when she notices that it's four in the morning, the yawn suddenly becomes very real. "Oh my God, I have to go," Sofia says in a slight panic and leans forward to stand.

"Wait, wait. I've got it," Dennis says, pulling her back to the floor.

"It'd better be good," she says, and swipes the glass of water out of Dennis's hand.

"I love you because you tolerate me . . ." he begins.

"Yes, I do. Okay, I'm going home." Sofia stands again, but Dennis is not finished.

". . . you tolerate me when I drive you nuts. You don't tell me I'm being silly, and you don't make me feel stupid or less than you for being a lame party promoter. I love you for answering my texts at two in the morning when I'm bored out of my mind with a tableful of models while guys twice their age try to fuck them, and I have to pretend that I don't feel like a pimp. I love you because you are my friend despite my series of missteps. I love you for making me believe I'm more than my mistakes. I love you for sitting here with me right now when I know the very core of you wants to dart out of the door because it's almost daylight, but instead you're here with me." Dennis stands up and meets Sofia's eyes and grabs her hand. "I love you like no gay man should love a woman. And that's all I got for right now . . ."

Before Dennis can say another word, Sofia leans in and kisses him hard, knocking his head clumsily against the wall. To both of their surprise, Dennis kisses her back passionately.

Dennis pulls away first and stares at Sofia silently. She doesn't take her eyes away from his. She rubs his tight muscular biceps with her hands, then moves her hands to his chest.

Whether it's the Ecstasy talking or the sheer passion of the kiss, he does not know, but Dennis asks, "Do you want to get out of here?"

The question hangs for what seems like an eternity. A million thoughts should be running through her mind, but only one comes out of her mouth: "Yes."

Dennis grabs Sofia's hand, and they maneuver their way out of the house party and into the elevator without saying a word. The elevator opens into the building lobby, and they walk out into the cold night air hand in hand.

As they wait on the corner for a cab, a gust of wind barrels through the buildings.

"It feels like snow," Sofia finally says aloud.

Dennis nods and helps her into the cab, giving the driver his home address.

said, what are you doing in my house, Christopher?!" Anna repeats. Her body is stiff and rigid, in complete contrast to the way it was three minutes ago when she was in the midst of kissing her biggest crush since . . . Christopher.

"A house that I paid for!" Christopher snaps back, staring at Tim.

"So typical," Anna says, completely annoyed.

Tim places his hand on the small of Anna's back, a move that Christopher quickly notices and can't avert his eyes from. Anna turns to face him, and Tim's hand slips to Anna's waist. Christopher shakes his head in disgust, but neither Tim nor Anna notices.

"Maybe it's best if I go," Tim whispers.

"No, you don't have to," Anna says, resigned.

"No, really. You guys obviously need to talk. But if you want me to stay for any reason, if you're worried . . ."

"Hey, pal, I was married to her. She's the mother of my

kids. You honestly think I'm going to hurt her?" Christopher shouts.

"I don't know you," Tim calmly, but firmly, fires back.

"Why are you here, Christopher? Answer me that," Anna says. Christopher stares at Tim, then back at Anna.

"I need to talk to you," Christopher says, resolved. Anna holds Christopher's stare, then turns around to face Tim.

"I gotta deal with this. Can we talk tomorrow?" Anna says.

"Call me," Tim says, and glances at Christopher one more time before descending the steps and getting into the town car.

Anna waits until Tim's car pulls away, then turns back to Christopher. "Go," she says, motioning toward the door. Christopher quickly walks into the house they used to share, with Anna trailing behind him. She notices an anxious Fabiana sitting on the couch.

"I think it's time for you to hit the sack, Fabi," Anna says.

"But Mom . . ." Fabiana begins.

"Fabiana," Christopher says.

In typical angst-ridden fashion, Fabiana rolls her eyes and hurls her body up from the couch. She stomps in Anna's direction, only momentarily stopping to quietly give her mother very specific orders: "Don't fuck this up."

Normally, Anna would immediately reprimand Fabiana for speaking to her in such a manner, but she finds herself too shell-shocked to respond. By the time she gathers herself, she can already hear Fabiana's door slamming shut.

Christopher perches on a chair nervously. Anna leans against the dining-room table, unsure of what's about to happen. She keeps a safe distance—not because she's worried about her physical safety, but for an emotional buffer.

"Okay, so let's get this over with. What did I do wrong now?" Anna says without a shred of sympathy. Same script, different day. The conversations about Ariel and how she was to blame for encouraging him to dress as a girl. They'd had this argument before. She'd bring up the suggestion of the child psychologist, she'd mention the journal articles, the gender-identity literature. He'd reply with gut and bluster. But tonight she is in no mood. She's spent, and her date was ruined by her ex-husband. She wishes she was still in some serious lip-lock with Tim at this moment, but instead she's in her living room ready, most likely, to receive an earful from Christopher about her parental failures.

"I want to give this another try," Christopher says shakily.

Instead of being stunned or flattered, Anna is angry. "Are you KIDDING me?" Anna steps out of her heels, so she can pace. "You want to what?"

"I want to give us another try," Christopher says, again nervously.

Anna feels vomit bubbling up to the back of her throat, and she gags. It's either the drinks at the Pierre or the bullshit being hurled at her that is causing such a violent reaction.

"I love you," Christopher says, and stands.

*It's definitely the bullshit.*

The words fall to the floor as quickly as they are thrown

out. Anna shakes her head. "What am I supposed to do with that?"

Christopher nervously unscrews the cap on an empty water bottle that was left behind by Fabiana. "Honestly, I don't know." He tries to take a sip then realizes the bottle's empty.

"Jesus, Christopher. Do you think I'm just going to say yes because you suddenly decide you want to come back? Are you that selfish? You *bailed*," Anna says, her voice growing louder with every word.

"I think we had . . . extenuating circumstances," Christopher says.

"That 'extenuating circumstance' is our child," Anna says.

"What do you want me to say? That I'm a horrible father? Do you want me to tell you that there are days that I think of taking a bottle of Vicodin because of the guilt I feel because I'm embarrassed of my own child? Do you have any idea how that makes me feel? My self-worth is about as valuable as that speck of dirt on the table. Or do you want me to tell you that since I moved out of this house—our house—I drink a fifth of vodka almost on a daily basis because I wasn't man enough to fix this. That I blame myself? Maybe I had some fucked-up chromosomes and it's my fault he turned out that way—or that I somehow did this to my own child. That if I'd spent more time with him, played with him more, then maybe he'd be different. Shit, Anna . . ."

*Breathe. Separate your heart from your head.* "What's changed?" she asks, not waiting for him to answer. "Ariel is *still* Ariel and will be for the rest of her life. That's not going to change. Every therapist and every article that Google can find will tell you the same thing. So what's changed, Christopher? Are you ready to fully accept your son as your daughter? If not, don't bother and just go."

Anna had played out this conversation in her head over a million times since Christopher left. Each time, her answer and her reasons were different—but the pangs in her stomach always felt the same.

"But what about your other two kids? You'll sacrifice them?" Christopher asks angrily. This sends a cold chill down Anna's back.

"I am a mother to all of my kids," Anna says calmly.

"I'm sorry. I didn't mean it like that," Christopher says sincerely. "I love you so much. And I don't know how to live my life without you," he says, his eyes filling with tears. And Anna knows he means each word. She knows, too, that she could have a relationship with him again. But she's not sure she *wants* one. And so she offers the only word that covers her uncertainty.

"No."

"No? That's all you can say?" Christopher says, amazed. "Can anyone else make you feel the way you feel when I touch you? Can you honestly tell me that you get a rush of adrenaline from that suit-and-tie guy? I know he doesn't give that to you like I can. Not with our history. We have something, Anna. I know you still love me. I can feel it."

"If that's the story you need to tell yourself . . ." Anna

says. She feels like she should cry, but when it comes to Christopher, she simply doesn't have the emotional energy left. Every last tear had been drained from her eyes. Or so she thought.

"We gotta figure this out. I know we can do this somehow. Don't you tell me we can't," Christopher says, moving closer to Anna.

"I can't go there again."

"No," Christopher says emphatically. "We gotta figure this out. Before . . ."

"Before what?" Anna interrupts. Christopher is silent and hangs his head, staring at the floorboards.

"Before what?" Anna repeats. Christopher is paralyzed.

"Before," Christopher whispers so softly that Anna doesn't hear him.

"All right. We're done here. I'm not doing this," Anna says, and shakes her head.

Anna walks to the front door, turns the knob, and opens it. A gust of wind blasts through the living room. She stands barefoot, still in the gown that JJ bought for her. Her hair is only slightly mussed: she is Cinderella rushing from the ball.

"Christopher. It's time to go."

"Before," Christopher repeats yet again, but this time loud enough Anna to hear. He raises his head, his face a mix of desperation and deflation. He walks to the door, where Anna stands. She averts her eyes from his.

"We gotta figure this out before what?" she says exhausted.

"Before I lose you for good," Christopher says resigned, staring at the woman he has loved for most of his life. Anna feels his eyes on her, but she cannot bring herself to look at him.

"I can't do this. Not again. I can't go there," Anna says. "You left us, Christopher. Things got tough, and you couldn't handle it. What do you want from me? I'm just done. I-I-I'm done," she stutters. The wind chills her arms.

"Anna, we can do this. We can figure it out. I can't lose you. I love you—and I think, I *know*, you still love me. They might be fading, but those feelings are still there, and if I don't try one last time . . . I'm afraid I'll lose you for good. I can't do that. I love you."

She looks up at him finally, their eyes together for the first time. And he presses his lips to hers and kisses her passionately—like never before. And finally, her hand on the door, the wind blowing through it, she lets go. She lets go of the arguing. She lets go of what's wrong and right. She lets go of thoughts of Tim. She even lets go of Ariel.

After a few minutes, he pulls his lips away from hers and stares into her eyes. "We have the power to change this. It doesn't have to be finished." A single tear blazes a stinging trail down Anna's cheek. Christopher wipes it with his thumb, then walks out the front door, leaving Anna standing motionless in the doorway, ignoring the cold wind. She's lost in the moment, still smelling Christopher's cologne on her neck until she hears the floorboard creak behind her.

She slowly turns around, fully expecting to see a defiant

Fabiana. Instead, she sees Ariel, standing quietly before her in princess pajamas. How long she's been standing there, what she's heard, and what she's understood Anna does not know. And the not knowing terrifies her. Anna calmly walks over to Ariel and picks her up in her arms and tries her hardest to smile.

"Hey, princess, what are you doing up?" Anna asks.

Ariel lets out a giant yawn, and says, "I missed you."

"You did?"

Ariel nods. "Yup. Can I have a snack?"

Anna laughs, then says, "Sure, but just this one time. It's late." With Ariel's arms wrapped around her neck like a monkey hanging from a tree, Anna walks to the kitchen.

"Thanks, Mommy," Ariel says.

"You're welcome," Anna says.

"Mommy?" Ariel says.

"Yes?"

"Can I live with you forever?" Ariel asks.

Anna's eyes well with tears, but thankfully Ariel can't see them.

"Sure," Anna says, her voice cracking.

"I love you, Mommy," Ariel says and kisses Anna on the cheek.

"I love you, too," Anna says.

# splat

A client of Sofia's for the past two years, Betsy Schiller first came to Impresarios when she was still single and hopeful. Today, she's married and bitter—and pregnant. Because lying flat on her back is nearly impossible and horribly uncomfortable, Betsy leans back on Sofia's table on her forearms, unable to see Sofia over her enormous belly, and lurches forward on the treatment bed every time Sofia says something of interest. Because Betsy's center of gravity is slightly off, Sofia fears Betsy might tumble to the floor. And with her wrinkled forehead—thanks to no Botox during said pregnancy—her brash and often curt delivery suggests a conflict between her own darting, snarky thoughts and her perfect Upper East Side appearance. Despite the bland matching maternity sweater set, there is still something feral about Betsy.

"So can you believe what this asshole says to me?" Betsy says loudly and in midthought.

"And by 'asshole' you mean your dear husband?" Sofia says, tending to Betsy's unruly garden.

"Yes, that one. Anyway, we were fighting about whether or not he was going to run to the deli on the corner to get me some Soy Crisps—hey, at least they're healthy," she says, interrupting herself. "And he bitches that he doesn't want to go. So I tell him he better get his butt out and get them for me. Well, he didn't like it . . . at all!"

"What did he say?" Sofia says, yanking one of the waxing strips.

"He said, you're lucky you bought low," Betsy begins.

"Bought low?" Sofia asks.

"You know these Wall Street assholes, always trying to be cute. When I met him, he was working some midlevel job. He didn't have a lot of money—but I was thirty-eight, and my options were seriously dwindling." Sofia shrugs and silently laughs at Betsy's comments. "He then says, 'You know, since you met me, my value has risen enormously,'" Betsy says in a northern New Jersey accent.

"No!" Sofia says, and peeks her head above Betsy's belly to show her shock.

"Yes, unbelievable this one. So I said to him, 'Well, maybe I'll just sell high then.' Screw him; I'll take the money. I'm already pregnant, and all I ever really wanted was the baby.

Him I could take or leave," she says in a nasally Fran Dre-scher voice.

"Betsy! You don't mean that!" Sofia says, doubting her own certainty.

"Wait a second, is that an iPod? It most be one of the originals it looks so old, my God!" Betsy says, examining Sofia's iPod sitting on the countertop. Sofia knows that Betsy doesn't mean anything by it, it's just Betsy's way.

"Anyway, where was I? Oh. Honestly, I do mean it. I could take him or leave him. It is what it is. He's so arrogant . . ." Betsy continues.

Sofia momentarily tunes out as she hears a commotion in the hallway. She even thinks she hears her name being called in the distance, but quickly dismisses it.

"So he then tells me how so many women at work would kill to be with him because he's such a hot commodity—again with the stock analogies, can you believe? So then I say . . ."

Sofia returns to waxing, then hears the commotion get-ting closer to her room. She hears a muffled voice and what sounds like doorknobs being jiggled and another female voice shouting closely behind.

Then she hears, "SOFIA!"

Sofia pops her head out from between Betsy's legs.

Betsy, however, is still lost in her own story. ". . . And all of this for a bag of apple cinnamon Soy Crisps!" she declares.

"Did you hear that?" Sofia asks.

"What?" Betsy asks.

Then the shout again, "SOFIA!"

"Oh my God. Who's screaming your name?" Betsy asks.

Before Sofia can answer, the door flies open and Dennis barges in. Thankfully, Betsy's back is to the door so nothing's on display.

"DENNIS! WHAT ARE YOU DOING HERE?" Sofia shouts.

"I HAVE TO TALK TO YOU!" Dennis shouts back.

Before Sofia can get another word out, Candace pushes in behind Dennis. "I tried stopping him!"

"This room is more crowded than the Barneys warehouse sale," Betsy says, and turns her head toward the trio. Sofia quickly grabs a towel and drapes it over Betsy to cover her. "Thanks, it was starting to get a little drafty."

"Do you want me to call the police?" Candace says, grabbing Dennis's arm and pulling him toward the door.

"Dennis, can't this wait?" Sofia asks.

"No, you won't return any of my calls, e-mails, or texts. I'm not leaving here until you speak to me," Dennis declares.

Sofia looks at Dennis dumbfounded, then turns her attention toward Candace.

"It's fine, Candace. I'll take it from here," Sofia says.

The shock and disappointment shows on Candace's face. "Fine, but I was ready to call the police."

"Thanks, Candace, if we should need New York's Finest, I'll be sure to let you know," Sofia says, and begins to shut the door.

"I'm going to tell Carolina," Candace says.

"Yes, I'm counting on it," Sofia says, and shuts the door on her.

Sofia turns her attention to Dennis, and says, "You need to leave—this is so far beyond the parameters of acceptable—"

"What did you expect me to do? You won't talk to me!"

"Good lord, honey, what did you do with this guy?" Betsy chimes in, still naked from the waist down and covered only by a small towel.

"You have to leave!" Sofia says, pushing Dennis toward the door. "I'll call you."

"No," he says as he steadies himself against the door-frame, "you won't."

"I'm with a client. What do you expect me to do?" Sofia says in a hushed voice.

"Talk to me in the hallway!"

"What—for the rest of the salon to hear you? Absolutely not!" Sofia fumes.

"Break room?" Dennis attempts.

"Nope," Sofia says flatly.

"Bathroom?" Dennis says.

"You can't be serious? We might as well talk over the PA system," Sofia says, and shakes her head. "Look you're just going to have to . . ."

"Oh my God. Just have the damn conversation here already. I'm pregnant and so very bored with Connecticut. I could use some drama," Betsy interrupts.

"Betsy, I couldn't," Sofia says.

"Look, whatever is going on is obviously very important. Just have the talk. Get it over with." Sofia tilts her head and holds her stare on Betsy. "Trust me, your discretion is assured. But you should be thankful Nancy Bitterman wasn't in here—then you'd be in deep shit," Betsy says, and lets out an abrupt cackle.

Sofia mouths "thank you" to Betsy and walks back to Dennis, who leans against the door, both in an attempt to keep Sofia from leaving and to balance himself because he's so nervous.

"You have 180 seconds. Go," Sofia commands.

"The other night at my apartment, I should have never let it go that far . . ." Dennis begins.

"Don't. We're both adults. Let's leave it there," Sofia says, and stares at the ground. She certainly didn't *feel* like an adult. She felt like a cheating high-school girlfriend. It all seemed so petty and juvenile. Sofia shifts her eyes to Betsy's gray cashmere sweater draped on a chair. It reminds her of the gray she wants to paint her kitchen—tangential thoughts of life with Scott explode in her mind.

"You DID sleep with him!" Betsy chimes in, her face pops back over her shoulder. "Oh my God!"

"Betsy!" Sofia says annoyed.

"Sorry! I didn't mean to. Go on. I'll just focus on my Lamaze breathing and close my eyes . . ."

"We stopped before that. We stopped before we did anything . . . irrevocable," Sofia says and stares into Dennis's eyes. The truth was that it was Dennis who had stopped Sofia from going all the way, something that had haunted her for two weeks. "So if you're coming to apologize, please, it's fine. Blame the Ecstasy. Blame me. Blame my mother."

"You did Ecstasy? God, suddenly I'm in an episode of *Intervention*—"

"BETSY!" Dennis and Sofia shout at the same time.

"I wanted to tell you . . ." Dennis starts. "Wait . . . your mother? What does *she* have to do with this?" Dennis asks.

Sofia is silent for a moment. "I finally get it. The passion, the lust. How she must have felt for those briefs moments. So alive. So special. So real," Sofia says, and tears up. "And then I tore it down the minute I realized. Not that I'm condoning it 'cause it's vile. But I did. I finally understood her affair at the moment when you kissed me on your bed."

Dennis is silent and takes a deep breath. "I don't think either one of us thought it'd actually go that far. I mean, come on, how many gay guys do you know that bring home their best girlfriend for random sex?"

"He's GAY?" Betsy screams in shock.

Sofia walks toward Betsy again. For a hot minute, it looks as though Sofia is about slap Betsy. Instead, Sofia grabs her iPod and shoves it in Betsy's hand. "Do you mind?"

Betsy takes the iPod from Sofia, places the earbuds into her ears, and repeats, almost to herself, "He's gay?"

"Yes, he's gay," Sofia says, and reaches across Betsy's lap and presses PLAY.

"I mean, you *are* still gay," Sofia says, for a moment back to her old self, "aren't you?"

"The last time I checked, yes," Dennis says, answering her tone with a nervous laugh. He cracks his knuckles anxiously.

"So let's just forget about this, okay? It'll be awkward for a while, but we'll get past it. And maybe less partying. You know, maybe just coffee or something. And dinners. The drugs don't . . ." Sofia says, rambling.

"That's not why . . ."

"And it's good. I should be at home more with Scott. It's not like he works every single night. We'll make more of an effort. We'll be fine," she says, primarily to herself. "And you," she says, smacking him on the shoulder awkwardly.

"Me?"

"You should be spending more time with that man of yours."

"Sofia . . ."

"That is, if this dream man really exists . . ."

"Sofia, would you stop talking for one goddamn second so I can say what I came to say?" His intensity stuns her, and she falls silent. "Because I'm not sure I'm going to have the strength to do this again, and I don't think I can afford bail money if I come back to this salon."

Sofia nervously fidgets and mentally prepares a standard response in case Dennis is about to tell her that he's fallen in love with her.

*I'm so flattered, really I am. But I'm married. If it would have been a different time in our lives . . . This is just a phase. You'll grow out of it. You'll be back to normal in no time.*

"Why are you closing your eyes?" Dennis asks.

"What?" Sofia says.

"You look like I'm about to smack you across the face, and you're anticipating the sting," Dennis says in his typically flippant way.

Sofia opens her eyes.

"It's about my boyfriend," Dennis begins.

*Bullet dodged.* "What's going on?" Dennis stares silently at Sofia, and the silence makes her crazy. "Dennis, what?" she says, breaking the silence. "Oh my God. He's cheating on you?"

Dennis remains silent. Sofia continues on. "Oh my God. He is. I'm so sorry—I'll take the rest of the afternoon off. Right after Betsy. I just really need to finish this up. I'm sure I'm already going to get an earful from Carolina. She will . . ."

"Sofia . . ." Dennis says, cutting off her rambling midflow.

"What?" Sofia asks, then suddenly gasps. "No. Don't tell me. You don't have . . ."

"What? No, no I'm not positive," Dennis says flatly.

"Okay. Well, can we continue this after Betsy, please?" she asks again. "Your boyfriend clearly is an asshole for cheating on you, and if I were you—"

"It's Scott," Dennis says quietly.

"Scott? What about Scott?"

"Scott is . . ." Dennis begins.

"God, Dennis, what? You're scaring me. What the hell are you trying to tell me about my husband?" Sofia demands.

"S-S-Scott is my boyfriend."

Sofia inadvertently breaks out into laughter, an obvious release of the fear of imagining Scott lying in the middle of Third Avenue after being struck by a delivery truck. "Oh my God. Thank you. I needed that." She sighs.

"Sofia," he says, barely able to see her through the tears gathering in his eyes. "Scott is my boyfriend. The one you've never met."

"Dennis, stop!" Sofia says, and spills laughter again, this time more manufactured than genuine. Dennis is silent. "Seriously, Dennis, stop," Sofia says, annoyed. Tears fall from Dennis's eyes and hit his jacket. "Scott is not gay. I don't know what kind of twisted bullshit you're trying to pull, but I think you really should leave," Sofia says, and backs away from him.

"We met fourteen months ago at Sweet Lorraine, this club on the Bowery that I was promoting. I was at a table with a group of Russian models, and Scott was with a table of suits. Within five minutes, the suits were buying the girls drinks—but not Scott. He stayed away. We hit it off immediately. I was open with him. I figured he was straight, so I didn't have to play the flirting game with him. By the end of the night we were all wasted, and everyone kind of split up, but not Scott, he stuck to me and he asked if I wanted to share a cab ride home."

Sofia's eyes narrow, and her mouth opens.

"We were both piss drunk and after about five minutes in the taxi, he kissed me."

"He kissed you," Sofia says defiantly.

"Sofia . . ."

"Go on."

"Sofia, you don't need to know every last detail—" Dennis cries.

"I said, 'Go on,'" Sofia says firmly.

Dennis hesitates, opening his mouth to speak, but says nothing.

"FINISH!"

"We, uh, we made out the entire cab ride to my place. And then he came into my apartment and . . . we, uh . . . Sofia—"

"Don't, Dennis. Don't you dare stop now. What did you do in your apartment?"

"We . . . we fucked," Dennis says.

With all her strength, Sofia keeps herself from punching Dennis in the face. "It was just that once?" Sofia asks through gritted teeth.

"I thought it would be. I honestly thought he was going to be just another random hookup. I've done it hundreds of times," Dennis says, and rolls his eyes. Sofia is frozen in shock. Silence fills the room when Dennis stops talking. "But then he began texting me at all hours, while he was at work, during the day, late at night. And then he started coming over, telling you he had to entertain his out-of-town clients."

"It's just sex. That was all. That's all it was with him. He doesn't love you."

"Maybe." Dennis begins moving closer to Sofia. "But it wasn't just sex. We'd go to movies together, have dinner together, lie in bed for hours," Dennis confesses. "He loves me."

Sofia pulls back her arm and slaps Dennis wildly across the face.

"I think I'm going to—oh my God, I can't breathe," Sofia says, swaying slightly and breathing heavily. She walks toward Betsy and steadies herself against her cabinets.

"Maybe you should sit," Dennis says, reaching to help her, his face red from the powerful smack he received.

"Don't you dare! Don't you dare EVER touch me!" Sofia shouts. Betsy continues to stare ahead obliviously. Sofia glances at the ground and tries to catch her breath. She sounds as if she's having an asthma attack, but this is even more deadly—this is sheer panic. Dennis stands a few feet away from her.

"Why? Why me? Why would you be my friend when you knew you were screwing my husband?" Sofia says, demanding an answer.

"You're screwing her husband?!?" Betsy says, and whips her head around to face Dennis.

"BETSY! PLEASE!" Sofia yells.

"It was between songs!" Betsy explains. She meekly turns back around to face the wall.

"He's leaving, Betsy. Give me two more minutes, then we'll finish up here. This one's on me. Actually, make that your next three appointments," Sofia says deliriously, in an attempt to keep some sense of normalcy in a very abnormal situation. Betsy cocks her head back in both surprise and delight. Sofia walks over to Betsy and rubs the top of her head sweetly. She gently presses the FAST FORWARD button on her iPod, then pushes PLAY.

"Speak," Sofia orders Dennis.

"I had to know for myself who he was going home to," Dennis says. "I had to find out."

"But you came here . . . He told you where I work?" Sofia says, exasperated.

"No. He was in the shower and his BlackBerry was on the bed. I was snooping around and saw, 'SOFIA WORK' in his phone. So I dialed it and got the reception desk. I made an appointment, but never thought I would go. I thought for sure I'd let it go or get cold feet. But my curiosity got me into the cab uptown. I had to see who my competition was. Who he was leaving me for every day? And then I met you," Dennis says, crying harder.

"You're a sociopath!" Sofia shouts. "Oh my God. You're seriously insane. Get out." Sofia grabs her phone off the counter and stares at the dial pad.

"It's so not like that. I never expected for you to be you. I hated lying to you. I wanted to tell you so many times."

"But you didn't," Sofia says curtly.

"I didn't."

"My God, I'm such a fool. The two of you in on this together. I'm the stupid one. I hope you got a good laugh after you fucked each other," Sofia cries.

It's too much for her to process. Sofia can't separate truth from lie. She wants to scream, she wants to cry, she wants to make him hurt.

"He doesn't know. I never told him my real name. I gave him my middle name, Ryan, the first night we met. He figured out I was lying about my name, but he didn't care. So he only knows me as Ryan. Scott is going to be devastated," Dennis says, trailing off. "He'll probably never talk to me again."

"You'll have to excuse me for not giving a shit!" Sofia snaps. Betsy moans from behind Sofia, but Sofia ignores her.

"Sofia, I never planned on any of this. I never planned on caring for you as much as I did, as much as I *do*," Dennis says, taking a step closer to her. Sofia quickly raises her hand, stopping him from coming any closer. "You're the best thing that's happened in my life," Dennis says softly.

"And the kiss? We almost slept together, Dennis. Could you have gone through with that?" Sofia asks incredulously.

"Yes. I mean, no. Honestly, I'm just as confused about all of this as you. I don't know what's going on. I've never had a friend like you before. The kiss . . . I don't know. It just felt nice. I felt connected to someone for the first time on a real emotional level. I went with it because I thought that's what you wanted," Dennis explains.

Sofia is momentarily stunned. She didn't think it was possible to feel even worse. "You thought that was what *I* wanted. So you were ready to sleep with me out of some twisted honor to our friendship? What a plan! Fuck me so you feel less bad about fucking my husband!"

Betsy moans again and shifts in her seat, this time calling Sofia's name. The iPod inadvertently slips out of Betsy's hand and crashes to the ground.

"One minute, Betsy," Sofia says, without turning around.

"I never meant to hurt you. This is not what I wanted to happen. But I couldn't lie to you anymore. I couldn't. I would kill myself if I thought it would make your pain go away," Dennis says, completely defeated.

"Of course . . . of course you would make this about you!" Sofia says coldly.

"Sofia," Betsy says louder.

"One minute," Sofia says, trying to remain calm. "Get out. If you come near me or MY husband again, I will kill you myself."

"SOFIA!" Betsy screams.

"I'm coming!" Sofia screams back and goes to adjust the iPod and notices it on the ground.

"Sofia, I'm sorry . . ." Betsy starts.

"No Betsy, I'm sorry. It's just an iPod," Sofia interrupts, bending down to pick up the iPod.

"No, I've been having contractions. I need to get out of here."

"Oh my God!" Sofia looks up at Betsy, just as Betsy's water breaks, drenching her face and shoulders.

"OH MY GOD!" Betsy screams.

Sofia waves her hands in front of her face in shock, unable to speak. Dennis rushes to the counter and grabs a stack of hand towels and starts patting Sofia down to dry her off, gagging at the thought of what he's actually wiping away.

"HELLO? Can you either hand me my FUCKING phone or call a goddamn ambulance yourself?" Betsy hollers.

Dennis jumps to his feet and fumbles with the salon house phone and dials zero. "Hello. Hi. I'm in Sofia Carnahan's room and you need to call an ambulance right away. This woman is about to—"

"ARGH!!" Betsy shouts in the background.

"—pop out a baby. And I don't . . . God, I don't know what to do about that, so call 911, like *now*!" Dennis yells, before slamming the phone back onto the receiver.

Sofia is still seated on the floor, caked in baby juice. Her face is covered with one of the small towels, and her shoulders move up and down as if she's sobbing. Dennis kneels down in front of her.

"I'm so sorry," Dennis says, patting Sofia down with another towel. He leans in closer to Sofia, and says, "Don't cry. Please don't cry."

Sofia lets the towel drop away from her face, and Dennis sees she's laughing hysterically.

"Sofia?" Dennis says in surprise.

"This is sick! So sick I can't even . . . Her water broke *on me*. Have you ever . . . ?" Sofia says, howling. Betsy joins in the laughter.

"I tried warning you," Betsy says, her laugh quickly turning into a scream of pain.

"They'll be here any second. Just hold on and breathe," Dennis says to Betsy.

"Says the gay home wrecker!" Betsy shouts, before another scream.

Sofia erupts in laughter and covers her face with the towel again. Dennis leans closer and attempts to absorb some of the liquid on Sofia's robe and neck. Sofia continues to cover her face.

In the few remaining moments, as they wait for the inevitable cavalcade of employees, gawkers, and eventually EMT workers, Dennis whispers to Sofia through the towel quietly enough so Betsy can't hear, "I wish I still believed in God." He briefly pauses, lost in thought and emotion. His eyes shift upward to a picture of Sofia and Scott on vacation. "Or hell, I don't know, Buddha, Allah, or something," he says, rambling and wiping tears from his eyes.

Sofia continues to keep quiet, leaving the towel on her face. Finally, Dennis turns away from the photo and stares at Sofia while wiping her hand.

"If I did believe, I would pray for a second chance with you," he says.

And at that moment, Candace and two EMT workers come barreling into Sofia's room, causing the towel to fall from Sofia's face. She momentarily locks eyes with Dennis, and somehow knows that this will be the last time she'll see him for a very, very long time.

n a navy corduroy blazer, gray T-shirt with the word WYOMING on it, a pair of baggy blue jeans, and a few days' growth on his unshaven face, Jack looks exceptionally stunning. He wanted to keep his "hot" moniker with the ladies at the salon even if they knew him as Mr. McLeery. He's surprisingly at ease in Carolina's pristine office as he sips on a Corona. It was only one thirty, but Carolina had a cold beverage ready in anticipation of his arrival. He sips on his beer as Carolina furiously types on her computer.

"So is the beer supposed to keep me calm while I watch you type, or is it to keep me from jumping over that desk and molesting you," Jack says and flashes her his trademark grin. But she misses it. She doesn't bother to look up.

"Carolina?" Jack says.

Nothing.

"Hey—you there?" Jack asks again. He remains fixated on Carolina. Her eyes, nearly covered by a black fedora, squint at her computer screen. Her blond hair creeps out from under the hat and rests on a pin-striped black suit jacket.

Carolina finally raises her head and meets his eyes. "Sorry. I have to finish these e-mails. Our WAXED product launch at Sephora is less than three weeks away. And it looks like production has just hit a major snafu, and we're supposed to ship to stores in one week," Carolina says, almost robotically.

Jack takes another swig of beer, then says, "Don't. Don't do that."

"What?" Carolina asks.

"Talk to me like I work for you. Talk to *me*. I'm right here. It's just me, you don't have to try and sound so businesslike."

"I didn't realize explaining the reason for my stress was 'businesslike.' I'm sorry I can't break it down into baby talk because you're so sensitive to 'business talk,'" Carolina says, her fingers shaping quotes.

Jack instinctually begins biting the side of his cheek. "Whoa, where is this coming from?"

"Coming from?" Carolina asks.

"You're being bitchy. But I'm not going to engage you," Jack says. He walks to the window and looks out onto Fourteenth Street.

"Ron and I are getting married," Carolina blurts.

Jack doesn't take his eyes away from the pedestrians shuffling down the street, in and out of the row of boutiques. "No, you're not."

"I'm not?" Carolina says.

"No. You won't marry him. You don't love him. You love me," Jack says flatly, the ultimate in masculine cool. "And you'll marry me."

"Marry you?" Finally, she looks up from the screen.

"Yup. You want to?"

If a year had passed, if she'd had some distance from her breakup from Ron, if she weren't pregnant—things might be different. But none of her "ifs" were realities.

"No," Carolina says, emotionless. "I don't want to. I'm marrying Ron."

As coolly as possible, Jack says, "I've gotten used to your face."

"Get used to someone else's," Carolina slices.

Jack remains stoic without revealing a single emotion. He looks outside again, this time pressing his forehead against the cold glass. It feels good on his suddenly flushed skin.

"You're serious, aren't you?" Jack says, moving his head back and forth against the glass.

"I am," Carolina says.

"I better get going," he says.

"I'm sorry," Carolina says, doing her best to remain emotionless. If she shows the slightest bit of emotion, Jack will call her bluff immediately, and she's not confident that she can continue the lie. Her emotions are too raw.

"Wow. Good luck to you. I guess you won't turn out to be like the stupid woman in the Cabiria movie after all," he says, calmly nodding while sporadically continuing to chew on the side of his cheek. "But let me remind you that she didn't have a happy ending either. She ended up alone," he says, not in a malicious way but more in a reflective tone.

"I cheated on my boyfriend with you. It's screwed up. We're all adults here. Let's call it for what it is. I wasn't happy in my relationship, so I found what I needed some-place else . . ." Carolina says.

"Don't do that. Don't cheapen it—"

"You just don't get it. I thought you would have after the night in the car," Carolina interrupts. "But not you. Your ego wouldn't let you. I have to know—why?"

Jack stares at Carolina. He's not sure if she's giving him a poker face or not, but either way he's ready to call her bluff.

"I'm going to be forty-five this year. Neither one of us has a lot of time to ponder the possibilities. Much like you, for the last fifteen years or so I catapulted myself headfirst into my work but have had no one to share my life with as fucking ridiculous as that sounds," Jack says, and shakes his head. Carolina remains silent, hanging on his every word. Jack continues. "And for the first time in a very long time, I want something and someone that's real. I'm tired of the bullshit, Carolina, and when I saw you that day in Queens, I knew it right then. Hell, I know we're off to a late start, but I want to share the rest of my life with someone. I'm not looking for you to give me praise or pity for realizing this, just give me a chance. That's all I'm asking."

Carolina looks him in the eyes and is on the verge of bursting into tears. She softly closes her eyes, and calmly says, "If it wasn't you, it would have been someone else. And the result would have been the same."

"NO!" Jack says loudly, and removes himself from the window and stares directly at her. "That is not true. You're being cold because you know—"

"You were a distraction," Carolina says, not meaning a word of it. "I'm better suited to be with Ron. He can provide me with a life that you can't possibly. And I don't mean that as a put-down to you, but Ron has a level of means that you never will. I don't need you anymore."

The minute the words leave her lips, she regrets them. It makes her physically sick to her stomach, and it goes against everything she feels and believes.

"MARRY ME! Goddamn it! Do not pull this shit again—"

"You should go," Carolina says. She stands up from behind her desk and walks toward the door. She isn't sure if this is going to be the answer to all of her problems or if it would completely emotionally destroy her. *Why are you staying? Please go. Go.*

"I don't believe you. This isn't you," Jack argues.

"Jack," Carolina says sympathetically.

"You'll come around. You will," Jack says emphatically.

"Jack," Carolina repeats.

"This isn't over. It never is really over. It wasn't over then, and it certainly is not over now," Jack says, moving within inches of Carolina's face. She can feel his breath against her cheek. She attempts to turn her head, but Jack reaches for her chin and turns her back to face him again. "Come on. I'm right here. Tell me what's going on. I won't beg. But this is your last chance. I'll stay no matter what's going on. It's only you and me, Carolina—right here, right now."

"Jack," Carolina says softly.

"I know it's not over," Jack repeats. "We're not to the point of no return yet. Don't make this mistake again, Carolina. Don't."

He grabs Carolina's face and presses his lips against hers— hoping for something, anything. But there is nothing.

Carolina gently pulls away. "I'm sorry," she says again. "We're done."

Carolina reaches for the silver handle on the door. What Jack didn't know was that she had been crying for the last week leading up to this. She'd known the day after she broke up with Ron what she needed to do about Jack. She didn't want the complications—not with a baby on the way. Right or wrong never entered into the equation. But she knew it was better to get all of the emotion out of the way before telling Jack in order to give a convincing performance.

"Don't bother. I'm going," Jack says, and marches toward the door. He's bitten the inside of his cheek raw and can feel the blood dripping down his throat.

Carolina hangs her head, not wanting to look him in the eyes.

Jack finally reaches the door, and Carolina opens it without looking at him.

"Good-bye, Carolina," Jack says.

Carolina takes a deep breath and exhales. She bites the back of her lip, then finally says, with a gentle calm, "Good-bye, Jack."

Jack walks out the door, and Carolina quickly shuts it behind him, her hand moving down from the handle to the carpet, as she collapses to the ground in tears. She knew that someday their paths would intersect yet again, but for now she has to go on assuming that it was the last she would ever hear from him.

Her office phone rings loudly. She thinks about ignoring it and letting it go to voice mail, but she can't stand the blaring noise that bounces off the bare white walls. The incessant sharpness pierces her eardrums. "STOP RINGING!" she shouts at her desk, and, as if on command, the phone suddenly stops. Carolina takes a deep breath and momentarily tries to collect herself. She picks herself off the floor, runs her fingers through her hair, and sighs loudly.

"Okay, you did it. It's over," she says to herself as she slowly walks to her desk. "You're going to be fine. You always are." She grabs her latte and is about to take a sip when her phone rings again. She reaches across the desk and picks up the receiver.

"What?"

"Hi. It's Candace. We have a problem. Betsy Schiller just went into labor."

"What? Where?" Carolina asks.

"In Sofia's treatment room. The paramedics are here. I thought you should know," Candace says.

"I'm coming down there now."

"Also, there's someone—" Candace begins, but in her haste to get down to Betsy Schiller, Carolina has already hung up the phone. She grabs her latte and races toward the door. But someone else opens it first.

"I came as soon as Anna called. You're pregnant!" the voice says loudly. The woman throws her arms around Carolina, who stands listless in a combination of shock and terror. Her arms pinned to her side, Carolina drops her coffee and it SPLATS all over her immaculate walls.

"Hello, Mother," she says in a muffled voice into Lunetta's shoulder.

'm up here, girly," JJ yells from somewhere on the second floor.

Anna walks up the steps lugging a small duffel bag. She guesses she's probably climbed these stairs well over a hundred times by now. She hears faint music playing on the speakers throughout the town house. She's unable to tell who the crooner is. Her first guess is Michael Buble, but he seems way too current for JJ. As she contemplates the music artist, she hears JJ's voice again—it's weak.

"Are you crawling? Come on. I'm going to be dead by the time you make it up," JJ says craggily.

"I'm almost there," Anna yells back while climbing the steps.

"Well then, speak up next time," JJ says, and walks down the hallway to the top of the stairs. She's standing in a pair of what looks like men's silk chocolate brown pajamas with a long lavender belted robe, and burnt orange Hermès slippers. She looks like a female Hugh Hefner minus the requisite centerfolds.

"I'm sorry. I didn't know we were on a schedule," Anna complains.

JJ rolls her eyes and walks back into the bedroom.

"Someone is grouchy today," Anna says, and follows JJ. Ever since the opening night of the ballet, JJ's health has deteriorated. She wouldn't tell Anna what was going on, but looking at JJ, the signs were there—her gray coloring, her constant naps, and her weakened voice.

JJ ignores her and walks farther into the giant bedroom.

"Where are we going today?" Anna asks in an attempt to stay optimistic. "I don't think I can do any helicopter rides today. Not unless you want to see what I ate for breakfast," Anna jokes.

"Charming," JJ snickers.

"So what's up? What are we doing after this?" Anna asks again.

"*We* are finishing *this* today," JJ says flatly.

"What do you mean?" Anna asks.

"We've nearly come to the end of the list," JJ answers.

"Just like that?" Anna asks, shocked by JJ's emotionless responses.

"Just like that," JJ says. "You need to get on with your life.

Raise your family. Take care of those two beautiful daughters and that handsome son. And let's be honest, you need to get laid," JJ says, and laughs before collapsing into a cough.

"Oh," Anna says, disappointed. "And you?" Anna asks, not sure she's ready for the answer.

"Me? I'll go back to my life," JJ says resigned.

"I call bullshit," Anna argues.

"I'm sorry, what?" JJ asks.

"Bullshit. You're not going back to your life."

"I most certainly am," JJ snips, and turns her back on Anna. She lights a match and moves toward a large, white pillar candle on a side table.

"No. You plan on dying alone," Anna says.

The bluntness of Anna's sentiment washes over JJ, momentarily paralyzing her, causing the match to burn her finger. "SHIT!" JJ shouts, dropping the match onto the table. "That was a cruel thing to say," she snaps.

"Tell me I'm wrong," Anna demands. JJ says nothing. "You want me to leave you alone so you can die, so it won't affect me. It's what dogs do. They get hit by a car, and they take off, so they can die alone. Honestly, I expected a little more creativity from you," Anna says.

JJ strikes the match against the box and finally lights the candle. "So can we do this, or do I have to call the salon and ask for another girl?"

"Oh God. Really? Another girl? So predictable," Anna says, taking the wax out of her bag. She begins to walk out of the room.

"Where are you going?" JJ asks.

"To heat up the wax," Anna answers.

"I had the housekeeper bring the microwave upstairs," JJ says, and points to the enormous walk-in closet. "It's in there."

Anna looks at JJ quizzically and zaps the wax in the microwave. She takes it out and walks over to JJ, who is still standing.

"So do you want to sit so we can do this?" Anna says, staring at JJ. She looks closer at JJ's face. It's gaunt, and the makeup isn't completely helping her coloring. "Honestly, your eyebrows look fine."

"We're not doing my eyebrows," JJ says.

"Your arms?" Anna asks and grabs JJ's forearm.

JJ quickly snatches it back. "No, you twit!"

"Well we took care of your moustache two weeks ago. So I'm not really sure what . . ." Anna stops midsentence, then says, "Oh."

JJ averts her eyes away from Anna.

"Are you sure you want to do *that*?" Anna asks.

"What? You don't want to see an old lady naked? I got news for you. It's going to be you before you know it," JJ says, and completely turns her back to Anna.

"No. I just don't get why now?" Anna says.

"Because it's the last," she says, and pauses. She turns around and faces Anna, her eyes are filled with tears—something Anna swore she'd never see from JJ. "Because it's the last thing on the list," JJ says, then takes a deep breath.

Anna always knew in the back of her mind that this day would come, but she'd always hoped it never would. She was lost in JJ's world and wasn't ready to go back to her own. The experiences were tangible proof that Anna's life had been transformed into one of risk-taking, adventure, and living her life authentically. Without JJ, Anna wasn't sure that she would be able to hold true to these newfound tenets. Anna glances at JJ, now sitting at the edge of the bed with her legs crossed. The room is silent despite the fact that only moments ago music played throughout the house. All Anna can hear is her head throbbing. It's too much for her to take in, and she walks to the giant window. She notices that the frost has kissed the windows. The sky is gray and serious.

"Well," Anna says in a shaky voice, "if we're gonna do this, you'd better uncross your legs."

## Thirteen

# waxed

e Metro is New York's latest addition to the constantly changing and ever-evolving nightlife scene. The *Observer* heralded it as the first legitimate contender to the current nightlife champion, Gramercy Park Hotel. Its nondescript door contains only the building number, adding to the mystique of this subterranean hideaway for New Yorkers in the know. Every trendy New York club has a gimmick, and this one is no different. Whether or not revelers recognize its European metro-line motif is unclear, but surprisingly, the design is carried out in a subtle and refined manner; white subway-tiled walls and a low, vaulted ceiling give clubgoers the illusion that they're waiting for the metro to take them from Paris to London. And tonight, the train is filled with models, trustfunders, publicists, media, and the rest of Manhattan's glitterati to celebrate the launch of Carolina Impresario's new product line, WAXED.

All aboard.

Instead of hip-hop, the club is playing a more sophisti-cated and down-tempo Bossa Nova song by Bebel Gilberto. Bikini-waxed society women and young heiresses branded with their lovers' initials flit among Impresarios staffers. Kiki and Candace are among them, passing judgment on every-one that struts past.

Carolina's publicist, Mia, a smoldering brunette, leads Carolina around the room, stopping intermittently for in-troductions and to offer sound bites to various reporters, columnists, and bloggers.

Sofia stands uncomfortably alone, fidgeting with her drink, surrounded by a hundred people watching her sister shine. This was exactly the type of event that Scott should have attended—she would have loved to have him within reach. She didn't need to hang on to him, but many eve-nings she had taken comfort simply knowing he was there. Normally, she could have smelled his peppermint Breath-Savers from a few feet away, and no matter who she was talking to, she could take a deep breath and feel him near her. Carolina's product launch was something they had of-ten talked about over the last few months. He had cleared his schedule for the evening to be certain he wouldn't have to be out with clients. *Clients*, she thought. *Right*. But she'd not seen or spoken to him in weeks, and he would not be here tonight.

Sofia's taken refuge at Carolina's, where her mother has also been staying. Fortunately, it had allowed Sofia finally to forgive Lunetta, to confront her face-to-face, and to heal wounds that had been painful and raw. She'd been grateful for the support of her family, but tonight, at this moment, she wants to be with Scott.

Instead of seeking to fight an all-out war, when Sofia returned home that horrific afternoon, she had packed three bags and walked down to the taxi, where Lunetta and Carolina were waiting for her. She had handed the luggage off and gone back upstairs to face the heartache head-on. She asked Dennis not to tell Scott of their conversation, and he had agreed—at least to her face. But when Scott returned home, he was frantic and pale. He knew that she knew. When he said her name, she put her hand up to stop the conversation before it could begin.

"Please don't. I will be there for you for the rest of my life. You are my best friend." Tears poured down Sofia's face, and she continued, "But right now, I cannot be here. You need to figure out what you want, Scott. You need to figure out who you are. And I need to do the same." She took two steps and collapsed into his arms. She sobbed, and he followed suit. After a few minutes, she pulled away and wiped the tears from her face. She pulled her sunglasses over her eyes and quickly walked toward the door, but abruptly stopped when she reached the small side table in the entryway. It was loaded with keys and loose change, unopened mail and matchbooks. It appeared as though she might turn to say one final word. But she did not. She placed one hand over the other and gently removed her wedding ring. It made the sound of a small coin as it landed in the glass dish. Then she opened the door and walked through it without looking back.

Back at the party, Sofia shakily stands amid the chaos, unsure of her next move. She takes comfort in knowing she doesn't have to decide, at least not right now. She feels a tug on her arm.

"Boo!" Anna says from behind her sister.

"Finally!" Sofia says, turning to hug her.

They stare at Carolina, who is being interviewed by a man with a digital voice recorder.

"What is she wearing?" Anna asks, giving Carolina the once-over.

"It's a cat suit," Sofia explains.

"A cat suit? I'm sorry, but maybe twenty-some years ago they were kind of in, but not today. They are just, hmm, they're just . . . No."

"You know Carolina, she's unapologetic when it comes to fashion. And I actually think I saw that same one on the cover of *W* last month," Sofia continues. Anna lets out a pouty exhalation as they continue to dissect their older sister as she is being interviewed. Carolina notices one of several displays of her home-waxing kits slightly askew and stops midinterview to readjust it.

"Is she already pitching a fit?" Anna asks.

"What do you think?" Sofia responds.

"Mom, can I go outside? I can't get cell service down here?" Fabiana appears, flanked by her two siblings.

Ariel is dressed in a mint-colored silk shift dress covered in pink and black polka dots. Her face beams as she holds her big sister's hand. Michael stands next to his two sisters, looking uncomfortable in his khakis and button-down striped shirt.

"No. You think I'm going to let you stand outside by yourself looking gorgeous? I already have my eye on you here. These men . . ." Anna says playfully.

"Gross," Fabiana snaps. She looks at her brother and sister. "Come on, guys, I saw three barstools open. Maybe Michael can shoot almonds out of his nose again because that was so much fun to watch for the last twenty minutes," Fabiana says sarcastically, before walking toward the bar.

"How's she doing with the Christopher thing?" Sofia asks.

"Oh, she totally hates me," Anna says plainly. "But it's now a low-level hatred."

"She's fifteen; of course she hates you."

"Please. There are some days I hate myself," Anna says, and stares at Carolina. She shakes her head, then adds, "What mother splits up her family?"

Sofia turns and faces Anna. "Don't do that. He's the one who left when things got tough. And now he wants to come back? No way. There's no going back—only forward." It's clear by her tone that Sofia isn't only talking about Anna's situation. "And you better stop playing that Sad Sally act because a very hot man is coming your way," Sofia continues.

Anna turns her head, and smiles. "Hi."

Tim smiles in kind and looks into Anna's eyes. Sofia feels like the proverbial third wheel and loudly clears her throat. "Oh. Sofia, this is Tim," Anna says.

Tim extends his hand, and Sofia shakes it. "Nice to meet you."

Before Tim can say another word, his BlackBerry rings. "Ugh. I'm sorry. Excuse me one minute," he says, and steps away from the sisters.

"How'd the date go?" Sofia asks as she watches Carolina and a woman with a clipboard talk near the front of the bar. A local camera crew waits on the sidelines.

"I'm not sure if you could completely call it a date, considering the kids came. But it went well, all things considered," Anna answers.

"All things considered?" Sofia asks curiously.

"Yeah, considering they had an old and practically dead lady as a chaperone," a familiar voice chimes in.

Sofia turns her head and notices JJ sitting in a wheelchair directly behind Anna. "Well, hello there," Sofia says politely.

JJ nods, then turns to Anna. "So when is Her Highness going to get on with this? This is not how I want to be spending my remaining hours. And why hasn't anyone offered me a drink for Christ's sake? What kind of shit-show is your sister running here?" JJ barks.

Like a true superhero, Tim appears from out of the shadows. "Let me take you to the bar. I'd get you a drink myself, but I don't want to take away the fun of berating the bartenders," he says.

"Finally, someone who gets me," JJ says, as Tim begins to wheel her away. JJ's eyes meet Anna's, and she winks and quickly flashes a half smile before anyone else sees. If it hadn't been for Anna's persistence and prodding, JJ could very well be gone by now. She might have grown physically weaker, but mentally she was as tough as ever, and Anna wasn't going to let her go down without a fight. And if there was one thing JJ knew how to do, it was fight. Tim wheels JJ to the bar and saddles up next to Anna's kids, who look painfully bored. There are several almonds on the floor around Michael's barstool.

Carolina walks away from the publicist and joins Anna and Sofia in the center of the room. She quickly grabs three champagne flutes off a passing waiter's tray and hands them to the girls.

Before she takes a sip, Carolina notices Anna's attire. She's stunning in a silk square-neck sleeveless green dress with a beaded waist that shows off her slimmer, tauter figure. Carolina moves her eyes down to Anna's matching green heels. "Well, you've come a long way from your Banana Republic suits that were two sizes too small." It was a quasi compliment, and the best that Carolina could do. It was enough, and Anna smiles in acceptance. "But her . . . look at her. Like a giant mango in heels," Carolina says, looking over at their mother, who is, not surprisingly, attempting to flirt with one of the waiters. Lunetta had not only taken a liking to the Florida sun, but had a particular affinity to its fashions as well. Her bright orange one-piece jumpsuit had a slight county-jail feel to it, the canary yellow belt with a gold-plated squiggle buckle adding a definite Palm Beach flair.

"The color isn't the worst part. The worst part is that our sixtysomething-year-old mother is wearing a pantsuit two sizes two small in an effort to get laid," Sofia says mystified.

"If my eyes could puke," Carolina says, "they'd be projectile vomiting right now."

"You're the oldest," Sofia says to her. "So you can be honest with me. I was adopted, right?"

"Sorry, not a chance. She," Carolina says, staring in wonderment at their mother, now attempting to make conversation with a man who could be her grandson, "is all ours."

Lunetta sees her girls together and rushes over to be with them.

"A city full of smokers and nobody can smoke anywhere," Lunetta laments as she plays with a lighter.

"Where did you get that?" Anna asks.

"That cute bartender gave it to me," Lunetta says, and turns back and smiles at the young man. Anna grimaces while her mother's back is turned.

"This is a real nice affair, Carolina," Lunetta says, turning back to her daughters. Carolina nods at her mother to acknowledge her compliment. "You really shouldn't be drinking with the b-a-b-y," Lunetta spells.

"I think we can all spell here, Mom," Anna says, and laughs.

"And I don't think we need to ever utter that word in public again," Carolina snips.

As the group stands in awkward silence, Mia, the publicist, and a photographer step in. "Can we get a group shot, Carolina?"

Mother and daughters turn and face the camera.

"Could you pretend like you actually like each other?" Mia laughs.

The women plaster on smiles, until Lunetta pipes up, and says through her teeth, "I don't know how you're going to explain a fat stomach. People are going to know."

The smiles instantly drop just as the photographer snaps the picture. Mia looks at the digital image, then back at the women. "Yeah. That was . . . hmm . . . It just *is*," she says before walking away.

Carolina shoots Lunetta a death stare. "What? I'm just saying?" Lunetta says innocently, and takes another sip of champagne.

"Is it wrong to say I'd always secretly hoped we'd all be under the same roof together again one day?" Sofia asks.

"Yes!" Carolina and Lunetta bark in unison.

"Honey, are you drunk?" Lunetta asks. Sofia rolls her eyes.

"Very, very wrong," Carolina says, wagging her finger.

"Oh, come on. Don't you remember when we used to have these conversations when we were kids? We were each going to have a wing in a McMansion. Remember, Carolina? Or have you blocked your childhood out of your mind completely?" Anna asks.

Carolina shrugs and motions her head toward Lunetta, as if to say, "Look what we had to work with!" But Carolina *did* remember those talks late at night in the family room. But those conversations were only theoretical—at least in Carolina's mind. She never actually thought her younger sister and her gypsy mother would be camped out in her loft—especially for an extended period of time. Lunetta insisted on "being there" for Carolina through her pregnancy, and until the child was a few months old. Carolina had still yet to come up with the right excuse to force her mother's early departure. *Maybe I could pay her to leave?* Carolina thinks as she stares at her mother.

"And *you*, my dear," Lunetta opines. "You need to get back out there." Sofia takes a sip of Veuve and turns slightly away. "You have to learn how to swim again."

"It's been three weeks," Sofia says flatly. Sofia rubs her fingers against her palms. She can feel the anger that was momentarily dormant start to fester once again. She tightens her jaw in anticipation of Lunetta's next move.

Lunetta places her hand gently on Sofia's shoulder in a somber fashion. "It's time to move on, dear."

"ARE YOU KIDDING ME?" Sofia shouts. A few startled guests turn around at the sheer volume of Sofia's voice.

"Sofia! Can we do the family talk-show segment some-place else?" Carolina says forcefully. She looks around at the random partygoers and smiles politely.

"My husband is gay and was sleeping with my best friend," Sofia says incredulously. "Give me a minute or two!"

"Well, then, you know to avoid the gay bars when looking for a date," Lunetta says, and puts her empty glass on a passing waiter's tray. "Who knows? Maybe we can hit a few bars together?"

"Mother!" Anna says.

"You, Mother, are not Blanche Devereaux, and this is not Miami Beach. I'd rather set myself on fire with that lighter of yours then go to a bar with you and watch you pick up a man," Sofia snips.

In one swift motion, Lunetta raises her arm in a theatrical manner, opens her fingers directly above Sofia's champagne flute, and plops the electric blue Bic lighter into Sofia's glass of bubbly.

"Burn baby burn!" Lunetta says just as more reporters approach Carolina.

Anna uses the distraction to pull Sofia away from her mother.

"What the hell will she do next?" Sofia says, and shakes her head.

"Who the hell knows?" Anna says and laughs.

"*She* is still standing here," Lunetta speaks up from behind them. "I am not escaped so easily."

"This we have learned well," Anna says.

"I guess that future is a bit uncertain for all of us," Sofia says, and sighs. Carolina turns away from an interview to see the threesome observing. As if on cue, Lunetta pulls the three women together and wraps her arms around Sofia's and Anna's waists. Slightly suspicious of her mother, Carolina stands on the other side of Anna just out of Lunetta's reach.

She says to the three of them, "Let me tell you something, my daughters: There are few things in life that frighten people more than the unknown. Many often prefer the status quo even if that means living an unfulfilled life, staying in a loveless relationship, or being in a constant state of denial. Until that one day when an awakening occurs, and suddenly it's time to take those first steps to a new life." Lunetta looks down at Anna's green heels, Sofia's black boots, Carolina's python Louboutins, and her own lemon-colored ballet flats, and says, "Just make sure to wear the right shoes."

"Oh God, that is such a bag of bullshit," JJ says from behind them. Tim stands uncomfortably behind her wheelchair.

"I'm sorry?" Lunetta says, pulling away from her three daughters.

"Shoes? Yuck. How many reruns of *Sex and the City* have you been watching? Excuse me while I go vomit what's left of those croquettes I was eating earlier."

"Okay, that's disgusting," Sofia says.

"JJ," Anna begins.

"No, let her finish!" Carolina interrupts.

"Life is more like the waxing you ladies do: Sometimes you have to go through a little pain to find the beauty," JJ says, and looks at Anna. "It's about putting on a brave exterior even when you think you can't take one more rip life has to give you. But, if you close your eyes and just breathe, you'll soon realize that the pain is momentary compared to the happiness that remains."

The Impresario women stand in silence, profoundly touched by JJ's words.

"Then again, don't listen to me. I just smoked some of that medical marijuana in the car ride over here," JJ says, and lets out her signature cackle.

"I'm going to the bar," Anna says, and smiles at Tim.

"I'll join you," Sofia chimes in.

"I liked my shoe analogy," Lunetta says as she follows behind her two daughters.

"Mother," Sofia says, annoyed.

Carolina and JJ remain staring at each other. It's the kind of knowing look that rarely happens in a person's life, but at that moment both women got it. Perhaps Carolina was looking into her future, and just maybe JJ was looking back at her past.

"All right, Tim, let's go. I've got the munchies."

When you're in the business of *spin,* how do you keep from *spinning* out of control?

Taylor Green, straight from the Midwest, lands a dream gig working for New York public relations dominatrix Jennifer Weinstein. Taylor soon becomes Jennie's right-hand man—but as the perks of his job increase, can he balance his own reality with that of her drug-fueled, high-intensity world?

**"A delightfully snarky and hilariously biting peek into the world of high-stakes public relations...You need two things in your beach bag this summer—sunblock and *Spin*."**

—Jen Lancaster, *New York Times* bestselling author of *Bitter Is the New Black* and *My Fair Lazy*

ST. MARTIN'S PRESS